OPPOSING FORCES

PRIVATE PROTECTORS SERIES

ADRIENNE GIORDANO

ALG PUBLISHING

Edited by Gina Bernal

Copyedited by Elizabeth Neal

Cover Design by Lewellen Designs

Author Photo by Debora Giordano

Print Edition ISBN: 978-1-942504-65-8

Digital Edition ISBN: 978-1-942504-64-1

PROLOGUE

GREG LEEDS KNEW IF HE OPENED HIS BALCONY DOOR, THERE'D be no turning back. His heart banged—*buhbum-buhbum-buhbum*—had to be five hundred beats a minute. He closed his eyes. Anything to block the emotions smothering him, sucking away what was left of his life.

Relax. Stop thinking.

He opened his eyes. One lone lamp on the side table lit the room and the sofa they'd bought last year, a white one, showed the abuse of their four-year-old. What the hell had they been thinking buying a white sofa? He and Marianne had laughed over that gaffe and chalked it up to a lack of parenting experience. He wanted to hope there would be more of those parental missteps. Wanted to.

Walk away.

If he had any sense, he would catch up with Marianne and sweet little Evan, who were on their way to the evening showing of Disney's latest 3-D flick. The pall of quiet over the house pushed Greg one step closer to the balcony and his heart tripped five hundred again.

For weeks he'd been at this routine. Teetering on this

fucking precipice of despair while eyeballing that fucking door with that fucking lock. Each time he'd backed away. Convinced himself he'd make things right.

Until this morning.

This morning it was made clear—there would be no redemption. Wanting only to provide for his growing family, he'd played the game and lost. His dream had been simple: get out of the tiny apartment and into a place with a yard where Evan would play with friends. Somehow, Greg had slipped off track. Or maybe he'd jumped.

At first, it was one small thing. A second of miscalculation. A minor error. Then it became a moment and the moments turned into hours and the hours turned into days and before he knew it, he'd fucked up good.

No turning back.

His scalp tingled and he absently rubbed the spot. Outside, darkness continued to descend on Chicago's streets.

He took one more step to the door, close enough to touch the handle. To unlock it. To open it. And then the burst of frigid early March air—thirty-six degrees' worth—blasted him. Somehow, the cold settled his nerves.

She won't want you now. Why would she?

From eighteen stories below, a truck horn, that long, piercing blare, sounded. Tail-end of rush hour. Pedestrians. He should check.

No. Didn't need to. He'd lived in this building five years. He knew the traffic patterns. He stepped onto the balcony and dragged the iron bistro chair next to the rail.

Minute by minute, hour by hour, day by day, he'd thrown his life away. He was the only one who knew. They'd know now. Marianne, his family, his friends. Evan.

They'd know now.

He closed his eyes, breathed in that frigid air and began to shiver. Fear or cold? Not sure, but his dress shirt offered little protection from the lake wind.

Stepping to the rail had been the farthest he'd made it in weeks. It must be the right thing if he'd come this far.

Across the street, half the units in the building were dark. Directly across from him, right in his sight line, one was lit. A bright light in a sea of darkness. There was his answer. The light.

He stepped onto the chair and his breath disappeared into another gust of wind. Somehow he'd started to sweat, and his mind looped. *Do it. Don't do it. Do it.*

Too late to think now. Should have done that earlier. When he could have stopped it. Tears streamed down his face. Crying was for sissies and screw-ups. Wasn't that what his father had always said?

Another car horn sounded and Greg stared at that lone light across the street. A shriek built in his chest, worked its way up his aching throat and bullied its way out.

Into the descending darkness, with the car horn blasting and his mind roaring, Greg hoisted himself over the rail and plunged to the street below.

1

JILLIAN DECIDED SHE MIGHT BE THE BIGGEST DINGBAT IN THE city of Chicago. Eleven o'clock on a Friday night and she should be doing things that didn't include schlepping to her office in a distribution warehouse on the South Side of Chicago. Just driving down the street on the South Side could get a girl slaughtered.

And yet, here she was, retrieving her beloved two-thousand-dollar camera. The one she'd forgotten in her desk drawer, thereby making her the biggest dingbat in Chicago. One thing she knew for sure, this would never happen again. All she could hope was that someone hadn't made off with it.

This camera was more than just valuable. It represented two years of what she could achieve when she set her mind to it. Pinching pennies, giving up lattes—whatever it took to accomplish her goal of owning a camera every amateur photographer would carve out an eye for. And that was saying something. Considering photographers needed their eyes.

She reached into the drawer and her fingers brushed the

soft leather of the camera case. Still there. To be sure, she unzipped the bag and found her precious baby, its lovely lens cover nearly smiling back at her. She snatched it out of the case, set it on her lap and gently ran her hand over the smooth surface. A grown woman shouldn't be so attached to an object.

Eh, why not?

Cameras didn't disappoint her.

Either way, mission accomplished. She sat back in her chair, ran a finger over her forehead. "You got lucky this time." She glanced down at the camera. "Let's get outta here."

She stowed the camera, slung the bag over her shoulder and kicked the bottom drawer closed. A sudden grinding of one of the loading dock doors shattered the eerie quiet outside her office.

A drug delivery at eleven o'clock on a Friday night?

It could happen, but being the assistant distribution manager for Stennar Pharm, she'd have known about it and she didn't remember seeing it on the day's manifest. Unfortunately, in the week since her immediate supervisor had thrown himself off his eighteenth-floor balcony not everything had gone smoothly. Since Greg's death, the VP of distribution, Ned Dillard, had been keeping abreast of the daily goings-on in the department. Even if she didn't know what this delivery was, Ned probably did.

Nothing got by him.

She moved to the doorway. At the loading dock, the growl of the truck engine calmed to an idle. A door slammed.

"Twenty minutes to unload and we're outta here," Cliff Henderson yelled.

Cliff, one of the distribution team members, had obviously been expecting the delivery. The ride down here and the flat-out creepiness of being alone in a huge warehouse must have zapped her senses.

She stepped out of the office, closed the door behind her and made her way to the loading dock.

"Hi, Cliff."

He spun toward her, his face stretched in that holy-crap look people get when surprised.

"Jillian. Wow." He half laughed. "You scared me."

"Sorry. I forgot my camera and had to come back for it."

He glanced at the case. "You don't want to leave that here."

She gestured to the truck. "What's this?"

"Delivery that was supposed to happen this morning. Truck broke down. Pain in the ass on a Friday night."

A delivery that hadn't arrived? She should have been made aware of that. Jillian glanced at the boxes neatly stacked inside the truck. "You're going to unload this yourself?"

"Not the whole thing. I'll be done fast."

"Can I help you?"

He waved the suggestion away. "Get on with your weekend."

"You're sure?"

"I got this. No problem."

She glanced back at the truck. "If you say so. Just leave the paperwork on my desk and I'll take care of it on Monday."

"Sure thing. Things have been nuts around here since Greg..."

Jillian stared straight ahead. "The poor man. I can't imagine being in such pain that he thought jumping off a building would fix it. I feel horrible for his wife and son."

Her own father would never win any parenting awards, but he'd never allowed his pain to drive him to suicide.

Cliff let out a long, streaming breath. "Let me walk you to your car."

For a week, the employees had been avoiding the subject. Everyone walking around sort of dazed, knowing their coworkers were thinking about Greg, but refusing to talk about it. The unspoken sorrow lay heavy on all of them, but, like the others, Jillian supposed it was better to not think too hard about Greg and his demons. "I'd appreciate that."

Cliff led her to the door and pushed it open. "Good thing the cleaning people don't come in until Saturday. Depending on the crew, you might have lost that camera."

"That's what I was worried about. And I need the camera for a class I'm taking tomorrow."

Another thing she'd pinched her pennies for—a one-day intensive with a world-renowned photographer. The class was only offered once per year and she'd been on the waiting list for four years.

"That sounds fun."

"I'm hoping so." They reached her car and Jillian set the camera bag on the floor behind the driver's seat. She turned to Cliff. "Thanks for walking me out."

"You bet. Be careful heading home."

"I'll lock my doors. Thanks."

Even self-sufficient women couldn't be too careful when it came to being alone at night.

JACKSON LYNX ADDED ANOTHER TEN POUNDS TO EACH END OF the weight bar and settled himself on the bench. On Saturday morning, the quiet of the gym in the Taylor Security building could only be considered heaven. No one yapping and wrecking his concentration when he wanted to focus on the day ahead.

Quiet. That's what he needed.

The gym door swung open and Vic Andrews—most likely the nation's loudest loudmouth—entered, wearing a ripped T-shirt that said I'm Just One Big Freaking Ray of Sunshine and a pair of gray basketball shorts. He tossed his gym bag on the floor and smacked his hands together. The clapping noise rocketed off the walls and destroyed the calm.

There goes the serenity.

Vic raised his arms. "Boy Scout, funny seeing you here."

The Boy Scout nickname had been around since their army days when Lynx, two years younger than Vic and fresh out of West Point, had joined Vic's unit as a Second Lieutenant. Vic, being Vic, was the only guy with balls enormous enough to call his superior Boy Scout. Somehow, they'd become friends. War did that to men. Bonded them. Gave them a common purpose and understanding of the insanity surrounding them.

Lynx lay back on the weight bench and gripped the bar. "Since you're here, you might as well spot me."

"Sure. How long you been here?"

"Forty minutes. Don't start."

"I'm not starting. I asked a question."

"Yeah, but I know you're gonna start."

In the five months since Lynx moved to Chicago from D.C., Vic had been nagging him to get out more. Meet some people.

Get laid.

All good things. Just things he wasn't yet ready for. He had someone in mind, though. Jillian Murdoch from his

Sunday morning yoga class. She was cute and lush but could derail his plan.

Twelve more days.

"But since we're on the subject," Vic said, "it wouldn't kill you to be spontaneous every once in a while."

"I don't like spontaneous."

"Really? Shocking."

God grant me the serenity to accept the things I cannot change.

Lynx let go of the bar and popped to a standing position. At six foot five Vic had four inches on him, but Lynx knew how to get large with someone without needing bulk. He folded his arms.

"I got an hour before my meeting. Let's make it peaceful. Yes, I should get out and have fun. You know what I'm doing. Don't fuck with my head. I have a plan. That *plan* requires me to stick to a routine. No slip-ups. No emotional upheavals. No pain-in-the-ass friends breaking my balls because I like to keep a schedule. Now, are you gonna shut up and spot me?"

Vic waved both hands at him. "I'm not the one running my mouth and wasting time."

Assuming his point had been made, Lynx dropped to the weight bench again.

Behind the bench, Vic waited for him to start his set. "All I'm saying—"

"I don't care what you're saying. And tell Gina to stop hinting at fix-ups."

"*You'll* have to have that conversation with my wife. She's on a mission to find you a woman and I'm not getting in the middle of it."

Lynx took a breath, held it a second and heaved the bar. His muscles groaned at the added weight, but he exhaled and fully extended his arms. He made it to eight reps before his arms quivered and he set the bar down.

Unaided. Not bad.

"I don't want to insult her."

"Then stop coming to my house for dinner every Friday night. She thinks you're lonely. Why else would a successful single guy be at our house every weekend rather than getting laid?"

True dat. "You don't think I want to get laid? This is no fucking picnic I'm putting myself through."

Without a doubt, there were nights he slept on his sofa to avoid climbing into his cold, barren bed. He was a man who enjoyed the feel of a woman next to him while he slept. In the time since he'd entered a thirty-day rehab for a prescription drug habit that turned borderline scary, he'd been following his program and, as the books advised, staying away from women. For three hundred and fifty-two-and-a-quarter days he'd been focusing on making himself well, on taking responsibility for his actions and more or less trying not to pummel himself for his mistakes. That meant attending regular support group meetings and concentrating on not relapsing. It had been some of the hardest work he'd ever done. He didn't need his friends testing him.

"Yeah. The big plan. The one-year mark you'll hit in what? Ten days?"

"Twelve. Asshole."

Vic laughed. "*I* get it. My wife isn't convinced. She thinks you need a woman. Can't say I disagree. Except, I don't think you need a woman to marry. You, my friend, need a woman to get busy with. You're like a goddamned monk."

"My life. My choice." Lynx set his hands back on the bar. "Second set."

"I'll talk to her. Tell her to lay off."

"Thank you. Tell her as soon as I'm ready, I'll let her know."

Vic sighed. "Boy Scout, I know you. You'll never *let* yourself be ready. You're so determined to have a plan that you'll make it a habit. Your life will become week after week of rigid schedules. Work every day. The gym every Tuesday, Thursday and Saturday. Recovery meetings every Monday, Wednesday and Friday. Yoga every Sunday. Am I close?"

Close? The fucker was dead-on. Lynx gave the bar a push and ripped off eight reps. Next time he'd shoot for ten at the higher weight. See how he did.

He set the bar back into its cradles and sat up. "I know what I'm doing."

"You need to get a life."

And now the next phase of the lecture would begin. What Vic didn't understand, and probably never would because he wasn't an addict, was that the life Lynx led now was one that kept him in control. To keep his sobriety intact and prove he could be the responsible person he'd been prior to getting hooked on pills. "I have a life," he said. "It's just not the life you think I should have."

2

By 9:30 Saturday evening, Jillian and her battered feet crawled into bed. Along with her came her camera. Ten hours of walking through the city for the much-anticipated photography class and she was downright giddy. She scrolled through a few photos she'd snapped in Grant Park, but her heavy eyelids begged mercy and she set the camera next to her. Too tired tonight. She'd download the pictures to her laptop tomorrow and analyze them more closely.

For now, she needed sleep. Blissful, much-earned sleep. She flipped the lamp off, curled under her covers and sighed. This had been a good day.

Hours later, in the early-morning blackness, she threw the bedcovers off and cursed her bladder. 3:45 in the damned morning and the thing couldn't make it another two hours? In her bladder's defense, the green tea before bed hadn't been a stellar idea.

She dropped her still-sore feet to the wood floor. The groove in the seams reminded her she hadn't saved enough to buy the throw rug she'd been eyeing. Soon she'd have it and her tootsies would fall onto chenille rather than cheap wood.

In the shadowed darkness, she moved toward the door and the refuge of the bathroom across the hall. A shaft of moonlight—her beacon in the I-need-to-whiz quest—shined through the tiny round window at the backend of her duplex and offered dim light. She stepped into the hall.

Breathing.

Not hers. To her left. By the stairs.

Every classic nerve signal—the tingling, the whooshing in her ears—sparked and her limbs stiffened. She turned her head in the direction of the offending sound. A man stood near the top of the stairs, his bulky form filling the space between the wall and the handrail.

Run.

The intruder blocked the stairs. She spun back to her room, slammed the door behind her. Bat. Under the bed. Years of paranoia about living alone had paid off.

Sweat and fear and anger overtook her, leaving the taste of metal in her mouth. She reached for her weapon, gripped it hard and shot to her feet. If the son of a bitch opened that door, she'd be ready.

She shifted sideways to the nightstand, grabbed the phone with her free hand and dialed 9-1-1. Would the police even get there in time? If not, she'd be forced to deal with the intruder herself. One thing she wouldn't do was be an easy victim. Not in her home. And if he had a gun, well, it would be over quick.

She put the phone on speaker, threw it on the bed and gripped her trusty Louisville Slugger.

"Operator 9-1-1. What is your emergency?" The female dispatcher's voice filled the silent bedroom and Jillian prayed the intruder heard the call.

"Send someone. Help me." Jillian kept her gaze on the closed door six feet away. "I have the police on the phone!"

At any second the prowler should be entering her bedroom. Coming for her. She might die trying to save herself. Simple as that. But no man would walk into her home, into her *life,* and think he could threaten her.

Not without a fight.

Please, don't let him come in here.

"Ma'am? What is your emergency?" the operator asked.

"There's a prowler in my house."

"Confirm your name and address please."

Jillian rattled off her personal info. Wait. A noise from the hallway. Doorknob turning? No. *No, no, no.* She held her breath, squeezed the bat. Sweat slicked the surface. *This thing better not fly when I swing.*

The dispatcher's voice pushed through the mental haze and Jillian closed her eyes. Only for a second. Just to calm the madness in her mind. "What?"

"Help is on the way, ma'am. We have a unit in your neighborhood. Where are you?"

She gasped and that bit of relief focused her. "Bedroom. Second floor."

Ready to crush this creep's skull. She stepped toward the door, far enough to be there when it swung open, and waited.

Nothing.

Sirens blared and a red light flashed against the window shades. Her knuckles throbbed. She eased her grip on the bat

"Ma'am?" the operator said. "Are you there?"

"I'm..." She cleared her throat. "I'm here."

"Can you get out of the house?"

"He has the stairs blocked. I could try the window."

"No. The officers are at your door. The sliding door is open. They're coming in. Where is the intruder?"

Tears filled her eyes and she blinked them away. Not now, dammit. Help was here and she was still alive.

"Jillian, I need your help."

"He was on the steps near the front door. When I saw him he was at the top."

"Okay. The officers are coming in. Stay where you are. When they get upstairs, I'll let you know it's safe to come out. Do you understand?"

What if the police trapped the prowler and sent him into a panic? Jillian secured her grip on the bat. "Yes. Please hurry."

Fifteen minutes later, she sat at her dining room table giving her statement to the responding officers. The blood rush from the last thirty minutes had long since crashed and her body ached with fatigue.

According to the officers, the prowler must have run out the back door after she'd discovered him. She silently thanked her weak bladder for waking her. Otherwise... Well, she wouldn't speculate.

She glanced at the desk where her personal laptop used to be. She'd have to do a full inventory, but she already knew her laptop and camera bag were missing. The lenses alone were worth almost four thousand dollars.

Now she was pissed.

From the time she was sixteen and interning at the local podunk newspaper, she'd been saving money for her camera equipment.

Where was her damned bat? If they found the SOB, she'd pummel him. Multiple times. Not only did she feel completely violated in her own home, she didn't have the satisfaction of getting a decent description of the guy.

"Okay, Ms. Murdoch," Officer Jacobs said, "we'll get someone in here to dust for prints. Maybe this guy is in the system. For now, you need to get a safety bolt for that sliding door. Slider locks are easy to bypass. It wouldn't hurt to get a security system either."

Jillian glanced at the open sliding glass door. She folded her arms and rubbed her hands over her fuzzy cotton bathrobe. It would take a month to melt the ice in her bones. "You're sure he came in through the slider?"

The one she'd been contemplating replacing because she knew—*knew*—it was an easy target. Purchasing the foreclosed home had left her strapped and she'd been forced to pace the many improvements needed. Still, at twenty-seven, she considered the purchase an accomplishment, and the idea of someone entering without her permission absolutely scorched her.

Where's my bat?

Officer Jacobs jerked his thumb toward the front of the house. "The door was still locked. No windows were broken or left open. No forced entry. Either the guy had a key and took the time to lock the front door on his way out or he ran out the back. Either way, he got in."

"Namaste."

"Namaste," the Sunday morning yoga class answered.

Lynx unfolded his legs and shook them out. Around him, his packed-in yoga classmates assembled their belongings, rolled their mats and made a dash for the door. After an hour of settling their minds into a calm, submissive state, they were once again off to the bedlam of their lives.

Lynx, however, would force himself to stay centered and present, as he'd done for the past three hundred and fifty-three days. Sundays were his day to chillax. Today he'd grab a preseason baseball game on television or wander the lakefront in his seemingly never-ending quest to acquaint himself with the city he now called home.

But first, his stomach rumbled. In a rather large, ominous way. Twelve hours since he'd given his body nourishment. His psyche knew the best damn meat lovers' omelet in the city awaited him not two doors down.

In the mirror along the studio's front wall, he spotted the reflection of Jillian gathering her things. Just the sight of her converted his omelet lusting state to a whole 'nother lustful state. With her, the rehab gods filled their quota of testing his recovery. Yeah, they really stuck it to him on this one. *Bastards.*

She looked up and busted him staring. How many times had that occurred over the last few months? Probably too many, but that's what happened when a man had been lacking female companionship for a year. Add horny as hell to the mix and he was screwed. Not in the way he wanted to be either.

"Hi," she said.

Lynx held his breath. Ten days and she was all his. Ten. More. Days.

"Hi, Jillian." He rolled his yoga mat. Anything not to look at her short auburn hair and big doe eyes. Why did she have to be so damned attractive?

Bastards.

"Do you have a minute?" she asked.

So much for quick escape. He'd have to suck it up.

He groaned, dropped the mat and stared into the eyes of the woman he simultaneously feared and hungered for. Tortured, that's what he was. Like a damned feral animal that had been caged.

"Sure. What's up?"

And then he saw it. The way her shoulders dipped. Relief. He took in the bit of luggage sagging under her eyes and his carotid throbbed. *Something's not right.*

"You okay?"

She nodded then tugged on a few strands of her pixie-cut hair. Nervous. "My house was broken into last night."

Whoa. "Were you home?"

"I woke up in the middle of it. Needed the bathroom. I walked out of my bedroom and there he was, on the stairs. I ran back to my room, called 9-1-1, and the guy took off."

Jesus. She must have been terrified. Half-asleep and—*bam*—bad guy in the house. Any number of horrific things could have happened. Tiny pinpricks dotted the backs of his shoulders. As detached as he wanted to be from Jillian Murdoch, none of it sat right with him.

This was the happy, carefree girl who marched into the studio every Sunday with a warm hello. Time and again, he found himself waiting for her and her infectious smile to give him hope that he'd find something good on the other side of recovery.

Except she tempted him in ways he shouldn't be tempted. Ways that would break his heart, wreck his mind and possibly send him running back to the numbing bliss of Vicodin. The last thing he needed was to get head over heels with a woman.

An addict is an addict is an addict.

Screw it. He stepped forward and risked nearly a year of sobriety by wrapping an arm around her shoulder. He'd probably regret it later, but right now, at this second, his body went berserk. Lightning zapped his limbs. He forced himself to stay loose and not panic. She pressed her forehead into his shoulder and he struggled to keep his hands still. The woman had been traumatized and didn't need him groping her.

Of course, given his lack of sexual activity, maybe he shouldn't beat himself up. The responsible thing would be to offer help.

He glanced around the now empty studio. At least they didn't have an audience. "What did the cops say?"

She stepped out of his grasp. "I'm sorry. I didn't mean to dump on you."

"Not a problem. I'll do what I can."

"The police told me I should get a security system. I remembered you told me you worked for Taylor Security. I thought maybe you could put me in contact with someone."

He grabbed his jacket off the floor and retrieved his phone from the pocket. "I'll make some calls. I don't usually work that end of the business, but I'll get in touch with someone. See if we can get you a system fast."

He'd start with Vic. Then Mike, CEO of Taylor Security. He handled running the company and the private security end of the business. Lynx was slowly transitioning into Vic's old job of working with government contacts who hired them to guard diplomats or other high-ranking officials. Then there were the off-the-books jobs. If the government wanted plausible deniability in the sudden demise of a terrorist or two, they called Taylor Security. All of it fell under Vic's—now Lynx's—to-do list.

"Did the thief get anything?" he asked Jillian.

"My laptop and a few camera lenses. I had the camera in the bedroom with me. The police think they were headed upstairs for jewelry. All in all, I was lucky."

Understatement of the year. "Jesus. Jillian, I'm sorry. That had to be terrifying."

"It was a shock."

The studio door swung open and three people entered. The next class making its way in. He turned back to her. "We need to clear out. I was gonna grab breakfast at Sal's. Why don't we head over there and I'll see if I can raise anyone at the office."

"Are you sure? I don't want to interrupt your day. All I need is someone to call about the alarm."

A vision of his calendar and the red X's on it popped into his head. He should put her in touch with someone and walk away. Walking away would keep him on his regimented recovery schedule.

Too bad he'd never been the guy who could walk away when someone needed help.

"Let's get something to eat. I'll call the guys on the way."

LYNX SAT BACK IN HIS CHAIR WHEN VIC STEPPED INTO THE Taylor Security conference room with his ten-year-old stepdaughter in tow. He halted on the other side of the table and folded his arms. His typical fuck-with-me-and-die stance.

"I'm guessing there's a good reason you're bugging us on a Sunday?"

"You guessed right." Lynx reached across the table and high-fived Lily. "Hi, Lil."

"Hi, Lynx."

Like the guys, she called him by his last name. He grinned at her, which was damned near impossible not to do given the level of cuteness she contained. She jumped into one of the leather chairs, gave it a spin and her curly dark hair flew. Oh, to be ten again.

Vic pointed at her. "Lil, take it easy on the chair." He brought his attention back to Lynx. "What's up?"

"You could have called me. You didn't have to come in."

"We got two teenagers and a couple of newborns at home. We're running from the carnage. I just picked up maxi pads. Kill me now."

Lily smiled, all giant teeth, and her cuteness doubled. "He made me carry them."

"I wasn't gonna do it," Vic said.

Jillian swung around the doorframe and her doe-eyed gaze landed on Vic's feet then slowly worked its way up the small mountain of him. Lynx nearly laughed. The guy's size alone scared the hell out of people.

"Sorry to interrupt."

Lynx waved her in. "This is Vic and Lily. Vic and Lily, meet my friend Jillian."

"Hi."

Vic slid Lynx a sideways glance. No doubt his mind had gone to the gutter.

Lily scrambled out of her seat. "Have you been here before?"

"No."

"Great! I'll give you a tour."

"I'd love a tour," Jillian said. A guy had to love a woman who indulged a little girl in her silly endeavor.

Ten more days.

Apparently Lily was the resident hostess with the mostest, because she latched on to Jillian's arm, dragged her to the door and pulled it closed as they left.

In typical Vic style, he waggled his eyebrows. "Finally? You're getting laid? Thank you."

"She's a friend from yoga. Her house got broken into last night."

Lynx's cell phone rang and he checked the screen. "Hang on. This is Mike." He hit the speaker button. "Hey. Thanks for calling me back. Vic is here."

"Is this about the car?"

Vic grunted. "Ix-nay on that, Mike. Haven't gotten there yet."

"What car?"

"Yours," Vic said. "It's a crapper. Mike wants you to get rid of it."

Now, that was offensive. He'd had that car ten years. It was a good, reliable car with low mileage, and he had no intention of getting rid of it. Change was not an addict's friend.

Mike cleared his throat. "We have a Mercedes in the garage. It's supposed to be Vic's, but he hates it."

"I don't *hate* it. I like my truck."

"So you're giving it to me?"

"If you want it," Mike said. "Otherwise, go lease yourself something. I don't care. Just get rid of the piece of shit you're driving."

"I like my car."

Vic rolled his eyes. "But you can't be sportin' clients around in that. You could use some new work clothes too."

Now it was bad clothes? "Until five months ago I was on a government salary. Forgive me if my suits aren't Armani."

Vic held his hands up. "Only an observation. And it wouldn't hurt to get laid."

Through the phone, Mike laughed. *Now I'm screwed.* Give Vic a responsive audience and he'd go into a stand-up routine.

"You gotta give yourself some slack on this one-year thing," Vic said. "Call it a done deal and go bang someone. The redhead would be a good choice."

Lynx poked his finger. "I've got a plan here. I'm in recovery. I'm focusing. Don't give me any shit."

"You're allowed to have fun. You're not supposed to make

any major changes either. Five months ago you blew that out of the water by leaving your State Department job and moving halfway across the country. I'd call that a major fucking change."

"The stress of that job was killing me. I made the change to better my quality of life."

"Exactly why you should get a new car, some good clothes and get laid."

Through the phone, Mike sighed. "Am I needed for this conversation?"

"No," Vic said.

"Yes," Lynx said. "I didn't call you about the car. I didn't even *know* about the car."

"What, then?"

"A friend of mine had a break-in last night. She lives alone. Can we get a security system installed for her today?"

Hesitation. "You realize its Sunday and I have to pay someone double time?"

Lynx had been ready for that one. "Take it out of my budget."

Vic whistled. "I taught you well, Boy Scout."

More silence and then, "I'll see if I can find you someone, but on an eighty-degree day in March, don't count on it. I'm out."

Lynx disconnected. Damned freakish weather was screwing him. "I guess I'll wait for a call back."

"I guess you will." Vic spun the chair Lily had vacated and sat. "Tell me about this redhead."

Not a chance. Vic would harangue him endlessly about whether or not he got laid. Forget it. Nothing doing. Lynx shook his head.

"Come on. I won't bug you about it." Vic held up two fingers and grinned. "Scout's honor."

The issue at hand was whether or not to believe someone known to keep a file of his friends' colossal fuck-ups. This guy was a terrorist at heart. If he got dirt on someone, he never let up. "What's to tell? We take a yoga class together. She asked for my help."

"But you like her?"

"Sure. Why not? If I was in the market, I'd ask her out."

"It's time for you to be in the market."

"No offense, but you don't know shit about my life. I have a plan. I'm working it."

"Wah, wah. I know all about your plan. That's good. I mean, you've been clean all this time. I'm guessing you've thought about going back on the junk, but you've resisted. You've done what you always do. You work the problem until you figure it out. That's who you are. You get shit done. Why do you think we gave you a job? Well, your government contacts didn't hurt, but the point is, we know you. *I* know you."

None of this was new information. Lynx prided himself on his networking abilities. He knew how politicians worked and understood the gymnastics involved in being awarded government contracts. Still, it never hurt to have those skills recognized. "Where are you headed with this?"

Vic leaned forward. "What will be so different about day three-fifty-five than day three-sixty-five?"

Lynx tapped his fingers against the edge of the table. This had to be a trap. "Huh?"

"Are you gonna have some big epiphany on day three-sixty-five? Some monumental thing that will convince you you're no longer in recovery?"

"I'll always be in recovery."

"That's my point. When do you start having fun again? You seem settled, you go to meetings, you take care of yourself, you're mindful of how your behavior affects others. You haven't just taken moral inventory, you've clubbed yourself senseless with it. If you ask me, you're ready to start living again. And I don't think it'll flipping matter if it's today or ten days from now."

The conference room door opened and Lily stuck her head in. "Uncle Michael's office is locked. I can't finish the tour."

"Sweet Pea, Uncle Mike doesn't want anyone touring his office. That's why it's locked."

"Oh. The tour is over, then. Can we leave now?"

Score one for Lily. She had just bailed Lynx out of this psych session. "Yes," he said. "Please do."

Vic stood and held his hand for a fist bump. "I'm just saying."

"Yeah, I get it. I'll think about it."

In ten days.

3

JILLIAN'S HOUSE WAS SILENT WHEN SHE AND JACK CAME through the front door. The last time she'd invited a man to her home it had been the oven repairman. What that said about her social life was downright disturbing.

Jack's cell phone rang. She wrapped her hand around one of the dining table chairs and pulled it out for him.

"Have a seat."

He slid into the chair and, after talking briefly—a conversation that didn't sound like she'd be getting a security system—dropped his phone to the table.

With one finger, he spun the phone around and around and around on the polished wood.

"No luck?"

"Mike can't raise anyone. He talked to a couple of guys, but they're out with their families. Someone will be here first thing tomorrow."

With time slipping into late afternoon, this wasn't a surprise. Still, it meant facing a night alone in her home minus a security system. The police who'd responded to her call had told her the thief had either picked the lock on one of her doors or had a key. Her mother was the only other person with a key, so she assumed the lock had been picked. For her own safety, she wouldn't stay there.

Jack continued to play with his phone, his gaze on it as it spun. All day he'd been lapsing into these brief silences. The man was a thinker. A strategizer.

"It's okay," she said. "I knew it was a long shot. Thank you for trying. I'm sorry I've wasted your entire day. I'll stay somewhere else tonight."

"You didn't waste my day. I didn't have plans. I was hoping to get this system installed for you. It sucks that you're being put out of your own house."

"It's only one night. Tomorrow, thanks to you, I'll be back in and will feel safer."

The phone spinning continued, but he jerked his head toward the cordless on the breakfast bar. "Call whoever you're gonna call. I'm not leaving until I know you have a place to go."

She patted his hand and held it to stop the mindless spinning. "I'll be fine."

His gaze remained on their stacked hands and the welcoming silence from just minutes ago became charged, a live wire snapping. At least until his fingers twitched. Then twitched again. He slid his hand from beneath hers. Somehow, her simple, meaningless touch sent them beyond the line of comfort.

She didn't understand. Particularly since she'd spotted him staring at her on numerous occasions. She couldn't say she minded. Not with his baby face and haunting blue eyes. There couldn't be a woman alive who would mind this man staring at her.

Just once she'd like to see his eyes twinkle. Jack Lynx was

always way too serious. At least in the minimal time she'd spent with him.

She dragged her hand back. "Sorry."

"No. I...uh..." He scratched his cheek. "I don't know."

"I wasn't—"

"My fault. I don't want you to think I'm manipulating the situation. That I'm hitting on you when you're vulnerable."

Seriously? Where did this guy come from? "I didn't think that. Thank you, though." She smiled. "For not hitting on me. I think."

Finally, he laughed and it transformed his oh so serious face into a tantalizing array of soft angles and bright blue eyes. So handsome when he smiled.

"You're welcome. What about family?"

"Huh?"

"That you can stay with tonight. Family?"

"My folks live in Evanston, but my dad and I are in a rough spot. I'd just as soon go to a hotel."

Things were bad enough today, she didn't need to step into the hot-ass mess of her father having fallen off the wagon. Again. Going there would surely suck her into childhood memories of him tucked into his favorite drunk chair with a bottle of scotch clutched in his greedy hands.

In front of her friends.

She'd had enough of that and even now, as an adult, knew to stay away from her parents during her father's drinking phases. Hot, flashing stabs settled in her shoulders. The never-ending guilt that came with estrangement. Still, by now she understood piling on her own drama regarding her father's disease did none of them any good.

And yet, she still loved the man. Complicated.

"Isn't there someone else you can call?"

How pathetic was this? She'd spent all these years slapping on her happy face, letting people think she was a well-adjusted, outgoing and friendly person when the reality was she'd worked hard to isolate herself. To keep the number of friends to a choice few. *This* was the life she'd built for herself.

Maybe she didn't love being alone, but loneliness brought the security that came with not risking people disappointing her. "Maybe my friend Mallory."

"Good. Get on it."

She pointed at him and circled her finger. "So pushy you are. Who knew?"

He grinned again. Twice so far. How about that?

"Just getting squared away here."

"Thank you."

She had to admit, it was nice having someone worry about her. Growing up as the makeshift adult in a house lacking maturity, she'd spent her time worrying about everyone else. She couldn't blame her mother, who simply wanted to survive and immersed herself into her alcoholic spouse's world. Years of therapy taught Jillian to stay away. Until her father accepted responsibility for his behavior, she couldn't be around him.

Harsh, maybe, but she refused to be unhappy because her father couldn't face his problems.

She grabbed her cell, called Mallory and was informed she could stay there, but the kids had the stomach flu. Thanks but no thanks.

"That didn't sound good," Jack said when she hung up.

"Kids have the flu. I'll go to a hotel."

Which, of course, would come out of her spending money for the week. There went the budget. It would be a week of lunches from home. No biggie.

"Are you sure you're okay with that?"

She leaned forward and rested her chin in her hand. "Sure. I've been on my own a long time. It's only one night."

"Yeah, but after what you went through last night, will you sleep at all?"

Probably not. "You're a worry wart."

"I like to think of myself as a fixer. Sometimes that falls into the worrying category."

"Well, Mr. Fixer, thank you. But go home. I'll pack a bag and find a hotel. I'm a big girl."

He drummed his fingers on the table and stared at her for a long minute. That same snapping energy roared back and her head pounded.

"If you wanted, you could stay at my place."

WHAT THE HELL AM I DOING? HE MIGHT AS WELL BE SUPERMAN inviting kryptonite into his bed. Definitely needed his goddamn head examined. But the idea of her in a hotel room? After she'd chased off a burglar last night? No one should be alone after an experience like that.

He'd go with that theory.

"I have a spare room," he said. "It's not fancy, but the bed is comfortable. If you're not alone, maybe you'll sleep. You could even lock the door."

She eyed him. "Can you be trusted?"

Not where you're concerned. "Mostly."

She laughed. "That's comforting."

"All kidding aside, I'd feel better if you weren't alone."

She glanced around the room, settled her gaze on the corner desk where she'd said her laptop should be. "It's an awful feeling. Knowing someone was prowling through my things while I slept. A total violation."

"I can imagine."

"I can't get hung up on it. If I do, it'll turn me into a lunatic. I want to feel safe here. I bought this place with my own money. It's mine. My sanctuary. My *place*. I can't let someone take that from me."

"And you won't. You'll get your security system tomorrow and take control again."

One thing he knew and respected was a person's ability to seize control. He'd been doing that for months now and had a stack of reasons why he shouldn't pursue this woman. Plus, he probably had ten years on her. That was a minor point. The biggie, the A-bomb, the one that scared the hell out of him, was that he couldn't risk swapping one addiction for the other. Jillian had taken up residence in his mind and wouldn't leave. That alone sent every caution bell in his body clanging. Theoretically, his compulsion to think about her could be a way to satisfy his dependency needs.

Ah, hell. He'd ignore his raging attraction. For another ten days. Maybe a few more to lock in his mental state. Then he could say he'd successfully completed a year of sobriety. He needed to hit that goal. Emotionally as well as physically. After that, who knew what he'd do?

Their gazes locked for a brief second while she thought about it. "And you don't mind?"

"Do you cook?"

She gawked. "Is that my boarding fee?"

"I don't want to be too forward."

"My tush," she said. "But I guess I can throw together a meal."

"Excellent. We can stop at the store on the way to my place. God knows I don't have anything in my fridge."

Jillian went upstairs to pack a bag while Lynx sat at the dining room table. He surveyed his surroundings. Thick, dark green drapes hung on the front windows and a cream upholstered sofa and two reddish chairs loaded with pillows in various shapes and colors filled the space. Even the greenish print rug under the coffee table accentuated the room. Jillian had made herself a nice, comfortable home.

Maybe she wasn't as young as she looked. In his experience, most working women in their mid-twenties couldn't afford to buy their own houses, much less tend to the details of decorating.

Terrific. If Jillian was older than he thought, his stack of reasons to stay away from her had just gotten shorter.

JACK LEANED BACK FROM HIS DINING TABLE AND STRETCHED his arms over his head. "Seriously, that was a hell of a steak."

Jillian twisted her lips to hide a grin. Silly man. "Then you must be deprived of good steak, because I'm not exactly a gourmet cook."

"You're a great cook. Besides, I'm a guy whose only home-cooked meals come from Vic's wife once a week. And those dinners usually involve screaming babies and grumpy teenagers. Give me a quiet home-cooked meal in my own place and I'm a happy guy."

He smiled at her, his lips parting into that boyish grin that instantly sparked something warm inside her. His smiles—or lack of them—could be one of the world's great tragedies. "You don't smile enough."

His focus stayed on her—something most definitely brewing in his mind—but if the last three months were any indication, he'd quickly look away. Hadn't that been his M.O.? To sneak glances at her during yoga and then, when she paid him any attention, look away. The man confused her. For someone generally suspicious of people's motives, this wasn't any great revelation. With him, she wanted to jump inside his mind and know his thoughts.

The silence around them lingered until he shot out of his chair, the legs scraping against hardwood.

History had indeed repeated itself.

He reached for her dirty dish but didn't look at her. "You cooked. I'll clean up."

Typically when he ran from her, he'd simply be gone and she wouldn't be faced with the awkward moment after. Sitting in his apartment left nowhere for either of them to run. She reached for the empty serving platter in the center of the table. "You helped cook."

"I stood there and talked."

"You handed me the salt and pepper. Doesn't that count?"

He shrugged. "I'll clean up." Without another glance, he spun and headed for the kitchen.

"I didn't mean anything by it," she called. "The comment about you smiling. When did the truth become such a horrible thing?"

He slapped the faucet on. "It's not a horrible thing."

Except you ran in terror. "Okay. Anyway, I'll go to my room and give you some privacy. Don't want to intrude."

"You're not intruding. And it's only seven. You can't stay locked in that room all night. We'll watch a movie or something."

"Fine. Right." She jerked her thumb toward the hallway and the safety of the bathroom. "I'd like to clean up and set my clothes out for tomorrow."

He scrubbed at the pan with enough force to fracture the thing. "No problem."

After all day together, a few—or thirty—minutes alone would do them good. As comfortable as she was with him, they were still casual acquaintances who'd only shared spurts of time together in yoga, or afterward when a small group ventured out for a meal or coffee.

Then again, this was obviously *his* issue and she couldn't take responsibility for it. Not when she didn't know how she'd caused it. She'd learned that lesson with her father. Right now, it was the main reason she stayed away from her parents. She couldn't be around them when Dad was off the wagon. Not when she'd get sucked into the emotional warfare.

She reached the bathroom, flipped on the light and closed the bathroom door behind her. Nice-sized bathroom. A little bigger than hers and it had that newly renovated look. No worn caulking or chipped grout. She liked the swishes of brown and blue in the tile. Strange color combination, but it definitely appealed to her. By next year, she'd have enough saved to update her bathroom. All things in good time.

A peek at herself in the mirror offered nothing spectacular. Eh, could be worse. She'd need an assistant to carry the bags under her eyes, but considering the night she'd had, she couldn't obsess over it.

Taped to the top of the mirror, probably eye level for Jack, was a small swatch of paper with a handwritten note. She went on tiptoes and leaned closer. The Serenity Prayer.

She blew out a breath. How many times had she said that damned prayer while dealing with her father's issues?

Or even in the quiet of her bedroom where she dreamed of a better life. A life like her friends had where daughters didn't feel nervous every hour of the day because their father could humiliate them any second.

And why did Jack have this taped to his bathroom mirror? Inspiration obviously. Plenty of people knew the

Serenity Prayer and weren't alcoholics. They just liked the prayer and found hope in it. She was one of them.

She tapped the faucet on and made quick work of splashing water on her face. She'd busy herself in the bedroom getting ready for tomorrow while giving Jack another few minutes alone. Maybe then they'd get back to the light, easy conversation they'd enjoyed over dinner.

Damned complicated man.

Eventually, she wandered out of the bedroom, turned into the hallway and saw him just outside the kitchen, one hand braced against the wall as he faced off with the calendar she'd noticed earlier. The one with the giant red X's marking off the days.

Upon hearing her, he straightened. "Hi."

"Everything okay?"

He flicked a finger against the calendar. "Thinking about my day tomorrow. Mike—my boss—called. Someone will be at your place at nine to install the alarm."

All day she'd been thinking about that alarm. Wondering how fast it would be installed and if she'd have to stay away from her home until it was. The knot in her stomach unfurled. "Thank you. I so appreciate you fast-tracking that for me."

"No problem. Happy to help. You'll have to be there for the install. Your boss won't give you a hard time, will he?"

Ned, her temporary supervisor until Greg's replacement was hired, was a reasonable man, but she'd only been there a few months and didn't like taking unexpected time off. "It shouldn't be a problem. I'll go in early to make up the time."

"I can meet you at your house and do the walk-through with you. Make sure everything's the way you want it."

She shook her head. "I can handle it. But thank you. Again. You've been great through this."

"All I did was make a few calls."

"Still."

The snapping energy in the room was back. *Here we go again.* Awkward silence drove her to a fit of arm tingles and she rubbed at them. *Should have gone to a hotel.*

He scratched the back of his head. "I'm...uh...sorry. About earlier."

"It's fine."

"No. It's not. I didn't want to make you to feel uncomfortable and wound up doing it anyway."

"It was a statement, Jack. You have a great smile. It would be nice if the world got to see it once in a while. I wasn't flirting."

Not really.

And then he smiled again. *Good golly.* If she only had her camera.

"Thank you for the compliment," he said. "I should have said that before. It's nice to hear. From you."

And once again we travel through confusion land. On your left is the tall, good-looking man who stares. On the right is the independent yet lonely woman who would like to jump him. "I—wait...what should I say?"

He grunted and banged his palms against his forehead. "I don't want us to have a perception issue. You're in my home. You've been through a trauma. I don't want you to feel like I expect something. You're safe here. With me."

Unbelievable. The last standing hero. "I feel safe. You've been nothing but kind to me for three months. And now, today, you've gone above and beyond to help me. Why wouldn't I feel safe?"

.   .   .

BECAUSE I DON'T FEEL SAFE. HE WAS COMPLETELY SCREWING this up. His body wanted to lock Jillian in his bedroom for a week and show her all the ways he could make *her* smile. His brain, though? That son of a bitch kept hissing at him, warning him he'd blow his recovery if he let this woman within three feet of his bed.

"I don't know," he said. "Thinking too much." He flicked his finger against the calendar. "The timing is whacking me out."

She glanced at the calendar then brought her gaze back to his before taking a step closer. He forced himself not to move. To stand there while she stalked him. Stalked? Really? Maybe *that* was excessive.

"I don't understand."

Me neither. He pressed his fingers against his forehead and scrunched his face. Massive headache.

"Jack?"

And damn, she'd stepped closer. He was so fucked. *Step back.* The damned hissing in his head continued and a prickling sensation skittered across the back of his neck. *Step back.*

But he knew what he wanted. What he'd wanted for months now, and she was here, in his place, and something told him if he made a move, she wouldn't run.

She was right there, her lips partly open and looking so perfect. All he needed to do was step closer and dip his head and...

The clunk of the automatic ice maker dropping a fresh batch of cubes sounded and Lynx flinched. Jeez, he was a mess.

A moment passed, a solid sixty seconds of her staring at him. Waiting.

"Why don't we just forget it?" she said. "We'll call it a temporary malfunction."

Good word choice. Maybe his body didn't think so, but his brain had finally stopped hissing. He needed all the crazy voices to stop and back the hell off. On top of all of this, he was now dealing with multiple personalities. For some completely asinine reason, that made him laugh.

Jillian did jazz hands. "Oh, yay! He's smiling."

He waved her off. "Yeah. I'm smiling. How about a movie? We'll chill out with popcorn."

"Deal."

"Good. Want something to drink?"

"I'd kill for a glass of white wine."

"Sorry, no wine. Iced tea or water. Or soda?"

Please don't ask me why I have no alcohol in the house. Having to explain that right now might hurl him off the scary fucking high wire he was balanced on.

"You East Coast people. We call it pop here."

He stuck his head in the fridge. "Blah, blah."

"I'll have water. Thank you."

Jillian moved into the kitchen to help him with popcorn and kept silent about the lack of alcohol in the house.

For now, he'd dodged multiple bullets.

4

By 8:00 A.M. JILLIAN HAD HER HEAD BURIED IN A DISTRIBUTION report when Ned stepped into her office doorway. A tall man with a fit frame, her boss wore tailored black slacks and a white dress shirt sans tie. Ned wasn't big on ties. Plus, this was mainly a warehouse so suits and ties weren't required. The management staff was expected to dress appropriately, though. No jeans. Not that she could ever picture Ned in jeans anyway.

They'd never discussed his age, but Jillian pegged him for mid-forties. He had that whole salt-and-pepper distinguished look going on. Everything about him telegraphed dependable, buttoned-up and good-natured.

"Good morning," he said. "You're in early."

"I came in at seven. If it's not a problem, I need to take some personal time today."

"Everything okay?"

"Yes. Well, it will be. I had a break-in at my house Saturday night."

Ned's eyebrows shot up. "My God. Were you home?"

"I woke up and scared him off."

He stepped completely into her office. "Jillian, I'm sorry."

"Thank you. He made off with my personal laptop—my work one was in the car—and some other items, but that's it. Anyway, I'm having an alarm system installed today. They're coming at nine and I need to be there. I came in early to make up the time lost."

Ned waved the statement away. "Of course. Go take care of it."

"Thank you."

"Do you need anything from me before you go? I'm heading into a meeting."

She remembered the delivery from Friday night. "Actually, yes. I had to come back to the office Friday night. I forgot my camera and needed it for Saturday. A late delivery came in while I was here, but I can't find any paperwork on it."

He frowned. "You sure? There should be something in the system on it."

"I can't find anything. Cliff said he'd leave me the paperwork, but it's not here."

"He might have put it in my box. I haven't checked it yet. I'll track it down and get it to you."

"Thank you. It feels like a loose end."

He smiled. "And you hate loose ends."

She laughed. "I do."

"We'll tie it up. I think we'll have a lot of loose ends until we hire Greg's replacement."

"Right. Any idea when that will be?" Not that she had any hope of being promoted in the short time she'd been at Stennar Pharm, but it would be nice to know when she might have a boss.

"Ted Ingrams will be here this afternoon to discuss it. I'll let you know after that."

Ted was the CEO but kept an office downtown. She'd met him exactly twice in the three months she'd worked for the company and each time he'd been professional and direct. Not in a condescending way, but focused. Something she liked in a CEO.

"Thank you."

Ned slapped his hand against the doorframe. "You bet. Go deal with your alarm."

JILLIAN OPENED HER FRONT DOOR AND FOUND ONE OF THE Taylor Security installers on the other side. Jack stood back a foot with a small tool bag dangling from one hand. *Hello, handsome.* It occurred to her that she'd never seen him in anything but jeans or workout clothes. The man could rock dress slacks and Oxford shirts.

Couple that with him taking time out of his day to help her and her stomach did a nutty flutter thing. Relief maybe, because she didn't have to deal with this alarm on her own. If nothing else, he could offer advice on the type of system she needed.

For once, she wasn't alone.

"Hi," she said.

"Hi back."

The two men stepped in and she closed and locked the door behind them. After introductions were made, she walked them through the house. Sam, the installer, took notes as he went along and she assumed he would ask questions if necessary so she forged ahead.

In the kitchen, Sam glanced up at the doorframe on the

slider. "You should put in a security bolt. When the bolt is engaged, the door won't open."

"Yeah," Jack said. "I picked one up. I'll install it while you do your thing." That was news to her. She stared at Jack maybe a second too long, because he threw his free hand up. "Not butting in. Figured I'd save you a trip to the store."

A warm *whoosh* of air surrounded her. He'd done that for her. Without her asking. When was the last time someone, anyone, had done something like that? A small thing, but —*wow*. For a woman who'd grown used to her solitary life, to handling difficult situations, to navigating life's ups and downs as an army of one, this meant something. What that something was, she couldn't be sure. But she liked it. Loved it, in fact.

Gently, using just his fingertips, he touched her arm. "It wasn't a big deal. I stopped on my way to work this morning. I thought we could take care of everything for you today."

The pit in her stomach widened, opened her up, exposing her. And she couldn't have that. *Get it together.* She blinked a couple of times, then glanced at Sam, who took his cue and wandered into the living room. Where the hell had all this emotion come from? Had to be exhaustion kicking in.

Had to be.

Once alone, she leaned closer to Jack. "Thank you. It *is* a big deal. To me anyway. This has been a nightmare. By the time we're done here, I'll feel safe again."

He backed up an inch, as usual, putting space between them. He did smile for her, though. Progress.

"That's the plan. Do you want to hang out while the alarm is installed? If you need to get back, we can call you when we're done."

Not only would he install that security bolt for her, he

would sit here while she went back to work. "I'm good. I brought my office laptop home with me. If I need to, I can work while I'm waiting. But, tell me, do you ever say no to anyone?"

He grinned. "Sometimes. This is supposed to be the year of no."

"I don't think it's working."

"I *know* it's not working. I'm better than I was." He shrugged. "I figure if I can help, why not?"

"Sometimes helping all the time gets to be a pain. You take on everyone else's crap."

"Comes with the territory. It's how I am."

Sam wandered back into the room. "How about I start upstairs?"

Jillian nodded. "Sure. Can I get you anything?"

"No, ma'am. Thank you."

He left again and she turned to Jack. "How about coffee? I'll make a pot. I could use the caffeine."

"I won't argue."

From the cabinet, she pulled the coffee canister and filters. She'd have to do one less scoop than normal. History had proved she was one of the few who liked sludge versus a typical cup of bold coffee.

Jack set the tool bag on her kitchen table and unzipped it. "I'm gonna get started on this bolt. I need to use the drill, so you'll want to go in the other room if you need quiet."

"It's fine. My emails will distract me. I'm waiting for some paperwork from a late delivery I saw the other night."

He fiddled with a drill bit. "Come again?"

"I went back to the office around eleven on Friday night to get my camera."

"You went alone?"

"I needed my camera for Saturday morning and I didn't

want to leave it there all night. It's my baby. Anyway, a delivery came in while I was there."

Drill bit firmly in place, he grabbed a measuring tape from the bag he'd brought with him and measured the doorframe. "Kinda late for a delivery, no?"

She set her laptop on the table and booted it up. "I guess it could happen. Anyway, my boss said he'd take care of the paperwork while I was out this morning. Usually he CC's me on stuff like that because I maintain the delivery schedule."

Jack snapped his tape measure closed. "Do you like this job?"

"I do. It's a step up for me. It's a little weird right now because my immediate supervisor killed himself last week."

Jack paused then faced her. "Holy shit."

"Unbelievable tragedy. He lived downtown and jumped off his balcony. Left a wife and a young son."

"Man, that sucks. Poor kid."

"In the interim, the VP of distribution and I are splitting the work and we're tripping over each other. We'll figure it out until they hire someone."

Jack went back to the door. "Why don't they give you the job?"

"I've only been there a few months. I honestly don't think I'm ready yet. But the company is growing. I'll wait my turn."

"Never hurts to have a plan. I love a good plan."

When the computer finished chugging, she clicked into her email and scanned the new messages. Nothing from Ned.

"Anything?" Jack asked.

"Nope. I'm so baffled by this delivery."

"Don't worry about it. Your boss said he'd take care of it."

The buzz of the drill being engaged forced her gaze from her emails. Somehow, she went from her computer to Jack's ass. It was, after all, right there in her sight line. And what a great ass it was. His body was lean and strong, but not overly muscled. Catlike. She tilted her head one way, then the other. Yep. Great from all angles.

"I'm a nut about the deliveries. When dealing with prescription drugs, we can't have loose ends. Not if I don't want the government showing up to check on us. Then it becomes my screw-up." She sat forward. "Ooh, there's one more place I could check."

Maybe Ned had logged the paperwork into the distribution system. She clicked on the icon and watched the hourglass swirl for a second. She'd already checked the system that morning, but maybe something had changed since she'd left.

At the welcome screen, she typed her username and password. The hourglass swirled again—nothing unusual there. The system was notoriously slow.

ACCESS DENIED.

She must have hit a wrong key. She tried again. Nothing. "Hmmm..."

Jack marked a spot on the doorframe and angled back. "You okay?"

She puckered her lips and focused on her laptop. Maybe because she was trying to remotely access the system something went flukey? "I'm fine. The system is fighting back. Won't take my password."

He stepped to where he could see the screen. "Did you have problems this morning?"

"Not in the office, but the software is temperamental. It's an in-house design and they're still working out the bugs. It'll wait until I get back to the office."

A soft *bleep-bleep* sounded—cell phone—and Jack dug it out of his pants pocket. For a moment, he stared at the screen, glanced over to her and, after the slightest hesitation, punched the button.

"What's up?" he said into the phone.

With the way he'd hesitated, could it be a girlfriend?

He didn't seem the cheating player type. And if it was a girlfriend, where had she been when another woman was sleeping at her man's house? *That* would be the bigger question.

"Slow down," he said. That fast, he'd refocused on the caller. "What happened?"

His voice stayed steady and calm. Commanding. *Interesting*. And really, she shouldn't be listening. Although, it was her house. He could go outside anytime he wanted.

"Don't. Where are you?"

He shot one of his cuffs and checked his watch. "You need a meeting. Do you know where there's a close one? I'll go with you."

A meeting. Her stomach knotted. The Serenity Prayer taped to his mirror loomed in her not so distant memory and suddenly it all came together. How many conversations had she overheard her father having with his sponsors from AA? How many times had she been disappointed when those sponsors begged him to go to meetings and he refused?

Enough to lose count.

Damn. She did not want this man to be an alcoholic. Well, she didn't want anyone to be an alcoholic. An alcoholic's life was filled with constant drama. One day they were promising themselves—and their loved ones—they'd get sober and by lunchtime they were holed up with a bottle.

A vicious cycle she didn't need. Dealing with her family was enough, and she refused—*refused*—to be one of those women who repeated her mother's mistakes. Her love for her mother, and even her father, remained constant, but she didn't need to live their life to prove it. Life was hard enough without the added stress of an addict. Or two.

Even if it sounded as if Jack was in recovery. Maybe a sponsor? Still, even sponsors had relapses and she hadn't spent her life battling the emotional disappointments that came with relapses to allow herself to get involved with someone at risk.

No, sir.

"I've got you," Jack said. "Text me the address and I'll meet you there. Go straight there. We'll be early, but we'll grab a coffee or something."

He disconnected, dropped his phone on the table and spun it. Round and round it went until he finally watched it slow to a stop.

Should she simply let the moment pass? Leave his business to him? He was in her house, and she *did* overhear his end of the conversation. She folded her hands in her lap. "That didn't sound good."

He peeled his gaze from the phone and studied her. Measuring. "It was a...friend. Having some trouble."

"You seem to be surrounded by friends in trouble. You must go through a lot of capes."

At this, he cocked his head, his eyes cloudy and questioning.

"Superman and his cape. That's you."

Barely a smile out of him. *Tough guy.*

"Superman, I'm not, but I've gotta go. I'm sorry. I *will* finish this bolt today."

"It's fine. Really. You've done enough. If you can leave the drill, I'll finish." She grinned. "I'll read the directions."

He shook his head. "I'd like to do it for you. I'll be back in two hours. Can you wait?"

"Sure. But that call sounded important. If your friend needs you, maybe you should stay with him. Or her." She smacked her lips together. What a completely lame way of asking if it was a woman caller.

"It's a him. Definitely a him."

She shouldn't care. "I'm guessing he's an alcoholic?"

Jack fiddled with his phone, flipping it side to side. "Recovering drug addict."

Moment of truth. She had to go for it. Sure she was being nosy, but he chose to have the conversation in her presence. Now she needed to know so she could convince her hormones that Jack Lynx would be off-limits. *I so care.* "And you're his sponsor?"

He blew air into his cheeks and let it pop free. "Not his sponsor. We're friends. I'm...uh...an addict. Recovering. Prescription pain pills."

Chill, hormones. It's over.

"I see."

"Nine more days and it'll be a year I'm clean."

A year. "How long were you an addict?"

"I tore my ACL two years ago. Six months after surgery I realized I couldn't get through the day without Vicodin, and it wasn't about the pain in my knee. I checked myself into rehab. A year later, I'm trying to keep my buddy from relapsing. He's worked too hard for that. If he relapses now, he'll go insane."

Never before did Jillian realize she had a thing for men and capes, but she might just be turned on. Which, of course, would be a complete disaster given her feelings about men with addiction issues. However—and this was a big however—before her stood a man taking responsibility for his own actions by sticking to his recovery. The fact that he was helping others do the same was admirable.

Still, she couldn't allow herself to get emotionally involved. Addicts sometimes couldn't help themselves and disappointed those who loved them. She'd learned that through experience and it was a simple fact she had no room for in her life.

Perhaps she should share that with him. Let him know where she stood on the topic. Yes, she was attracted to him. Nothing could change that. But what was the point if they had no future together? She simply could not risk being disappointed if he relapsed. At that moment, it sounded harsh. Bitchy even. And she wasn't sure how to make him understand in the brief minutes he had before leaving.

Pouring out her emotional sludge wouldn't do either one of them any good. She'd save it for later. "You should go. Tell your friend he should be proud of his ability to stay sober. You too, you know. Be proud that you've made it through. A lot of people don't."

Like my father.

"I am proud. My problem is I can't believe I ever let myself get there in the first place." He paused. "Anyway, I have to go. I should be back in a couple hours. Or, if you need to get back, I can do it after work."

She grabbed a scrap of paper from the holder on the counter. "Call my cell if you'll be more than two hours. Otherwise, we can work on the bolt tonight. I'll even make you dinner for helping me. How's that?"

I so care.

He stuck out his bottom lip. "If you're throwing in

dinner, I'm doing it after work. You know how I feel about home-cooked meals."

Damn, why did he have to be so charming? "A home-cooked meal it is then. I'll see you after work." He ripped off one of those killer smiles and Jillian gave him a thumbs-up. "You're getting good at this smiling thing."

"I guess it all depends on who I'm smiling at."

The man had a way about him, all blue-eyed and baby-faced, yet so intense. A deadly combo slowly chipping away at the number one reason she shouldn't allow herself to get emotional about him.

BY LATE MORNING, JILLIAN RETURNED TO THE WAREHOUSE. Two deliveries were being dealt with in bays one and two. Due to the small size of the truck in bay two, it must have been a local delivery. She'd double check the schedule to make sure.

She unlocked her office door, flipped the light on and fired up her laptop. A slam, then a curse sounded from the warehouse. *Whoops.* Someone dropped something they weren't supposed to. Finally, the whirring laptop quieted and she clicked the icon for the reporting system.

With great care—assuming she'd fouled up earlier and one more mistake would lock her out completely—she typed her password.

More whirring as the hourglass on the computer spun.

ACCESS DENIED.

Grrrr. Obviously, the problem didn't pertain to remote access. She scooped up her desk phone and called the IT helpline, affectionately known as the no-help desk.

"Help desk. This is Dan."

"Hi. It's Jillian Murdoch. I'm getting an access denied

message on the distribution database. I was just in there this morning."

"Hang on."

Jillian hummed along to the hold music. Tina Turner should never be relegated to hold music. Just criminal.

The music stopped and Dan came back on the line. "Jillian?"

"I'm here."

"I'll transfer you to my supervisor."

Now this is interesting. "Um, sure."

A second later, the IT director, a guy she didn't know well but who had always been cordial, picked up. "Jillian, hi. We're making adjustments to the system this morning. You're temporarily locked out."

She picked up a pen she'd left lying on the desk and tapped it. "I need access to the system to monitor the schedule. How do I get my access back?"

"The changes are coming from Ned. Maybe there's been a mix-up. I'd start with him."

She hung up and grunted. The no-help desk lived on. In order to do her job, she'd have to waste her boss's time by whining about an IT issue.

She strode down the corridor to Ned's office. Just inside, in a small outer office, sat his assistant. "Hi, Mary."

The older woman glanced up. Mary was one of those women who might only be fifty-five, but wore her hair teased and cemented into a beehive that made her look ancient. Plus, she carried an extra thirty pounds that added to the matronly mystique.

Mary offered her usual welcoming smile. "Hi, Jillian."

"Is Ned in?"

"He's in a meeting." She leaned forward and whispered. "It's with Mr. Ingrams, but I think they're finishing up." She walked to Ned's door and lightly knocked. After exchanging a few brief words, she waved Jillian in.

Good. A chance for face time with Mr. Ingrams. Maybe she'd wait on her IT issue. Nothing like whining in front of the big cheese. She stepped into the office and nearly smacked into Mr. Ingrams's chest. At five foot seven she wasn't exactly short for a woman, but he stood a good seven inches taller. His dark blond hair had more than a bit of gray at the sideburns and temples. Between his height and the graying hair, the man's presence spoke of strength and power.

"Hello, Mr. Ingrams." She stuck her hand out. "Jillian Murdoch."

He nodded. "I remember. Ned tells me you're doing a great job during this horrible transition."

She glanced at Ned and smiled a silent thanks. "I'm always ready to do my part. Greg was a nice man. It's a tragedy."

"That it is. But thank you for your efforts. I do appreciate it." Ingrams turned back to Ned. "I'll speak with you before I leave this afternoon."

He exited the office and Jillian let out a breath. It was never a bad thing when the big guy complimented one's work.

"What's up, Jillian?"

She brought her attention to Ned, still behind his desk. His office had that lived-in but neat vibe going. Stacks and stacks of papers lined the outside edges of his imitation cherry desk. Even the credenza behind his chair was smothered with file folders.

"Sorry to bother you. I'm having an IT problem. They're telling me I'm locked out of the distribution database and I should talk to you about getting my access back."

He nodded. "I meant to talk to you about that, but you were out dealing with the problem at your house. How did that go, by the way?"

"It's fine. All set."

"Good. Glad to hear it. About the database, the company is moving toward tightening up who has access to what."

A light thumping nagged her right eye. Somehow, she knew she wouldn't be happy about this.

Ned held up a hand. "It's a companywide initiative. Certain information will now be filtered through the department heads. It'll be a need-to-know basis rather than everyone-knows-all. Does that make sense?"

On some level, yes, it made sense. As it pertained to her performing her job? Not one bit. "I understand, but I don't know how I can do my job if I don't have access to the system. Vendors call me all day wanting to know the status of deliveries. If I can't get into the system, how do I help them?"

"I understand. I do. I'll email you updated reports. If you get a call from a vendor and the information is not on the reports I've emailed, refer it to me. My assistant will handle it."

His assistant had access but not her? Putting her in a time-out would have been a more subtle hint. In her experience, the best way to handle these situations would be to lob it out there. Just ask the question. If she knew what the issue was, she could fix it. "Did I do something wrong?"

Ned's mouth dipped into a frown and he drew his eyebrows together. "Not at all. As I said, it's companywide, not just our department." He shifted right and pulled a folder from his desk. "I've scheduled a department meeting this afternoon about this, but since you're here, I'll tell you about it."

From the folder, he pulled a sheet of paper with copy on both sides. "Part of this new initiative is protecting our proprietary systems."

"Like the software?"

"Exactly. We're asking all employees to sign a confidentiality agreement." He handed her the form. "Basically, it requires that you not share proprietary information with anyone outside the company."

"I see." She took the paper from him, glanced at the front then flipped it over. Single-spaced, front and back. A lot of reading here. And if he thought she'd sign it on the spot, he didn't know her at all. One good thing about not trusting people she was supposed to be able to trust was that she didn't get screwed all that often. "This is quite a bit of material. How about I read it and get back to you if I have questions?"

"Sure. We're expecting the employees won't have any issues with it."

Whoa, Nellie. Way to make this form sound harmless when he was really telling her she didn't have a choice. "You're saying if I don't sign this, I'll get fired."

As she watched his lips curve into a smile, the nagging thump behind her eye went to a full bang. That smile was all wrong. Too tight. Pinched. She set the paper in front of her on his desk and sat back.

He did the same. Must have gotten the hint that his little document tripped every one of her danger sensors. "Jillian, this isn't a big issue. It's a simple document that protects the company. Just read it. If you have questions, let me know and we'll discuss it. I think you'll find it fairly standard."

Standard? She'd been working since her sixteenth birthday, including a stint at a major pharmaceutical company, and she'd never been asked to sign any agreements.

No sense in arguing until she read the form. "Fair enough. I'll read it and get back to you. Regarding my access to the database, if I need information, do I speak to your assistant?"

"Start with her. If she can't help you, I'll get on it. And, Jillian, nothing is set in stone. If we find you can't perform your job without access, we'll work something out. We don't want to destroy our efficiencies. Okay?"

So not okay. But she'd be the dedicated employee, the good little worker bee, and slap on her perfected happy face. "No problem. Hopefully it won't be an issue."

JACK RANG JILLIAN'S DOORBELL AT EXACTLY 6:30. PUNCTUAL. *Of course he is.* Superheroes. Always on time.

She swung the door open, happily anticipating his presence on the other side. After the odd day at work, she found herself craving company. Something she typically didn't need. That alone could have been enough to send her into her emotional cave. To withdraw to her safe zone, reinforcing the layers of cement around her untrusting heart. Alone time always refocused her. She'd grown to thrive on it, but lately, as her twenty-eighth birthday loomed, she'd started to resent her self-imposed oneness.

Except tonight, Jack stood on her doorstep wearing Levi's, an unzipped leather jacket and a faded blue T-shirt that made his eyes sparkle. Being alone suddenly didn't seem like such a good idea. The man should wear old shirts more often. 24/7, in fact.

"Hi. Am I late?"

"Right on time. Come in." He moved through the doorway and for the second time today, she snatched a glance at his perfect ass. What was it about Levi's that made a man's ass look so good?

Heat shot up her neck and she stuck her head out the open door for air. *Whew*.

He turned to her, his eyes questioning. "Everything good?"

If everything looks like your ass, it's more than good. "Yep. Just checking the temperature. Outside."

Not in my body. That temp would fry a thermometer.

He followed her to the kitchen.

"Chicken tonight. I'll make some mashed potatoes and salad with it. Sound good?"

"Oh, yeah."

The drill he'd abandoned earlier in the day remained on the floor where he'd left it and he squatted to retrieve it. "How'd the rest of your day go?"

It sucked.

She set a tomato on the carving board and sawed through it. When the thing disintegrated into a squishy mess, she decided to move on to the cucumbers until she could control herself and not destroy the last-standing tomato. "My day was...odd."

One perfect cucumber slice. Very good.

Jack marked a spot on the top inside of the doorframe. Obviously, he knew what he was doing. Handy around the house. A plus for a growing list of pluses.

"Odd how?" he asked.

Another perfect slice. Excellent control. "I went back to the office and discovered my password for the distribution system still didn't work."

"You said it worked this morning."

"At 7:00 a.m. it worked. Not at 11:30. I called IT and they told me my access had been changed."

He finally looked at her. "Really."

"Yep. I went to my boss and he said the company is realigning who sees what. I still have access, but only to certain things. I was told not to worry about it and that he would funnel any important reports via email. Oh, and I get to work with his assistant." She waved the knife. "His *assistant*. I know we're experiencing turmoil right now with Greg's loss, but how they expect me to keep track of all the deliveries without having access to the system, I have no idea. And what if there's a problem with a shipment? I have to run to Ned every time I have a question."

Jack picked up the drill, gave the trigger a test squeeze and the motorized sound filled the kitchen. He let go of the trigger. "That's dumb."

Another cucumber slice. This one extremely less than perfect.

"During the same conversation, I was told the company is also asking all employees to sign confidentiality agreements."

With that, Jack abandoned the drill and walked to where she stood at the counter. Another slice. *Smack.* Dead cucumber. One for the garbage. Fearing for the safety of the remaining vegetables, she set the knife down. "I'm killing this food."

The crushed tomato she'd set aside drew his attention and he scrunched his nose at it. "Have you been asked to sign anything before?"

"No. I told him I'd look at it and get it back to him. I'm not signing anything until a lawyer okays it."

"We have a corporate attorney on staff. Give me a copy of the agreement and I'll have him look at."

Superhero. "I'll pay for his time. I just don't know any lawyers."

He waved the suggestion away. "No big deal. Did you read it? Is anything jumping out at you?"

"Besides the whole thing?"

He rolled his eyes. "Yes, besides the whole thing."

"Sorry. I'm irritated. I read it, but it's legal speak. The gist is, I'm not to discuss anything—there's a specific list in the document—regarding company business with anyone. So, if I sign this thing, the conversation we're having right now could get me in trouble. I mean, what is *that* about?"

"Was everyone asked to sign this agreement?"

"Yes. Ned called a meeting and told everyone they'd receive a copy. I didn't want to make a stink so I didn't talk to anyone about it. That place is a gossip mill. If I ask someone, before I know it, I could be labeled a troublemaker. I'd rather play it safe and wait for someone to come to me."

"Not a bad plan."

"I can't help thinking I did something wrong."

Jack whistled. "And they call me King of the Paranoids. You said everyone has to sign the agreement. What about the restricted access? Is that everyone?"

"Ned wasn't specific about who'd be affected, but, yes, there were others."

"I wouldn't worry about it, then. Trust me, I've worked in politics. Crazy shit happens in the workplace and there's no explaining it."

She supposed that was true. He definitely had more experience in this area. She went back to assembling the salad. "I guess for tonight, you install that bolt, we have dinner and I get to pretend I haven't been through a meat grinder these past few days."

5

THE GRINDING OF JILLIAN CONTINUED THE FOLLOWING morning. By 10:00 a.m., she was half out of her mind. She'd been sitting at her desk since eight and literally had nothing to do.

Not. One. Thing.

If she couldn't get into the database, she couldn't work on her month-end report for Ned. Nor could she check the delivery schedule for the day or do the myriad of other things that required her to log into the system.

How was she supposed to do her job under these conditions? With her luck, she'd get in trouble for lack of performance and wind up losing a position that could fast-track her career. Then there was the importance of health insurance and paying the mortgage. With the economy being what it was, she couldn't be out of work.

She glanced at her laptop as the rainbow screen saver swirled. What could be going on in the database that she wasn't permitted to see?

For kicks, she'd try getting into the system again. Couldn't hurt. Maybe Ned had changed his mind about revoking her access. She clicked on the icon and punched in her password.

ACCESS DENIED.

So much for Ned changing his mind. Not that it would deter her. She'd visit Mary and see if she could pull a report for her. Maybe the phantom delivery from Friday night would finally be logged into the database.

She wandered the long corridor lining the epicenter of the warehouse. A truck was being loaded and, once again, because she couldn't get an updated report, she had no idea where that truck would be headed.

Well, she'd remedy that. She found Mary sitting at her desk.

The no-nonsense secretary looked up from the note she was jotting. "Hi, Jillian. Ned is at a meeting."

Even better. "Actually, it's you I need."

She set her pen down precisely at the top of her blotter. "Of course. How can I help you?"

"I can't print the latest distribution report. The one I have is from Friday. Would you mind pulling up the report for me?"

Mary spun sideways to her keyboard. "Certainly. I'll print it for you."

Perfect. By the time Jillian had gotten around the desk, Mary had already started typing her password. Out of the corner of her eye, she caught the last two digits. The letter *A* and a capital *Y*.

Quickly, she averted her gaze. Being locked out of the system was not productive, but snooping over Mary's shoulder wasn't the answer.

"Here it is," Mary said. "Do you want to look at it or just have me print you a copy?"

"It would be great if you could sort it by date and print it.

I can get what I need from the report."

"Sure thing." Anticipating the printer spitting out the report, Mary set her hand on it. "Ned mentioned you took a photography class the other day. Was it fun? My husband is an amateur photographer."

Jillian thought back to Saturday and the time spent with her beloved camera. "It was amazing. A long day, but one of those once-in-a-lifetime experiences. The instructor has one scheduled for the Colorado Rockies next year. I put myself on the waiting list."

If she got into the class, she didn't know how she'd pay for it, but she'd make it happen.

"Good for you." Mary handed over the report. "Here you go."

"Thank you. I appreciate it."

On her way back to her office, Jillian stopped in the kitchen to grab a pop and found Debbie, one of the HR assistants, pouring coffee. Debbie had been the first person Jillian had met when she interviewed with Stennar Pharm and, although they couldn't be considered close friends, they occasionally grabbed lunch and chatted about the mundane trappings of life.

"Hey, Jillian. I was wondering where you've been. I stopped by your office yesterday, but you were out."

"I had to deal with something at the house."

"Is everything okay?"

"Just an installer. Did you need something from me?"

Debbie dumped sugar into her cup and stirred. "Nope. Just thought we could have lunch one day this week. The weather has been so nice. It'd be good to get out some."

Given the current goings-on, it couldn't hurt to make nice with HR. "I'd like that. I'll email you and we'll set it up."

Minutes later, behind the closed door of her office,

Jillian scanned the first column of the report, her gaze traveling down the list. *Wednesday, Thursday, Friday.*

Friday.

She grabbed a ruler, lined it up on the spreadsheet so she could check the Friday deliveries one by one. Two asthma drug deliveries. Those she recognized. One was a high-blood-pressure medication they didn't do much of. The last two deliveries of the day were for an anesthetic and Baxtin, a blood thinner that had grown significantly in sales over the past year. She checked the times for both deliveries. The anesthetic came in at 4:30 p.m. That was the one the warehouse crew had been unloading when she'd left on Friday.

Which meant the Baxtin came in after she'd left for the day. That delivery had not been on her earlier report, but here it was. *Delivery time: 11:10 p.m.*

She pushed back from the desk and tapped her foot. The phantom delivery wasn't so phantom after all.

JILLIAN HAD JUST WALKED IN HER DOOR AND DUMPED HER briefcase on the kitchen chair when the doorbell rang. She glanced at the clock. 6:15. Probably Jack. He'd called an hour ago and said he'd be by in, yes, an hour, and here he was. One thing she could appreciate about this man was his courteous nature when it came to being prompt.

She strode to the front window and, just to be safe, peeped out the curtain. Jack stood on her porch with a brown paper bag that she assumed was the takeout Chinese he'd mentioned.

As expected, the little explosion in her chest happened. She stepped back from the window. *He's a recovering addict.* Her reminder to herself seemed to be happening with greater frequency in the last couple of days, but her hormones didn't necessarily care. They couldn't give a lick about what her brain thought. They were only interested in what her body thought, and her body thought quite a lot of Jack.

She swung the door open and he stepped through. He wore gray dress slacks and a white Oxford. No tie. He'd mentioned he rather enjoyed the no-tie look after working at State where his boss insisted on a suit and tie each day. Along with the outfit came his typical brooding look.

Jillian held up her hand. "Wait. Step back."

He drew his eyebrows together. "Huh?"

"Out the door."

Turning, he did as she asked but stopped on the outside landing. "What?"

"Okay," she said. "Now, slap a smile on and let's try this again. The world is a better place when you smile. Right now, I'd like my world to be a better place, so give me a little."

He didn't just smile, he *laughed.* One of those rich belly laughs that caused an entire room to let loose. Her hormones were no exception.

Why do I like this guy so much?

She grasped his elbow and pulled him into the house. "See? I feel better already. That wasn't so hard, was it?"

Before she knew it, he'd dropped the food and the bag toppled and crackled against the hardwood.

"Yow," she said.

She bent to pick up the bag, but he placed a hand on her shoulder to stop her. Slowly, he backed her against the wall, his gaze focused on her mouth. Oh, boy, he was coming closer and—*whammo*—he kissed her. She discovered his lips were great at things other than smiling.

His kiss was warm and gentle, but with a hint of fierceness that left her more than gooey. Particularly when his tongue slid along her bottom lip. For half a second—maybe a quarter—she contemplated easing away from him. Her brain begged for it, pleaded for it really. What her brain understood that her body didn't was that kissing Jack just might be deadly.

Before her impending death, she decided getting naked —fast—would be a good idea.

Emotional homicide. *Call 9-1-1.*

Suddenly, he stepped back. Not just one step, but three or four. What was that about? He gets the horse saddled up and then runs from the barn?

He rubbed his hand over his face. "I'm sorry."

She straightened. "Um, you may have noticed, I didn't mind." To this, he smiled. "Be careful, Jack, that's twice you've smiled in the last five minutes."

"Could be dangerous."

She raised her eyebrows at the challenge. "Could be a lot of things."

"I have eight days left."

Of all the rejections she'd received in her life, what day it was had never been mentioned. The memory of him faced off with his calendar flooded her mind. *The red X's.* She scrunched her nose. "I don't understand."

"In eight days, it'll be one year I'm in recovery. One year of...uh...*solitude.*"

And, oh my, her trips to Al-Anon taught her this lesson. The first year had to be about healing himself first and then his relationships. "People in recovery shouldn't start new relationships during the first year."

He nodded. "It depends on the person, but it's not advisable."

"So, that's why for three months you've been sending me mixed signals?"

He winced. "Ouch. Sorry."

"No apology necessary. At least I know I'm not insane." She waggled her finger. "You had me going there."

He pounded his fists against his head. "I lost it a little bit with that kiss, but damn, the whole thing at the front door was a rip and—*boom*—I needed to have at you. For the record, I'd like to do more of that. I want to. Badly. *Very badly.*"

She held her hand up. "Stop talking. I get it." *More than you know.* "You have a plan. You've said you like plans. Eight days and you hit the one-year mark."

He had no idea how much she understood. And appreciated it. Her father had never once hit three hundred sixty-five days of sobriety.

This is a good man. A man who kept his word. Or at least tried to. All the reasons she should run from him faded. No, they didn't just fade, they dropped off her emotional survival list like bricks from a tall building.

But she had to be smart about this. Had to take it slow and give her mind time to absorb what her body so desperately wanted. She breathed in and stooped to pick up the bag still on the floor. "I love Chinese food. Apparently, you're on a mission to steal my heart."

"I took a shot."

"Bull's-eye."

He touched her arm. "Thank you. For understanding. In eight days, I'll be all over you. I swear."

She bumped him with her elbow. "I will eagerly await the swarm."

Ach. Sometimes her quick wit, usually such a source of pride, got her in trouble. She wanted to believe it was a slip

of the tongue, a *Freudian* slip even, but somehow, she knew
her resolve when it came to Jack was weakening. Even if she
couldn't quite grasp the logic of eight more days making a
difference, she admired his steadfast dedication to reaching
his one-year goal. Eight days wouldn't be a horrible thing
for her either. It would give her time to contemplate aban-
doning her rule about getting involved with an addict. Never
would she have imagined that. Never.

She pointed to the kitchen. "Let's eat. If my mouth can't
be busy doing other things—kissing you for instance—it
might as well eat."

He fell in step behind her. "How was your day?"

"Fine. I think. The phantom delivery showed up on the
distribution report."

Jack stopped at the doorway. "That's good, right?"

"Yep."

At the counter, she unloaded the bag and the aroma of
mixed spices made her stomach rumble.

Jack grabbed a container, opened the lid and started on
the next while she assembled the necessary silverware. The
two of them worked in tandem, making all this domesticity
seem easy. Or maybe comfortable was the right word. All
she knew was she liked it. A major change from the quiet
life she'd built for herself.

"How was your boss to you?" Jack asked. "Normal?"

"He's fine. I've barely seen him. His assistant has been
quite chatty. I see her all the time now."

Jillian transferred everything into large, colorful bowls.
When she was a kid, her mother had worked nights. On the
nights she didn't work, they'd often made meals together.
But on the evenings her mother was gone, with her father's
issues, Jillian had often been left to fend for herself with
either microwave meals or takeout. All those meals were

eaten straight from the containers. A trend that ended when Jillian moved out on her own and took control of her life. Now, she simply refused to have paper products on her table. Home and security meant sturdy plates and bowls that wouldn't shatter with a bump or nick.

Jack carried two of those sturdy bowls to the table and came back for the remaining ones. "I like these. Nice touch."

He noticed. "Thank you. I think so too."

"What do you mean about the assistant being chatty?"

"Every time I need something, I have to ask Mary. I guess we're BFFs now, because she asked me about the class I took on Saturday. She said Ned mentioned it."

She stopped, focused on the bowl in front of her. *Hang on.*

Jack took the bowl. "What?"

"I don't know that I mentioned the class to Ned."

"Yeah, but you said you told the guy from the warehouse the other night. He probably told Ned."

She shrugged. "I suppose. My paranoia continues. Speaking of which, I have a question about the alarm." She pointed to the keypad by the slider. "The two buttons on the end are the panic buttons, right?"

"Yes. Press both keys and hold for five seconds."

"And what about the glass-break sensors. How sensitive are they?"

He picked up the decorative vase, the one with the bright colors that added a festive touch for people entering through the back door. These days, the only people coming through her back door were burglars who wanted to terrorize her, but hey, they'd get a colorful greeting.

Jack held the vase up. "If this falls, the alarm will go off. As long as the alarm is on, any breaking glass will set it off." He studied the scrollwork on the vase. "This is a nice piece. My mom likes stuff like this."

He flipped it over to check the name on the bottom and his eyebrows shot up.

"It's just a cheap thing I bought at the consignment shop. I thought it was pretty."

He glanced at her, back to the bottom of the vase, then around the kitchen, his gaze furiously darting in all directions.

"What?" she asked.

He set the vase down and held his fingers to his lips before tearing off to the living room. What the hell was he doing? Aside from acting like a ninja assassin. She followed him and, once again, he turned to her and held his finger to his lips.

Yeah, I've got it. No talking.

Gently, he ran his fingers along the white trim around the windows and doorways, then dropped to his knees and looked under the furniture. What was he looking for? A minute later, he lifted his head and pointed at the lamp on the table. The one with the hollow base. He unplugged it, took the shade off and began dismantling the part that held the lightbulb. With the lamp in two pieces, he ran his finger along the inside of the base. His hand stilled.

"Shit," he mouthed.

She moved toward him. "What?"

He pointed inside the lamp where a tiny black device— an ear bud maybe?—sat. She stared at it a moment. What the heck was it?

Setting the lamp down, Jack waved for her to follow him

back to the kitchen but didn't stop there. He went out the sliding glass door to the yard. When she joined him on the patio, he slid the door closed, grabbed her by the sleeve and led her to the farthest corner of the lawn.

"You're not paranoid," he said. "That was a bug. Someone's listening."

6

JILLIAN STARED UP AT LYNX WITH THOSE BIG BROWN EYES THAT reminded him he'd been without companionship for almost a year. He'd love to look into her eyes every morning and that, for various reasons, scared the hell out of him.

She tugged her sweater around her to block the cold air. "Someone is spying on me?"

Sugarcoating it wouldn't help. Besides, she didn't seem the type that needed coddling. "Yes. Based on what's gone on with you this weekend, and then the nonsense at work, you must have seen or heard something you shouldn't have."

She held her hands out. "The only odd thing, aside from the systems lockdown, was the weird delivery the other night. But that's been resolved. I saw it myself on the spreadsheet Mary gave me."

"Yeah, but it happened right before your house got broken into."

Pausing for a second, she squinted. "Right after that, I was locked out of the system and asked to sign a confidentiality agreement."

Two paranoid people could be quite the conspiracy theorists. He might be in love.

"No," she said. "That can't be."

"We need to figure out what that shipment was."

What the hell was he doing inserting himself into this? The year of no was an epic failure. His counselors all warned him about taking on everyone's problems. When his life became a mass of people dumping their shit on him, he'd be overwhelmed by the weight of it all. That excess weight was a free ticket to the numbing bliss found in a bottle of pills.

If he helped Jillian, who else would he help? Then who else after that? Worse, he was *attracted* to Jillian. So, A) she needed his help and B) he hadn't gotten laid in almost a year and wanted nothing more than to pound himself into her body.

The odds of him getting through this shit storm without relapsing were not good.

"It was Baxtin," she said. "A blood thinner."

He focused on her moving mouth. Great lips. A little crooked and full. *The year of no.* "Did you see the actual boxes?"

"I didn't. If the shipment is still in the warehouse tomorrow, I can check the paperwork that's with it." She dug her fingers into her hair and tugged. "What do I do about these listening devices? For God's sake! They're spying on me."

"You ignore them."

"*What?*"

"You have to. If we pull them, they'll know you discovered them."

"Yes. Then I can talk to Ned and figure out what the hell is going on."

Rather than tell her she was nuts, he considered it a

moment. "You don't wanna do that. If they've gone to the trouble to plant bugs, they're not just curious about what you do at night. They're scared."

She smacked her hands over her face.

Terrifying her may not have been his smartest move. He grabbed her arm and pulled her close so he could slide an arm around her. "Sorry. Sometimes I forget I'm not dealing with hardened politicians or mouthy spec ops guys."

She rested her head against his chest and he quietly inhaled her lavender scent while fighting to control his raging body. The one that had been without a woman over a year.

"All I wanted was a good job and to take care of myself. I'm twenty-seven years old and building a great career. What have I gotten into?"

He shook his head. Maybe to answer her question, maybe to clear it. He couldn't know. Not with his erection about to announce itself to Jillian's lower region. *Ignore it.* Right. "I don't know. But I'll help you figure it out. Okay?"

And maybe, while he was ignoring his hard-on, he'd disregard the fact that he had nine years on her. *Twenty-seven.* The old-man jokes would be in full swing at the office. Might be fun, though.

She snuggled in closer and the sex-starved man inside him snapped. *Time for action.* He nodded. Complete agreement on that one. No doubt. Except, it wasn't time yet. He had eight more days before the horny bastard could run amok.

Jillian glanced up. "Okay."

At this, he had to laugh.

"What's funny?"

"The horny bastard inside me is reminding me I haven't

gotten laid and...well...you're standing close. And you smell good."

Most women would take the hint and step away. Or maybe smack him. Most women. This one? She stood there. Completely *not* moving. The hole inside him filled. All that emptiness that had kept him focused and alone and craving female company disappeared, and he wasn't sure what the hell to do about it.

He cleared his throat. "Here's what we'll do. We'll go inside and have dinner. We have to eat that food or whoever is listening will know something is up. We'll talk like nothing happened. They know you've told me about the confidentiality agreement, so maybe we'll continue that conversation. It's out there. We have to give them enough to make them think we haven't found the bugs. After dinner, I'll search the rest of the house. Tomorrow, you go into work like it's any other day. Just act normal. Don't talk to anyone about the bugs. Let them think you don't know."

"I don't know if I can do that."

He shrugged. "What choice do you have?"

"I can call the police."

"And tell them what? That you saw a weird delivery the other night, at a place that gets deliveries every day, and now your house is bugged? You can't prove who bugged the house. As it pertains to Stennar Pharm, there's no probable cause for a search warrant. At the very least, you calling the cops will get back to your employer. If they are guilty of something, you'll lose your job—or worse—because you brought heat to them."

She took a second to absorb what he'd said. He was being a prick. Not exactly what he wanted, but she needed to hear it. Sometimes cops brought more trouble and he knew for damn sure she wasn't ready for that. "I'm sorry. We don't know what we're dealing with yet. Let's find something to bring to the cops."

"I see your point. It stinks, but I get it."

"It's one of those shitty things in life. No way to win."

She stepped toward the house, but stopped, then turned back to him. "Unless we find the evidence."

JILLIAN MARCHED INTO HER OFFICE, SMACKED THE LIGHT ON and checked the digital clock on her desk. 8:15. She was early. Just as planned. No sense letting anyone think she was on to their dirty, scheming ways.

The day ahead would be beyond emotionally draining. How was she supposed to pretend she didn't know her employer had bugged her home?

Assuming it was them. But who else could it be?

Three bugs. That's how many they'd found. Well, Jack found them. She'd sort of wandered behind him in a state of numb shock that left her screaming inside her head. No listening devices were found on the second floor. Her guess was the intruder she'd found on her stairs had been placing them and hadn't yet gotten there.

Her shoulder twitched and she rolled it. All night she'd been up. Even with the alarm set, she'd barely managed an hour of sleep. Jack had offered to let her stay with him, but she didn't think it a wise move.

On several fronts.

Aside from the possibly cataclysmic sexual attraction they shared, she was a homebody. Whoever was listening probably knew that. Breaking her pattern would only compromise her more.

Yet she still had no idea what it was she'd landed in.

Something big or they wouldn't be breaking laws to find out what she knew. Which would be exactly zippo.

Today's goal was to somehow get around the thick plastic strap on the totes from the phantom delivery and see what was inside. Maybe it wasn't the drug stated on the tote? Perhaps not a drug at all.

Ned swung around the doorframe and into her office. "Morning."

She took in his golf shirt and navy Dockers. They were a casual workplace, but the executives were more often in dress clothes. Other than his mode of dress, nothing about his demeanor was off. Utterly confounding. If he were involved in the bugging of her house, wouldn't there be some kind of tell? Some subtle change in his behavior? Anything?

Or did the lack of a tell mean Ned wasn't involved? That he knew nothing about this? She simply didn't know.

She slid her bottom desk drawer open, shoved her purse in and plastered on a smile. "Good morning. Did you need something?"

He leaned against the doorframe, settled in for a chat. "Nothing urgent. Wanted to let you know you're getting new digs."

"I'm sorry?"

"We're giving you a bigger office."

More changes. "I don't understand."

"I know it's a surprise. Ted Ingrams will be working out of this location until we fill Greg's spot. Ted's secretary needs a desk. Since this office is next to Greg's old one, we have to move you upstairs. It'll be better. Your new office is bigger and will give you enough room for a couple of filing cabinets and guest chairs. You won't be so crammed in."

The second floor? The only thing up there was storage. Sure there were offices, but no people.

"Wow," she said. "So many changes around here."

"Change is good. The guys will be here this morning to move your stuff. Get packed up."

Panic fired and her legs twitched. Why were they in such a hurry? "Which office am I going to?"

"The one on the east corner of the building. Not a great view, but it's the biggest office up there. Eventually we'll move some others, but you'll have gotten to the best office first."

She attempted a smile but wasn't sure it worked. Her body was suddenly leaden. "Thank you for the bigger office. Who else will be moving?"

"We're still working out the list. Maybe a couple new hires."

Hardly an answer to her question. Realistically, she didn't need an answer. If they wanted to get an employee out of the way, to isolate them, the best way to do that, short of firing her, would be to move her to the absolute farthest office from any activity.

He boosted off the doorframe and smacked his hand against it. "Congrats on the new office. I'll see you at ten for the staff meeting."

Jillian stared at the space Ned had vacated. In the span of two minutes, during a simple conversation with her boss, all the words he didn't say reached her.

They wanted her out of the way.

BARELY SHY OF NOON, LYNX SAT AT HIS DESK SCROLLING through his phone contacts when Vic strode into the office. Recently, Vic had spent most of his time overseeing the progress on Taylor Security's training center an hour outside of Chicago. The training center was his baby and his daily focus, despite the grind of newborn twins at home, had been bringing his dream to fruition. Given his experience in black ops, he wanted the center to be a place where operatives could practice or learn new skills once they left the military.

"I'm grabbing some chow," he said. "You coming?"

"No. Thanks."

"Why?"

Only Vic would ask why rather than just take no for an answer. "I'm hitting a meeting."

"Again? You just went to a meeting yesterday."

Was he his wife now? "Listen, sweetheart, don't nag me. I'm going to a meeting." Lynx went back to scrolling. People without addiction issues didn't always understand. Even if he'd just been to a meeting, it didn't mean he wouldn't need another.

"Why?"

Lynx tossed his phone on the desk. "Because you're making me nuts, that's why. Because of you, I'm about to dive into a bottle of Vicodin. Happy?"

A smile spread across Vic's face. He found this amusing. Of course he did. "Take it easy. It was an observation. Two meetings in two days is outside your routine. And you, my friend, like routine."

True dat. Before Sunday morning, he'd been obsessed with his finely crafted schedule. Now, with Jillian and the crazy shit surrounding her, his paranoia about relapsing ran hot and deep and he wanted the insurance of an extra meeting. Plus, he'd kissed her last night. And what a risk that was considering his looming one-year mark.

Seven more days.

The only way he knew how to deal with the change in his environment would be to attend meetings and be around people on the same journey. So, yeah, he was going to a meeting today.

He picked up his phone again and starting scrolling.

"What's up with the phone? You're like a mad scientist."

"I'm figuring out who I know on the Oversight and Government Reform committee."

Vic raised his eyebrows. "What the hell for?"

Now he's curious. The not so subtle hints for Vic to leave, to vamoose, to *vacate* were a bust. "I'm helping Jillian on something."

"The redhead?"

Her hair wasn't red. Not totally. Sort of auburn. Except when sunlight hit it. Then it looked red. Indoors, more brownish red. "Yes. She works for a drug distributor. Something is going on there. Don't ask what because I don't know. All I know is she saw an after-hours delivery Friday night, her house was broken into on Saturday and now the company has locked her out of their database."

Vic whistled. "Crazy-assed few days."

"Now I'm gonna see if the company is on a watch list somewhere. Or being investigated by Oversight."

"That shouldn't be too hard for you, Boy Scout."

Years as an aide to the secretary of state came in handy at times. The idealist in Lynx had loved that job. Dealing with high-powered politicians, believing that, regardless of the political maneuvering and bullshit, on some level, he was contributing to making this great country better. That gave him a rush.

Until the lines blurred and the job started to define him. Night and day he'd been on call. The stress was constant. And draining. The first four years he'd thrived on it. Everything was looking good. His successful, beautiful lobbyist girlfriend had moved in with him and together, they'd reach all their goals. Professionally and personally. A D.C. power couple.

Then he'd ripped his knee apart in a pickup basketball game and his world went with it. The surgery sucked and rehab sucked and the pain in his knee sucked, so he'd pop another pill. Why not? When he took a pill, he stayed numb to the pain and Julia's frustration over his mood swings. At work, if the stress ramped up, eh, he popped a pill.

"If I find the right guy on Oversight, I can do this quietly. Could be nothing." He scrolled past a name. *There it is.* "Watkins. He's the one."

"You trust him?"

"I don't trust any politician. This guy, though, he always seemed straight up. I'll keep it light. See if he knows anything about Stennar Pharm."

"What if he does?"

"Then you can finally stop calling me King of the Paranoids, because my paranoia will have turned out to be warranted." The phone in his hand rang and he checked the ID. Jillian. "I gotta take this. Beat it."

"You don't have to be an asshole about it."

"Yeah, I do. I've been trying to get you out of here for five minutes. Now leave." He hit the button before it went to voice mail. "Hang on," he said into the phone. When Vic didn't budge, Lynx rose from his chair, walked to his much larger friend and shoved him out the door. "Nice talking to you."

Then he shut the door with Vic still standing in front of it. Just in case, he flipped the lock.

"Hey. Sorry about that. Vic was being his usual self."

"Hi," Jillian said in a rush. "Can you meet me for lunch?"

Not when he needed a meeting because his horny self was contemplating breaking his celibacy. "Uh..."

"If you're busy, it's okay."

But something in her tone—that tight, stressed-out resonance—told him differently. "Something wrong?"

"Outside of the fact that I'm calling you from the ladies' room because I'm afraid my boss is spying on me and I just moved into my new office? The office where not one other person will be joining me."

"Come again?"

"Ned came by this morning and congratulated me because I was getting a bigger office. They've moved me to the second floor. Where there is nothing but storage. They're freezing me out."

Lynx strode through the door at the Seville Restaurant, one of those ancient diner-type places in Fuller Park with a twenty-page menu and portion sizes that would keep fad diet companies in business for decades.

He surveyed the half-filled room until he found Jillian near the floor-to-ceiling windows lining the facade. She looked up from her menu and waved, but her face remained...frigid. This woman could never hide her moods. For months he'd watched her swing into yoga class with her glowing cheeks bunched into a smile. Today, she sat in that red vinyl booth with skin the color of ashes.

In the days since she'd come to him with her security issue, she'd been robbed of not only her sense of safety, but that energetic, happy quality that was so much a part of her.

That alone pissed him off.

He slid into the booth. "You okay?"

"I had to get out for an hour. Suddenly you've become

the voice of reason. Stinks for you and I'm sorry, but right now, I need every ounce of reason I can find."

A waitress came by, took their drink order and was off again.

"What happened?"

"Ned said the owner of the company will be working out of our building until they hire Greg's—the guy who died—replacement. His secretary needs a desk and my office is next to Greg's old one. They've moved me to an area of the building where I'll be alone. Completely alone. As in, no other people. Anyone could march up there and I wouldn't know it. If I screamed, they wouldn't hear me. I keep thinking that. No one would hear me. It's like some kind of corporate terrorism."

Lynx sat back in the booth and folded his arms. "That's exactly what it is. You need to start keeping notes. Them wanting you to sign that agreement, the limited access—start writing it all down. "

"Why?"

"Because even if they're not doing anything illegal, you might have grounds to sue their asses for constructive dismissal. They're bent on making you miserable so you'll resign."

She shook her head. "I don't want to sue them. I want to do my job. That's all I've ever wanted."

Lynx studied her. Stalling and hoping he, by some miracle, developed an idea that might help. Nothing. Screw it. "Are there any entrances leading directly to the second floor?"

"No. But the stairwell is just inside the warehouse door. And in that neighborhood? With all the drug dealers? Anyone could wander up there."

"Tell your boss you have concerns about the security. I'm

curious what he'll say. Don't be surprised if you get a call from HR."

"If they think I'll let them pick on me, they're wrong. This is crap. I don't know what they're up to, but I'm gonna find out."

The waitress cruised by, set their drinks down, grabbed her notepad and pen out of her apron and took their order. Lynx waited for her to scamper off. "I'm working my contacts in Washington to see what I can dig up. I know a senator on the Oversight and Government Reform committee."

"You know a senator?"

He smiled. "My years at State garnered a nice contact list."

"That cape of yours is something else."

"Not really. I know how D.C. works. I'm good at politics. People, a lot of them, owe me favors and I have no problem cashing in."

She grabbed his wrist and squeezed. "I knew I liked you."

That wrist squeeze? Not a bad thing. At least the horny bastard inside him didn't think so. "It's a long shot, but if Stennar Pharm is being investigated, it's probably happening via Oversight."

She pulled her hand back and he was instantly crushed.

"I haven't heard about anything hinky," she said. "Plus, I checked the company out before applying there. From what I'd heard, there have never been any infractions."

"Doesn't mean anything. They might be on the government's radar for price fixing or off-label marketing."

Jillian made a *pffting* noise. "Please. Off-label marketing is common practice. It's just a matter of whether they get caught. And the drug companies would rather pay the fine than stop selling off-label. The fine is cheaper than giving up the revenue."

This, Lynx knew, was true. He'd experienced it right after his surgery when the doc prescribed him an antide-pressant for his pain. The drug wasn't FDA approved for treating pain, but doctors are free to prescribe it if, in their professional opinion, it's a viable alternative. Where the manufacturers got into trouble was when they actually directed their sales team to market drugs for purposes that hadn't been approved.

He shrugged. "I'm looking into it."

In fact, he'd have Janet check with her IRS sources about the company's finances. If Stennar wanted to start a reign of terror, he'd give them his own special brand of it.

Jillian stared down at the table and tapped three fingers against her glass. "I'll be interested to hear what your friend says. I left a decent job to work for these people. I wanted to grow. To make the leap into management."

Beating herself up over it wouldn't help. He knew that firsthand, but the do-gooder in him understood her penchant for it. "We'll find out. Go back to work and talk to your boss. I'll wait for the call from my guy and we'll compare notes tonight."

Except, he needed a meeting. The one he wanted to attend at lunch. He pulled his phone, checked his calendar for all the local meeting times. There was one in the Loop at six. "Can we meet about eightish? My place. We can't talk at yours."

"Sure. Will you have eaten?"

"I'll grab something."

"No. I'll put something together. Least I can do."

He grinned. "You're on. You keep feeding me homemade meals and you may never get rid of me."

. . .

JILLIAN STARED AT HER DESK PHONE IN A DESPERATE telepathic attempt to make the blasted thing ring. Not only had she been banished to the second floor, the phone hadn't rung all afternoon. Typically she needed to forward all calls to voice mail in order to get her work done. Today? Nothing.

She lifted the handset and checked the dial tone. Still there. They hadn't cut off her phone service. She checked the clock on the phone's display. 2:15. Not one call since she'd returned from lunch.

Time for an efficiency test. She snatched her cell phone from her purse in the bottom drawer and walked to the ladies' room. She'd be damned if she'd speak freely in her office after finding listening devices in her home. The ladies' room was probably safe. Probably.

The no-nonsense secretary at Taylor Security answered and put her on hold. A minute later the hold music—a nice jazzy number—disappeared.

"Hi," Jack said.

"I need you to do a test for me."

"*O*-kay."

"By the way, hi, how are you?"

"Jillian, it's okay. You're obviously on a mission here. What do you need?"

How she loved low-maintenance men. Made life so much easier. "Dial my office number. Please."

"Why?"

"My phone has been oddly silent. Usually I get calls all day. I think they're screwing with me again. And, in case you're wondering, I'm aware of how delusional I sound."

"Vic calls me King of the Paranoids. You got nothing. I'll call you."

"Thank you."

She charged back to her office and waited. Thirty seconds passed. Nothing. Maybe he'd gotten another call. She'd wait. Jeopardy's theme song floated in her brain. "An insanely paranoid distribution manager," she muttered to herself. "Who is Jillian Murdoch?"

Her cell phone rang. Jack calling back. "Hi."

"They're routing your calls through Mary. She just gave me the third degree, then told me you were away from your desk and took a message."

Sneaky schmucks. Why were they doing this to her? She rested her head against her free hand. The weight of it equaled a cement block. So freaking exhausted. "I guess I'm not delusional."

"Not by a long shot. What do you wanna do?"

Part of her wanted to simply walk away and forget about Stennar Pharm. It might even be the smart thing. The safe thing.

She couldn't do that, though. Not if it meant running in fear from the fight. Fear, she'd learned long ago, could hold a person captive. Besides, she'd never been good caged.

First thing she would do is log this episode in her diary of suspected corporate terrorism.

She cracked her neck and stood. No cowering. Not today. "I'm going to poke the tiger."

"Jillian—"

"It's nothing crazy. I'll play dumb and ask them to check my phone. I want them to know I'm suspicious."

Silence. The superhero didn't like her idea. Too bad. "How will that help?"

"They'll know I'm not crawling into a corner whimpering."

"Wait. Please. I have a call in to Senator Watkins. I

should have something by end of day. Then we can make a plan."

Sometimes plans were overrated. It would be good to know if the government was keeping an eye on Stennar Pharm. Still, she didn't want to wait. She was done with not fighting back. "I'll be careful."

Mostly.

After hanging up with Jack, she unplugged her phone from the wall and walked down to the first floor. She passed the loading dock. A truck was being unloaded. If she had access to the system, she'd know what shipment that was.

Schmucks.

She entered Ned's outer office. Mary sat at her desk sorting the day's mail. "Good afternoon, Jillian." The secretary gestured to her hand. "Is that your phone?"

Nothing like an imaginary broken phone to open a dialogue. She set the phone on Mary's desk next to one of the mail piles. "I think there's something wrong with it. It hasn't rung all afternoon."

Mary didn't flinch. Not even a blink. "I don't understand."

"Me neither. It worked fine yesterday and I can make calls out, but I haven't received one call all afternoon, which is *highly* unusual."

For a brief moment, Mary simply stared at her. Jillian knew the feeling. Standing on the edge of knowing something, but not really knowing anything at all. At least she wasn't the only one.

"I suppose I could put a help ticket in for you."

Yes, and I could steal the remainder of your password.

Interesting what a difference one day could make. Yesterday, Jillian stood in this same office feeling guilt over peeking at Mary's password. Now? Forget it. No guilt. These people had invaded her privacy and made her feel unwelcome after she'd done nothing but work her ass off.

They started it.

Determined not to miss the password again, Jillian scooted around the desk. "That would be great. I can only imagine the calls I'm missing."

Mary cleared her throat. "This is certainly a bizarre problem. We'll get you a new phone right away."

Her fingers flew over the keyboard as she typed in her username. Jillian focused without making it obvious, a challenge on a normal day, never mind when a girl found herself in the middle of corporate espionage. Mary smacked the tab key with her pinky and—*here we go*—A-g-5-z.

A-g-5-z-a-Y.

Got 'em.

Jillian folded her arms and tapped each finger against her biceps as she silently repeated the password. Mary had more clearance than ninety-five percent of the employees, and Jillian now had her password. Access to the distribution system and employee files would be hers, but she'd have to avoid using the password in the office or even at her house. A library maybe. Or a coffee house.

Someplace where she could snoop without getting caught.

7

LYNX STRODE INTO HIS APARTMENT, HIS MIND CENTERED AND the horny bastard living in his body relatively under control. Normally after an evening recovery meeting, he'd go right to the calendar on the kitchen wall and mark a red X for having completed another day.

Except, this day wasn't over. Not nearly. With Jillian showing up in the next fifteen minutes, this might be the hardest part of his day. Horny men should not be allowed to be alone with attractive women. The temptation was too great.

Silently, he recited the Serenity Prayer. He needed to stay on track, to look at his calendar and take pride in the multitude of giant red X's. Soon he'd reach that one-year mark. Goal attained. That's all he wanted.

That, and three days of nonstop sex.

Why stop at three? Six days of nonstop sex. Ten days. Whatever. There'd better be a lot.

He fiddled with the string attached to the red marker hanging from the wall. If he marked the day, maybe it would keep him from doing anything stupid. *Can't change it once it's marked*. No do-overs when a permanent marker was involved.

That would be cheating, though.

His conscience would know what he'd done. He'd have to get through the remainder of the evening and then mark it.

His phone rang and he checked the ID. Watkins calling back. He punched the button. "Senator Watkins, how are you, sir?"

The senator grunted. "Fuck the formality. I got no one at State anymore."

Poor baby. A native New Yorker, Watkins had a knack for pissing people off with his frank summations of everything from school lunches to the death penalty.

"I'm sorry to hear that."

"My ass."

Lynx laughed. "Thanks for returning the call."

"Always, my friend. Always. How've you been? Everything good in Chicago?"

He surveyed the barely furnished apartment. It wasn't what he'd had in D.C., but he had no qualms about it. This was his home now. "Yeah. Everything is good."

And he meant it.

"Excellent. Why are you bothering me?"

"A drug distributor. Heard anything about Stennar Pharm?"

Watkins stayed quiet for a minute. "Not ringing a bell. Why?"

Lynx would have to be careful here. "A friend works there. Wants to make sure it's a place she'd like to stay. Think you can quietly ask around?"

"Sure. I'll see who knows what. Anything else?"

"Your secretary said you're coming to Chicago."

"I am. We'll have lunch."

Lunch with Watkins could only help Taylor Security. "I'm at your disposal, Senator."

"Then find someone at State who loves me."

Lynx smiled. "I'll see what I can do."

The apartment buzzer rang just as he hung up. That would be Jillian. Right on time. He loved punctual people. He hustled to the intercom. "Jillian?"

"It's me," she said.

"Come on up."

From his spot near the door, he hit the button that would unlock the street entrance and let her into the building. The one containing his apartment. Where he lived alone. Where he had yet to get laid. In his new bed.

Okay. Time for a pep talk. He walked back to the kitchen and faced off with the calendar. For added confidence, he crossed his arms. He was the one in control here. "Don't fuck with me on this."

Should it concern him that he was speaking to a calendar?

Most likely, but desperate people did desperate things. Jillian knocked on his door. His lack of sanity would need to be dealt with later. He swung the door open and found Jillian holding an insulated food carrier.

"Oh, hey, let me grab that. Sorry, I would have met you downstairs."

"It's not that heavy."

Still, he took it from her and brought it to the kitchen. "Man, this smells good. What is it?"

"Roast beef and rosemary potatoes. Nothing fancy."

Didn't need to be. Fancy he could get in a restaurant. What he craved was the comfort of home-cooked like his mom always made. Home-cooked, for him, meant family and being settled into a routine all things that balanced him. In the kitchen, he unloaded the roast and potatoes, then grabbed plates from the cabinet.

"Cutting board?" she asked. "I need to slice the meat."

Cutting board. Did he even own one? He pointed to the cabinet next to the oven. "Check there."

She bent over to open the cabinet and Lynx helped himself to a nice long look at her ass. Not his fault if it was right in front of him. Sort of.

"The only thing I see is a questionable-looking cookie sheet."

She turned and busted him staring. All he could do was laugh. "Sorry."

"For the cookie sheet or staring at my ass?"

"Both?"

She rolled her eyes. "Good one. I'll use a plate, but we'll have to do some shopping for you."

They worked in the kitchen together, Jillian slicing and transferring meat to a serving dish while Lynx finished assembling dishes and silverware.

"How'd the rest of your day go?"

"Not bad. I checked on the shipment from the other night and it's gone."

Not surprising. "Do you know where?"

"I do. I had Mary print me the latest distribution report. I also nabbed her password."

"Good work."

"The shipment went to another distributor in Iowa."

Lynx set the silverware down and focused on Jillian. He needed to concentrate. "Another distributor? Is that normal?"

She shrugged. "Sure. They'll just send it on to the client

or maybe even another distributor. Eventually it'll get to its final stop."

"But we don't know where."

"No. I should have checked those totes the other night. That was stupid."

And he thought *he* was hard on himself. She didn't pull punches either. "It wasn't *stupid*. It looked like a normal shipment, right? Nothing tampered with? "

She sliced off a small piece of meat. "No. I checked them. It looked like the original seal." Taking one of the forks he'd set out, she stabbed at the sliver of meat and held it to his mouth. "Taste it."

Hell no. She was not feeding him. For him, there had always been something innately sexual about that. He suddenly had a vision—or twelve—of Jillian stretched on his bed naked and feeding him.

He cut his eyes to the calendar on the wall. *Fucking thing.*

She waved the fork at him. "Open up."

"Tell you what," he said. "I'll let you feed me, but then I get to kiss you."

"Is that supposed to be the rotten end of the deal? Because I'll let you kiss me anyway."

He opened his mouth and she popped the fork in. Damn good—even if he'd barely tasted it before swallowing. More important matters to tend to.

"Did you like it?" she asked.

"Very much."

"You didn't even taste it, did you?"

He smiled. "Not really. I'm thinking ahead."

She tossed the fork into the sink, shoved the meat aside and boosted herself to the counter. "Well, then, bring it on."

He stepped closer, slid between her legs and kissed her. Slowly, her hands moved up his arms to his shoulders and she pulled him tight against her. Months of need tore into him. He deepened the kiss. Nothing too crazy, but enough that she couldn't miss what he wanted.

Eventually.

In seven days.

She ran her tongue along his bottom lip then pulled back. "I like kissing you."

He waggled his eyebrows. "I like kissing you too."

Her gaze wandered to the wall behind him. The calendar with all those red X's. "Today isn't marked off yet."

"Not yet."

She pulled him close and hugged him. He breathed in and out, savoring the contact, and her scent—something flowery today—lingered for a minute before she met his gaze. "I think we should eat so you can mark the day off without any further distractions."

Without a doubt, he could love this woman. Somehow she understood his determination to hit that one-year mark. "Thank you."

She patted his cheek. "It's all good, handsome. Now back up so I can take this food to the table. You grab the plates and tell me how *your* day was?"

"Status quo." He laughed. "Whatever status quo is. One of the guys got shot overseas. Asshole rebels trying to attack an ambassador."

"My God! Is he okay?"

"He's fine. On his way home. I had to juggle the roster and send someone else. It happens, but it throws everything off. I did speak to Senator Watkins. The one from Oversight."

She glanced at him, her eyes wary. "What did he say?"

"He hasn't heard of Stennar Pharm. He's gonna check for me. If there's anything, he'll sniff it out."

"What did you tell him?"

"That a friend worked there and wanted to know if she should stay."

She set the meat and bowl of potatoes on the table then moved them another inch. "That's not a lie."

"I told him what he needed to know."

When she finished arranging the dishes, all two of them, she grabbed the plates and fussed with setting the table. He let her do it. Why not? He missed watching a woman make herself at home in his space. His iPod sat in the dock on the counter. A little music wouldn't hurt. He punched the power button and went to shuffle. Creed blasted into the room. *Whoa.* He left the song but turned it way down.

"Glasses," Jillian said. She went to the kitchen for two glasses and came back. "You're good at figuring out how much people need to know, huh?"

He half smiled. In D.C., knowing how much to tell people was a basic survival technique. Leaking too much information could end a career. Not giving enough could end a career. It was all about balance. "Between my time as an officer in the military and my years at State, yeah, I'm good at it."

"How long were you in the military?"

"I graduated from West Point and went into the army. Did that until I was thirty-two and went to State."

"Did you like the military?"

He shrugged. "I liked the order of it. The discipline. It fits with my personality."

"How did you get to the State Department?"

He thought back on the assignment that, when he'd first gotten it, repelled him. It hadn't escaped him that the secretary of state was female and he had the all-American looks that made a photo op a slam dunk. But good soldiers do what they're told and don't bitch. Whatever the mission, a soldier does it, even if it meant playing babysitter. "The secretary of state visited the base I was stationed at. I was her liaison."

Jillian took one of the napkins, folded it into a triangle, shoved it into one of the glasses and fluffed it. She had to have worked at a restaurant at some point. She repeated the process with the second napkin. "What's with the napkins?"

She stared at them a second, gave one another fluff. "When I was a kid, we never had a fancy table or ate as a family. I like a nice table." More fluffing. "Did the secretary fall for your boyish good looks?"

"That's exactly why they gave me the assignment. Made me nuts."

She reached across the table and squeezed his arm. "I was joking. I'm sorry. Didn't know it was a sensitive spot."

He hesitated. She slid her hand away and he wasn't sure how he felt about that. "It is. Maybe too much so. The rumor at first was that I'd gotten the State job because I was sleeping with the secretary. She warned me that would happen. I didn't care. I wanted the opportunity and dealt with the bullshit. I worked night and day. Whatever time, my phone was always on and I always answered. Always. Even on a stretcher and half whacked out on Vicodin."

He grabbed one of the chairs and pulled it out for Jillian. As soon as her butt landed, she whipped the napkin from the glass. Bizarre. What was the point of the napkin sculpting if she was going to trash it seconds later?

She smoothed the napkin into her lap. "That's not a job you leave at the office."

"Not ever."

"Is that why you left D.C.?"

"Yes and no. I loved the job. There's honor in it. I considered it my way of serving even after I'd left the military. But there are sacrifices."

"Like not having a life?"

He smiled. "Exactly. When I blew out my knee, I was dealing with a crumbling relationship and a high-stress job that afforded me little sleep. I had surgery and recovered fast. Except, I still needed the painkillers. I just wasn't sure what pain I was killing. I needed to get healthy again, physically and emotionally, so I checked myself into rehab."

She leaned forward, propped her chin in her hand. "You should be proud of that. The self-acceptance."

He eyeballed the potatoes. "Proud would be not getting hooked on the pills in the first place. After rehab, I went back to the insanity of my job and an empty apartment because the already rocky relationship couldn't support a recovering addict."

"She left you?"

Did he want to be talking about this? Spectacular way to kill a mood. He reached for the potatoes. "She did."

"But you got help. How could she leave you?"

Because she didn't sign on for addiction.

"There was a reason we'd been together for years and had never gotten married. On paper, we were great. The lobbyist and an aide to the secretary of state. After a while, we'd more or less become roommates who cared about each other. Rehab was bad for both our images. She couldn't have that."

He passed her the potatoes, but she set the bowl down. Obviously, Jillian wasn't lured off course when she didn't want to be.

"Did it feel like a betrayal?"

If he started in on the meat, maybe she'd get the hint. "Actually, I was relieved. Halfway through my rehab stint, she called to tell me she'd moved out." He dumped some roast onto his plate. "She'd been putting pressure on me about the constant work interruptions so I knew she wasn't happy. I couldn't blame her. But that's the job and there wasn't a lot, aside from quitting, I could do about it. I thanked her for letting me know and that was it. Haven't spoken to her since."

Finally, Jillian put some food on her plate. With any luck, she'd eat and he wouldn't have to dig into the bowels of his monumental screw-up.

"Wow," she said. "It seems so...I don't know...cold? To have it end like that? No discussion?"

Could he not get a break here? "We both knew it was coming, we just didn't know how to end it."

"Then what? You went back to work?"

"I did. At least until I got stressed out and reached into my desk drawer for the pill bottle I used to stash there. There was nothing there, but if I'd found one, that would have been the end of my recovery." He shrugged. "I needed to make a change. I called Vic, told him I needed a job somewhere other than D.C. and here I am. But Jesus, who moves to Chicago just before winter?"

Jillian laughed. "I guess you do. Any regrets?"

He grunted. "I regret this conversation."

"Why? I'm getting to know you? What's the big deal?" She stood. "I need a pop. What do you have to drink?"

Perfect escape. He waved her back down. "Sit. I'll get it."

At least the foray into the kitchen would give him a minute to think.

"You still haven't answered me."

Forget the foray. He poured two glasses of soda and headed back into the shark-infested waters. "No regrets. I feel like myself again. Vic harasses me constantly, but he's always been that way. It feels normal. And I hadn't had normal in a long time."

"I think old friends are good that way. They remind us why they care."

"Where Vic is concerned, that's a scary thought."

She waved him off. "Oh, hush."

He laughed. Another thing he hadn't had an abundance of in the past year. With Jillian it came easy. She had that sassy, determined way about her that made the teasing side of him beg for action. Another part of him begged for action too, but he'd have to wait it out.

Talk about a buzz kill. All he knew was that if he ever got Jillian into a bed, she'd need a helmet.

"Oh, hey," she said, her gaze skittering over his face. "*What* are you thinking?"

He raised his eyebrows, but didn't answer.

"You've got the look of the devil. Whatever it is, it must be wicked."

This might be fun. Dangerous, but definitely fun. "I was thinking if I ever got you into a bed, you'd need a helmet."

For a second, she stared at him then pursed her lips and —yeah, that was sexy. He ticked off the seconds. By the count of four she'd let a laugh loose, all sultry yet sweet. As usual, it made him think about all the places—bedroom, shower, his *office*...and holy hell what did that say about him?—he'd like to be with her while hearing that laugh. Pretty much, he wanted to do Jillian in any available place he could find.

"What kind of helmet?"

Most women would be embarrassed. Or at least pretend to be. Jillian wanted to explore it. "A helmet helmet," he said. "What's the difference?"

"There are different kinds. Would I need a bike helmet

or say a football helmet that gives total coverage? I think this is an important point."

Okay. He'd play. He leaned forward, propped his forearms on the table and tapped his fingers. "You'd need full coverage. We're talking major impact here."

Her mouth opened partway and she blew air through her lips. *Yes, sweetheart, you heard me.* She wasn't the only one who'd heard, because he got hard. There'd be no getting up from this table anytime soon.

She leaned toward him, right into his space, and drilled him with a hot look. "I love major impact. There's something about the rush of skin against skin and the wild need for release. All hands and mouths and chaos. I think that's great fun."

Seriously, she was doing this to a man who hadn't gotten laid in over a year?

Then she rose out of her chair, stretched across the table and got nose to nose with him. "What do you say to that, helmet boy?"

She was jerking his chain. Or perhaps something else. With any luck.

He grinned. "Right now, I'll say anything you want me to."

But he kissed her first. Softly this time. No pressure. He needed it. Needed the contact. Needed to feel like a man who could drive a woman to insanity like his old self used to.

In a flash, his mind went to the calendar on the wall. *Fucking calendar.* With great effort, he backed away from Jillian and opened his eyes. She remained half on the table, her big brown eyes focused on him, the curve of her cheek hinting at a smile, and he was *gone.* Not just a little gone either. Gone as in if she broke his heart he'd happily crawl into a bottle of pills to make the pain go away.

And he couldn't have that.

"You scare the hell out of me," he said. "I want you in a way that makes me willing to sacrifice everything. That's not good for a recovering addict. Before the pills, I'd have been all over you. You'd have never wanted to leave my bed. That's how good I'd have been to you. I can't risk that all-consuming thing."

She sat again. "Why?"

"Because it'll drive me straight back to the oblivion of painkillers."

"You'll spend the rest of your life in neutral? That sounds miserable. Don't you think?"

Two minutes ago they were having fun. *Now she decides to make a reasonable point?* He pounded his open palm against his forehead. "Of course it's miserable. I've been living this way for a year. Can't get too excited about anything because, God knows, if I suffer a disappointment I could fall off the wagon. Then when I'm bored out of my skull, all I want is to do something that won't make me think about blowing my sobriety because I'm bored. It's a goddamned vicious cycle. I need to find the midpoint between bored out of my skull and euphoria."

Jillian rolled her lips in. Hiding a smile. Terrific. In addition to being an irresponsible addict, now he was a head case. He wouldn't blame her if she set the floor ablaze trying to get the hell out. "You can laugh. Trust me. It's the only thing to do. I make myself insane."

"You think too much."

This was news? "Of course I think too much. It's part of my DNA. I've *always* been a planner. I like details and order and goals."

"Which is all good."

"Except when it whacks me out."

"Well, yes."

"Like now."

She laughed. So did he. "What the hell am I even talking about?"

Jillian swung around the table to stand next to him. "Why are you so brutal to yourself? You're human. You're allowed to have setbacks. And I'm not talking about going AWOL on recovery. Not every plan will work. It doesn't mean it's a bad plan. It doesn't mean you'll fall off the wagon."

"But I'm so close to hitting that one-year mark. I'm determined to make it. That's the plan and I'll see it through." He grinned. "Even if you try sticking your tongue in my mouth again."

"I rather enjoyed sticking my tongue in your mouth."

"I'm sure you did. Plenty more where that came from. You just need to wait seven more days."

"I'll wait."

He tilted his head, took a chance on wrecking his mind by running his finger down the side of her cheek. Damn, he loved touching her. "I'm hoping so."

He stood, smacked her on the hip with the back of his hand and headed to the kitchen where he'd mark an X on his calendar.

Another day down.

Barely.

8

THE FOLLOWING EVENING, LYNX HAD JUST HIT SEND ON AN email when Jillian walked into his office with a black leather briefcase slung over her shoulder. She wore gray slacks, a pair of spike heels and a silky black button-down blouse with the top few buttons undone. Damned shame about the tank under the blouse, but he supposed walking around with her blouse half unbuttoned wouldn't make the HR people happy.

Not that anyone in her office seemed happy with her anyway.

"Hey," he said, still staring at the buttons on that blouse.

Six more days.

"Hey, yourself." She set the briefcase on one of the chairs in front of his desk and propped her hands on her hips. "You're thinking about my tongue in your mouth again, aren't you?"

"Now you're psychic too?"

Swinging around the desk to where he sat, she propped a hip on the edge. "You had a look about you."

"What look is that?"

"The one that screams you need a boinking."

He burst out laughing. "I'm a guy. Every look screams that."

"Good point." She motioned to his laptop. "Tell me about your senator friend."

Lynx had called her cell earlier in the day to let her know he'd received more information on their "project" and could she stop by his office after work. Her home being bugged left it off-limits. Unless they planned on feeding information to whomever was listening.

Lynx pulled up the password-protected files Watkins had sent him. "He emailed me some files." He glanced back at her. "We're not supposed to have these. It'll seriously screw me up if anyone outside of us knows about them."

Her right hand went up. "Swear."

Someone knocked and in walked Janet Fink, all five feet and barely a hundred pounds of her. Accompanying her was Gavin Sheppard, the former FBI hostage negotiator who now ran Taylor Security's hostage negotiation division. The large number of expatriates overseas lent itself to kidnap and ransom cases, and Mike Taylor, being the sharp businessman he was, had seen an opportunity to grow his business by luring Gavin to the private sector.

For the purposes of this meeting, they'd be utilizing Gavin's FBI knowledge.

"Good timing," Lynx said. "Thanks for staying late. Jillian, meet Janet and Gavin."

Hellos and handshakes were exchanged and they all sat at the small conference table in the corner.

Janet slid into the chair by the window. "Gavin's sugar is crashing. He's crabby."

The look Gavin gave her, that maybe-I'll-kill-you-now

glare, could have cracked cement. "I'm not crabby. I'm hungry."

She rolled her eyes. "It all equals the same thing."

On an assignment last summer involving the kidnap and ransom of Mike's pregnant wife, Janet and Gavin decided to *explore* the chemistry firing between them. At least that's how Vic had put it. By the time Lynx had come to Taylor Security, it was common knowledge that Janet and Gavin were a couple.

Lynx didn't much care that Gavin was an executive and Janet wasn't. As long as they kept their relationship private and didn't bring it to the office, he couldn't give a crap.

Lynx turned to Jillian. "I forgot to ask if you like Thai. I bribed them with dinner."

"It's fine," she said, but if he'd learned anything about woman-speak, that meant she hated Thai. He filed it away.

"I'll get you something else when we're done."

She aimed those doe eyes at him and her amazing lips— just a little puffy, but not too much—slid into a half smile. Oh, yeah, the things he'd like to do to make that smile a little bigger.

All he could hope was that she'd been helmet shopping.

Gavin cleared not only his throat but the fog of lust distracting Lynx, and he straightened up. "I've briefed Janet and Gavin. Gavin worked for the FBI and still has friends there. Janet is our resident computer geek."

"I've only found one system I can't hack," Janet said, "but I'll get it."

Jillian stuck out her bottom lip. "That's handy."

"Understatement of the year," Gavin said.

Lynx glanced at Janet then Gavin. "I heard from Senator Watkins today. He's on Oversight. This conversation stays in the room."

"I love the cone of silence." Janet cracked.

"I know you do. Here's what we've got. Stennar Pharm is not actively being investigated, but they're on the government's radar."

Jillian's eyebrows went up. "And I thought I'd checked them out."

"You did. There's no way the average person would know this. A group of hospitals contacted the ranking Democrat on the House Oversight and Government Reform Committee regarding price gouging on a blood pressure medication."

Jillian inched closer to the table and folded her hands. "Unfortunately, this is not uncommon. Distributors buy mass quantities of drugs and when there's a shortage, they jack up the price. It drives hospital pharmacists crazy because surgeons don't like being told they can't have a certain drug. Then the pharmacy has to figure out how to get it. Sometimes that means going to gray market distributors, where the pedigree of a drug might be questionable."

Janet raised her hand, a habit Lynx found undeniably adorable considering her diminutive stature. "Pedigree? As in the origin?"

"Yes. The pedigree documents the drug's trail from the time it leaves the manufacturer to when it gets to the pharmacy. Without it, the drug could have come from anywhere. Sometimes shipments pass through several distributors before reaching its destination. It could even be stolen and then sold back into legitimate distribution channels."

Gavin nodded. "The Bureau has a task force assigned to pharma thefts. It's a problem that runs into the billions."

"Hang on," Lynx said to Jillian. "How the hell does it get back into the legitimate market?"

She gave him a look like he was the poor naïve idealist in

the room. "It's not difficult. A warehouse could get robbed or maybe a truck is hijacked. The thieves sell the stolen drugs at a severely reduced price to a distributor. That distributor forges pedigree documents and the drug is then sold back to a legitimate distributor."

Lynx thought about that a sec. "What about the manufacturer? Don't they have to recall the stolen drugs?"

Gavin shrugged. "Some of them don't."

"Why?" Janet asked.

"Because," Jillian said, "the expenses surrounding recalls —and don't forget the public's confidence in the manufacturer—threatens the bottom line. Entire lots are rarely stolen and there's no way to figure out which pills in the lot are the bad ones. Manufacturers can only hope if the stolen drugs enter the supply chain, someone will catch it."

Given his intimate relationship with prescription drugs, Lynx could see how profitable the illegitimate drug market would be. The people in his meetings spoke all the time about backdoor pharmacies and how they never had a shortage of drugs. "That's disturbing."

"Welcome to the pharmaceutical world," Jillian said.

Gavin made a note then slapped his pen down. "What else have you got?"

Lynx sat back. "Outside of the complaint from the hospital group, there's nothing to prove any illegal activity. Yet."

"Does Oversight think the blood pressure drugs are stolen?" Gavin asked.

"They don't know. Think about this." Lynx pointed to Jillian. "She saw a delivery at a weird time last week. Since then, her house has been broken into, Stennar Pharm has isolated her and asked her to sign a confidentiality agreement—by the way, our lawyers said you shouldn't sign that.

No kidding there." He went back to Gavin. "And we think they were the ones who bugged her house."

Gavin's head dropped forward. "Jesus. Who found the bugs?"

"I did."

"Did you get rid of them?"

"No," Jillian said. "We agreed I should leave them. Someone at my company is listening. I think it's my boss. His secretary knew I took a photography class this past weekend. She said our boss told her."

Janet smacked her hand on the table. "And you didn't tell your boss."

"Nope."

"She told another guy that might be involved, though. We're not sure."

Gavin made another note on the pad in front of him. "Let me talk to my buddy at the Bureau. He's worked with the pharma task force. Maybe he can get us some intel. He'll be quiet about it."

"Thank you," Jillian said.

She turned to Lynx and the light hit her face, revealing the shadows under her eyes. He inched closer and squeezed her hand. "You look tired."

Her eyes glistened and, hell, if she cried, he'd...he didn't know what he'd do, but he'd find a way to fix it. That was a definite. He squeezed her hand again. "It's okay."

Throwing her shoulders back, she nodded. "I know. It's been a hell of a week."

He pulled his hand back before she construed it as pity. The woman in front of him didn't want his or anyone else's pity. "Sure has."

Janet raised her hand. "What can I do?"

She craved getting in on the action. If hacking into

someone's system meant working toward the greater good, she did it without compunction. She got shit done and Lynx loved it.

"Can you get into Stennar Pharm's network? See what's sitting out there?"

Jillian tore a corner of paper from his notepad. "I snagged my boss's secretary's password. I can give you that."

Janet smiled. "A girl after my own heart. I probably won't need the password, but you can leave it with me, just in case. What am I looking for?"

JILLIAN STARED AT JANET WHILE ABSORBING THE IDEA THAT A week ago, she'd been a career woman, doggedly chasing her future. Now she was running from whatever insanity existed within the confines of Stennar Pharm. What if she just walked away? Turned her back on the whole thing and forgot about it.

No harm, no foul.

Why bother amusing herself with that thought? She'd never be able to do it. Not after her bosses had come after her this way. Stealing her hard-earned possessions, listening in on her private conversations, screwing with her ability to perform her job. All of it added up to one pissed-off career girl.

"We're looking for any shipments that look odd. Weird delivery times, funky payments, inflated sales numbers, anything."

"Any particular directories I should look under?"

"Start with Ned Dillard's files. He's my boss. There are databases only he has access to. I've been told those directories contain payroll information, but it could be anything."

Janet nodded. "I can do that."

"Most of the software is company developed. I don't know if that matters."

She only smiled. Right. *Silly me.*

Jack touched Jillian's arm to get her attention. "Are you okay with this?"

"I have to be. These people are screwing with me and I can't let that happen."

Janet's cell phone buzzed and she checked it, her body moving in a swift, compact efficiency that seemed to define her. "It's security. Our dinner is here."

"I think we're done. You guys eat. I need to get Jillian food she actually likes." Jack turned to her. "My bad."

"You didn't know."

Gavin stood. "I'm beat anyway. Let's take the food home with us."

Janet grinned at Jillian. "He just wants to get naked with me."

"Do I need to hear this?" Jack asked.

Gavin let out a huff. "How about we not do this in the office?"

"It's Lynx. He doesn't care."

"Trust me, I care."

Janet rolled her eyes and smacked Gavin on the ass. "Blah, blah. Let's go, Sexy Galore. I'll make it up to you."

"*And* it gets worse," Jack said.

Finally, Gavin gave up the fight and laughed. Fascinated, Jillian watched them go, their banter echoing in the hall. "Funny couple."

"I can't figure it out. I always think their relationship shouldn't work, but there's a weird balance with them."

"Your boss doesn't care that they're a couple?"

"No. Janet works for me. Gavin isn't her superior."

"And you won't get in trouble for having her help me?"

He studied her a moment, his blue eyes so focused that it rattled her, caused a little zip in her spine. "The hacking you mean?"

"Yes."

"No. As long as it's not done on company time, I'm not worried about it. Besides, she won't get caught. Mike stole her from the CIA. She knows how to fly under the radar."

The CIA. Who the hell were these people? And how did Jillian wind up lucky enough to have met all of them? "Thank you. For this. All of it."

He held her gaze and even if she wanted to turn away, to ignore the tension buzzing between them, she chose not to.

"You're welcome," he said. "I couldn't leave you on your own with this. Something isn't right."

"You're a good man, Jack Lynx."

Too good. Frighteningly good. A recovering drug addict with a big heart. In her normal way of thinking, these concepts, the drug addict and big heart, were in direct opposition. Given her experience with her father, addiction represented selfishness. An unwillingness to self-heal and protect loved ones from destruction.

And yet. Here was Jack. A man who continually put others ahead of himself.

"I don't understand," she said.

"What?"

"How you became an addict."

His head snapped back. "Why do you say that?"

"Because you're so giving."

"And that means I can't suffer from a disease?"

She was screwing this up. Quickly, she shook her head. "Not what I meant."

Tell him. This was her opportunity to come clean about her family. After all he'd done for her, he deserved the truth.

"Then what did you mean?"

Telling him required opening up. Allowing him into the twisted world she came from. Something she rarely did. She'd refused to let people into her barricaded life. A certain vulnerability came with such an admission and right now, she was vulnerable enough. A basket case, she would not be. Not in his eyes.

She dug her fingers into her forehead. Anything to stop thinking about all the things she should and shouldn't do. "I don't know what I meant. I'm sorry. I'm not judging, though."

He leaned back in his chair, feigning relaxation, but his shoulders inched up. "I didn't think you were judging."

"Good. I respect what you're doing. You'll never know how I admire it. I'm just trying to understand how a man like you, a responsible, dedicated guy who has it all together, falls into addiction."

He stood. "First, I didn't fall. I walked. At the time, all I knew was I liked how it felt. I've always been the over-achiever and when I was stoned, I didn't feel pressure."

"And why is that? That you feel so much pressure?"

"I was raised by good parents. My father built a career in law enforcement. He's the chief of police in my hometown and my mother is a schoolteacher. They've spent their lives serving. I decided to do the same."

Freaking Mayberry. Just what she needed. His parents would tsk-tsk the dysfunctional catastrophe that was her childhood.

"I see why you like wearing the superhero cape."

He laughed. "I totally like wearing the cape. Unfortunately, the cape comes with asphyxiating responsibility. It's like an elephant sitting on my chest. After my knee surgery, the drugs took away the elephant. For the first time, I didn't feel the pressure. There was freedom in that."

"Do you miss it? That feeling?"

"Every damned day. It wouldn't be an addiction if I didn't. I understand that now. I've accepted it. That feels better than the numbness that came with pills."

"I love how open you are about this."

He shrugged. "I don't walk around telling people, but I owe it to you. For months, I've unintentionally sent you mixed signals and I wanted you to understand why. I can't help myself. There are times when all I want is to look at you. I could spend the whole damned day staring at you and that scares me."

"I'm not a painkiller."

"In a lot of ways you are. I get that same calm feeling from you. I'm afraid it's an artificial high. You could be the drug I shouldn't have."

Who the hell tells a woman she gives him an artificial high? She smiled. "If that's a come-on, you need to work on your approach."

"I know. That's the problem. I'm trying not to hit on you. Have been for months and it's completely foreign. Not that I'm a player, but it's an unnatural state. No companionship, no sharing—"

"No sex."

He tilted his head. "There is that. And the more I look at you, the more I want to spend time with you. And then I wonder why you would want me."

If he only knew.

He stepped closer, looked right into her eyes. "I blew up a good life in a spectacular way. Who'd want a guy like that?"

Me. The thought came without warning. All this trying

to convince herself she couldn't be with Jack because of his issues was like standing at the top of a greased slope craving the leap, but being too afraid of the ride.

Inching closer, she slipped her finger between the two middle buttons on his shirt and tugged. "You're looking at this all wrong. You may have blown up your life, but you put it back together. In my experience, it's a lot harder to reassemble the pieces." She inched even closer, letting one finger skim the surface of his undershirt. "Don't you think?"

He looked down at her fingers tucked into his shirt and blew out a breath. "I think I hope you're helmet shopping."

Then he kissed her—another one of those *whammo* deals where his mouth crushed hers—and he clung to her, pulling her closer and closer. She wrapped her arms around his waist and held on. Nothing about this kiss was gentle. Not one thing. She didn't care. What was happening here personified untamed, and the ever-guarded part of her loved the sensation, the uncontrolled fury of it. His tongue slid along her bottom lip—cripes, he was a master at that— and she sighed.

Save me. Who was she pleading to? She'd never been one to shy away from something she wanted. She'd also never been one to rush headlong into something she knew, *knew*, would suck the emotional fortitude from her life. She'd always been the safe one. Cautious to a fault when it came to relationships. But now? Heaven help her, Jack made her want to take a flying leap onto that greased slope.

She backed away from the kiss, but he moved along her jaw, down the side of her neck, softer this time, slower, and her body gave in to the heat.

He'd be good in bed.

She felt it to her core. The one burning like a forest after a six month drought. She stared at the ceiling, closed her eyes and, for a change, enjoyed a little reckless pleasure. "Do me a favor."

No answer. More kisses, though. Nothing to complain about. Not with his hands under her shirt and his fingers skimming the underside of her bra.

"What?"

"Screw me blind."

"Can't."

"How many days?"

"Six. Then you'd better get that helmet on."

AFTER BUYING JILLIAN A PROPER DINNER AT MASTRO'S, LYNX'S new favorite steak place, they walked the three blocks back to his office. The damp wind bit into them as a sea of red taillights lit the wet, darkened street. He loved this city, but the weather sucked in March. One second it was raining, the next snowing. Or vice versa. He zipped his jacket higher and glanced at Jillian in her buttoned-up coat. She'd pulled her knit hat around her ears and tied a scarf around her neck. *Someone* had prepared for the cold. And it wasn't him. "Are you warm enough?"

"Toasty. You need to learn how to dress for a Chicago spring. I never put my coat away until June. That's how crazy it gets here."

"I'll keep that in mind."

His cell phone rang and he checked the ID. "It's Janet." He grabbed Jillian's elbow and ushered her into the entry alcove of an office building. "Hey, Janet."

"Is Jillian with you? I'm into a file here and I think I've got something."

"Hang on."

He held the phone between them so they could both

listen. The faded scent of Jillian's perfume—*lilacs, that's what it is*—reminded him too much of how extremely satisfying being close to her could be. He dipped his head closer. One way to get rid of the cold icing over his balls.

Jillian—just to be a pain in the ass and torture him—linked her arm through his, snuggled up and blew him a kiss.

Killer.

"Hi, Janet," she said, her gaze still on his. "What's up?"

"I found a folder under a private directory and it shows a list of shipments from the last year. I've only spot-checked them, but a few of these shipments aren't on the main distribution list."

She straightened and focused on the phone in his hand. "Excuse me?"

"Three shipments from the past month don't exist in the company's main database. They're only in this file."

"What's the drug?"

"Two of them are Baxtin."

That's no coincidence. Jillian glanced back at him with raised eyebrows.

"Is one from last Friday night?" Lynx asked.

"Yes."

"When is the other delivery for?"

"It came in at 11:55 last night. Another late one."

Jillian inched closer to the phone. "Can you copy that file for me? I can cross check it by item with what's in the main distribution database."

"Sure thing. I'll get it to Lynx in the morning."

"Thank you," Jillian said. "Who does the file belong to?"

"D. Smith. Do you know him? Or her, I guess."

"No."

"Thanks, Janet," Lynx said. "See you in the morning."

He clicked off then waggled the phone at her. "Interesting. What do you think?"

"I don't know. I want to compare the lists and see if there are any commonalities. I don't understand why they wouldn't be on the main list. It's very odd. Particularly if the shipments are large."

"Could this D. Smith be skimming from the company? Maybe keeping the money from the drug sales?"

"If he—or she—is embezzling, there are other people involved. Every shipment is logged. When it comes in, it's logged. When it's shelved, it's logged. When it goes out, it's logged. Then there are multiple checks and balances when it comes to invoices. It would be extremely difficult to hide a shipment."

"Sure," he said. "But there's a reason those shipments haven't been entered in the main database."

"I'll make a list of all the drugs in the questionable shipments. See if anything is common among them. As soon as you get that list, you need to give me the location of where last night's shipment is stored. I want to get a look at the totes they were shipped in."

How he hated his next idea, and if he could do it himself, he would, but she'd have to do it. It didn't sit right with him, not for a half second, but they needed to explore all options. "Would you be able to snap some pictures of the labels? It'd be good to have a trail."

She made a gagging sound and scrunched her nose.

"I know," he said. "I hate it too."

A cabbie sat on his horn and they both jumped at the sudden blast.

"Jerk," Jillian said, then turned back to Lynx. "During the day it'll be too risky. If I wait until everyone leaves, I should be able to do it."

"You can't stay there alone."

"Well, it's the only way to do this without getting caught."

"I don't like it."

She leaned in and bumped him. "I know you don't, but you can't strap on your cape this time. I need to do this alone."

He jammed his icicle fingers into his jacket pockets. "And, if you get caught snapping pictures, what are you gonna do?"

She set her gloved hand on his cheek and patted. "I don't know. I guess I can't get caught."

9

JILLIAN SETTLED INTO HER NEW CHAIR IN HER NEW OFFICE AND stared at her new door and the empty hallway just beyond.

Total isolation. Being alone had never been an issue before. From an early age she'd savored moments of solitude. Moments when her father wasn't passed out and her mother wasn't ignoring the disaster that had been their home life. As an adult, Jillian thrived on singularity and preferred the quiet that came with it.

Except now.

This current isolation offered no comfort. It created nervous energy that kept her on edge, watching and waiting and wondering.

She battled how that energy made her temples throb with anticipation. How it brought her back to her tiny childhood bedroom, huddled in her closet reading a book and dreaming of escape.

How it made her weak and small.

That's it. She smacked her hands on the desk, marched toward the door and slammed it shut. "No, sir. Not gonna stare at that empty hallway."

On her way back to her desk, her cell phone rang. Considering her phone issues at the office, her cell phone had become Jillian central. It also offered a much needed distraction. She grabbed the phone and spotted Jack's name.

"Hi," she said. "And thank you."

"For what?"

No sense going into it when her office could be bugged. "Just thank you."

He laughed. "You're welcome. I've got your list."

She glanced at her desk clock. 10:30. "Good. Can you meet me for lunch?"

"It would have to be around 11:30. I have a one o'clock meeting."

The empty surface of her desktop gleamed. *Not terribly busy here.* What with the phone not ringing, no access to company files and having an entire floor to herself. Her stomach pinched. So flipping irritating. "I can make that work."

After killing the hour, Jillian entered the Seville Restaurant, from here on out known as *their* new place, at exactly 11:30 and found Jack sitting in a booth in the far corner. He waved to her and she marched toward him as he slid from the booth and held one arm out for a hug.

Instantly, the ball of tension in her stomach evaporated. Somehow, he always knew how to help her. She snuggled under his arm and propped her chin on his shoulder. A simple hug could do wonders for a girl. "I needed this."

"I figured. Have a seat."

She opened her eyes and found the patrons in the next table watching them. An audience. Slowly, she backed away and scooted into the booth.

She scanned the remainder of the restaurant where the

early lunch crowd filtered in and the noise level slowly rose. It wasn't enough to drown out their conversation, but in another half hour there'd be no discussing anything confidential. Not unless they planned on customers at the three tables surrounding them hearing.

Jack passed a stapled report to her. "Here you go."

A waitress came by and dropped off two pops. "I ordered you a soda," he said. "Hope that's okay."

"That's perfect. Thank you." She flipped through the pages on the report. "This is quite a list."

Jack leaned forward. "It's all the deliveries over the past year. I put it on a thumb drive for you so you can sort it. Didn't want to email it."

"Definitely not. For all I know, they've got spyware on my laptop." She shook her head, squeezed her eyes closed for a second then opened them again. Her gaze connected with Jack's and held. "Just smile for me. Throw me a bone. Please? That smile always makes things better."

The corner of his mouth lifted. Half a bone. Maybe a quarter. "That's all you've got? Really?"

His lips quirked another inch. Tough customer. She'd deal with it. "I need to check these deliveries against the company database. Which I now have Mary's password for."

"I'll split the list with you. We'll log in from somewhere with free Wi-Fi and go through it together. How about after work?"

She nodded.

"We'll use my laptop," he said. "We won't even load it onto yours. Just in case."

"Good idea. I think we should sort it by drug. Then we can see if there's a particular brand that shows up more than the others."

She eyeballed the report, but no particular drug stood out. Line by line she checked the entries until she came to the shipment from two nights ago. The storage location had already been entered into the spreadsheet.

"Before I leave work tonight, I'll sneak into the warehouse and find this latest shipment of Baxtin. I have my camera in my trunk. I'll snap some photos. The tote will be sealed so I won't be able to get into it, but I can get pictures of the labels."

"Can I help you?"

"A strange guy walking around the warehouse is more of a red flag than me doing it." She gripped his hand. "I'll be fine. We need this. I'll just wait around until everyone leaves."

He slumped back. "I don't love this idea."

"I know. I don't either. I've spent my life being cautious and suddenly I've abandoned that concept."

"For good reason."

"Still. It's different. Kinda like you not being able to don your cape."

He rolled his eyes.

"I'm not being snarky. I'm just explaining how this feels. You're used to rushing in and helping. You can't do that now and I know it's bothering you. I have that same feeling, only mine comes from having to do something risky."

"Why is that?"

"What?"

"That you're so cautious?"

She waited. Pondered. Calculated. He'd given her the opening to share her childhood and why she obsessed over stability. He, of all people, would understand the groundwork that led to her being a self-sufficient woman with an aversion to chance.

But he's from Mayberry.

She glanced at a passing waitress, hoping the woman would check on them, but no luck. Waitresses were like cops, always around when you *didn't* need them. She looked back at Jack. "I like stability."

"We all like stability to a certain extent."

She shrugged. "I suppose."

His phone beeped. A text coming in. He scooped it from his jacket pocket. "Crap."

"What?"

"I'm sorry. Mike just moved our meeting up. I gotta go."

Temporary reprieve. "It's fine." *Exceedingly fine.* "I have what I needed." *And I skated from telling you about my screwed-up family.* She held up the report. "Why don't you keep this until tonight? I don't want anyone at my office seeing it."

"Will do. Call me later and let me know what time you want to meet."

With that, he stood, adjusted the cuffs on his shirt and bent over to peck her on the lips.

Hello.

He shot straight, all stiff officer-in-charge, and his gaze slid left and right. She held up her hand. "Don't freak. A simple peck is not going to blow a year of hard work."

"Jeez, I can't believe I did that."

"A hug *and* a kiss. I liked it, Jack."

Maybe a little too much.

"Hell, so did I. I don't want you thinking—"

"Stop. I'm not thinking anything. Don't analyze. We both enjoyed it. Go back to work."

Finally, he smiled—the trailblazing one—and she sighed dramatically. "Just for that, kiss me again before you leave."

. . .

ANOTHER AFTERNOON OF MIND-NUMBING BOREDOM TICKED BY
and at 6:30, with Jillian an inch shy of blowing her brains
out, she was sure everyone had gone home. She'd been
sitting behind her locked office door for over an hour. If
anyone checked the door, they'd assume she had gone
home. She'd even parked her car in the adjacent lot when
she'd come back from lunch so it wouldn't be noticed in the
Stennar Pharm lot when the staff left.

To make sure all was clear, she'd do a quick bit of reconnaissance before going downstairs. Slowly, keeping her
steps light against the cheap, cracked linoleum up here in
the dead zone, she walked to the office at the back of the
building and peeped out at the parking lot. *Almost empty.*
Only one car remained.

Darn.

She gnawed her bottom lip. Perhaps the person was still
in the building. Or maybe they'd gone out to dinner with
one of the other employees and went in one car? No way to
know.

Why sit contemplating when she could take the five
minutes she needed to snap photos and be done?

She'd have to risk it. Back in her office, she grabbed her
camera case and purse from the bottom drawer. Using her
normal gentle care, she unzipped the camera bag, pulled
the lens cover off and checked the settings. Her intention
was to get down to the warehouse, snap the pictures fast and
get the hell out.

If someone stopped her while she poked around the
aisles, she could say she was checking a shipment on her
way out.

Easy-peasy.

Except sweat pooled on the back of her neck and her pulse hammered.

"I can do this."

Just a few pictures. Hopefully the security cameras wouldn't catch her.

Jeez-o-Pete. She had to think of that now? Not that it mattered. Her butt was square in the middle of this thing and she wanted to know why. What was Stennar Pharm trying so hard to hide that they'd terrorize an employee for it?

Time to find out.

At the stairs, she stepped down on tiptoes so her heels wouldn't smack. The main warehouse lights had been turned off, but the industrial-looking sconces that dotted the walls remained lit and provided enough illumination for her to see.

Once on the warehouse floor, she glanced around at the row of closed office doors. So far, so good. Rather than stay in the main area of the warehouse, she darted down the first row so she could cross to the back end and stay fairly hidden.

In the silence of the cavernous building, she swung down aisle seven, her gaze drifting over the location numbers on each column. Halfway down the aisle, she located five boxes of Baxtin. The large plastic totes, as expected, were sealed with plastic straps. Fingerprints had been left in the dirt and grime on the outsides of the containers. The totes saw a lot of action in and around the warehouses and their condition was an indication of how long they'd been in service. The grime didn't necessarily mean anything. The dents on the durable plastic were the tells. More dents meant older totes. These totes might be middle-aged.

Fastened to the sides of the totes were pockets containing barcode tickets. Barcodes told the story. At each location, scans would be done to create an electronic trail of where the totes had been. After delivery, all totes were sorted and a printed manifest given to each driver prior to leaving Stennar Pharm. Once the order was delivered to the outside location, the driver would scan each barcode. The receiving company would compare the number of totes in the delivery to the electronic signature pad and the paper manifest. After the electronic and paper manifests had been signed off, the driver retrieved the empty totes and left.

Jillian pulled the label and the crackle of paper in the silent warehouse triggered a blood rush. She glanced around. No one in the area.

She went back to the label where she saw the Stennar Pharm address, the route, order number and the barcode containing all the pertinent delivery info. She focused the camera. *Snap.* Next box. *Snap. Snap.* Up one box. *Snap. Snap. Snap.* Seven shots later, she had what she needed and slid the camera strap over her shoulder.

Mission accomplished. Time to go. She returned the barcodes to the side pockets on the totes and darted down the long aisle. A shipment of boxes waiting to be dealt with sat at the end of the row.

And then the bay door creaked and rumbled to life and Jillian's head damn near exploded.

A male voice sounded from two rows down and she froze, her arms and legs deadening.

Two men rounded the end of the row. One was Cliff.
Move.

Without thinking, she dove behind the pallet of boxes and her sweaty palms slipped on the cold cement floor. Her elbow took the brunt of her landing. Jabbing pain shot through her shoulder. She drew air, holding it for a second until the initial sting wore off.

"It's the one on the end."

That sounded like Cliff. Coming her way. Obviously in search of the boxes she hid behind. If she hadn't panicked, she would have simply walked around the corner and told Cliff she'd been checking on something on her way out.

Hadn't that been the plan?

Too late now. She swung her head left and right, searching for an escape route. Anywhere but here.

Nothing. Even if she made a break for it, they'd see her.

She heard a truck backing to the loading dock and then the squeak of brakes.

"Let's just load it by hand." Definitely Cliff.

"Awright. I'll grab the dolly."

The swish of sliding cardboard came from above her head and that same blast of panic shot through her as the top box was moved off the stack. Jillian, back on her haunches, curled into a ball, making herself as small as possible. Her arms trembled and she slammed her eyes closed, praying she wouldn't be seen. *Do something.*

Another box slid off and she crouched lower. Time to get serious. One more box and—hello, boys—she'd be seen.

With the camera.

How would she explain this? She couldn't. Not reasonably. Sure she took the camera everywhere, but after the week she'd had, the break-in, the listening devices, they'd never believe she wasn't up to something.

SD card.

She should take it. If something happened to the camera, she'd have the SD card. She flipped the tiny door open, ejected the card and shoved it in her bra where it wouldn't get damaged.

She hoped.

Her chest ached from the clotting air trapped there. She backed against the box and rapped her knuckles against her chest. *Can't get hysterical now.* Slowly, she drew a breath and let it out.

Directly in front of her was a long aisle. If she created a distraction that would draw Cliff and the other guy away, she could run.

Phone.

She dug her cell phone from her purse. All she needed to do was set an alarm then slide it to the right. When the men went in search of the noise, she'd bolt. If she got caught, she'd say she returned to the warehouse to find her phone that she must have dropped on her way out.

Not a great plan, but it would do.

The red message light on the phone blinked and she touched the screen. Jack. They'd made plans to meet, but he'd have to wait.

"I've got it!" The second man's voice boomed in the near vicinity. *Here they come.*

Quickly, she pulled up her calendar, missed the button and squeezed her hand closed. *Steady now.* She tried again and managed to set an appointment. Then she locked the screen. Just in case someone got nosy. Silently, she slid the phone in the opposite direction of her intended escape route. The stupid thing only went twenty feet. *Damn.*

It would have to be enough.

"What the hell is that?" Cliff said when the phone began chirping.

Please, please, please.

"I thought everyone was gone," the other guy said.

"They are."

But Cliff's voice was more distant now, moving away. Toward the phone.

Realistically, she had about five seconds before they located the phone and stepped right into her sight. Now or never. Keeping crouched behind the remaining boxes she gathered her camera and purse and scooted across the aisle, her low heels *click-click, click-click, click-clicking* against the floor. Towering stacks of boxes swept by in a blur. Her purse and camera drooped off her shoulder and she gripped them tighter. The end of the aisle was in sight. She could hang a left and bolt out the emergency exit just a few feet down.

Four more steps and she'd be at the end. *I've got this.*

Two steps.

On the last step, a man came flying around the corner and rammed into her. *Caught.* Crushing weight knocked her over, her right knee hitting the floor first followed by her head.

"Ooofff."

An explosion of pain filled the side of her face. A warm trickle of something, blood maybe, seeped down her cheek and she brought her fingers up to check. Yep. Bleeding.

She lurched forward, her shoes slipping on the cement. No traction. The man grabbed her blouse and his fingers scraped along her back. He gripped harder and crumpled the material in his fist to rein her in.

"Stop," the man said. "Don't make me hurt you."

"Hey," Cliff yelled, his voice not far behind her. "She works here."

The truck horn blared and, with the pounding her skull had taken, it blasted like cannon fire, the sound gonging inside her head and reverberating. Her vision blurred and she drew her hands up to cover her ears. Knifing pain bore into her and her stomach flipped. *Need to get free.*

Vomit gurgled in her throat and she concentrated on each inhalation of breath.

Too late.

The end of the aisle seesawed. For a second, she heard a *fffoom*. Must be her mind playing with her. Or maybe shutting down the pain.

10

LYNX CLIMBED THE LAST STEP ON VIC'S BACK PORCH AND THE door swung open. The big man stood in the doorway with one of the twins, Ava if the pink sleeper was any indication, asleep in his arms, her chubby cheek resting against his chest.

"Wake her up," Vic said in a barely audible voice, "and I'll rip your jaw off and shove it up your ass."

Helluva greeting.

"Wow," Lynx mouthed.

Vic waved him inside. "You can talk. Don't be loud. She's been screaming for two hours. Gina gave in half an hour ago. She may be upstairs killing herself. I'm not sure. At the very least, I know she's got a bottle of scotch up there."

"Where's Justin?"

He grinned. "My boy? Sleeping like a champ. As usual, the women in my life are being a pain in the ass."

Lynx laughed. "You know you love it."

Glancing down at his daughter and her little bow mouth, Vic tilted his head. The look on his face, all...well... peaceful, made Lynx wonder if he'd ever have kids.

Last thing a recovering addict needed to throw into the mix was a screaming baby. Still, he wouldn't mind looking at someone like that.

Vic eased the door shut, making sure the lock didn't snick and wake up the baby. He waited three seconds, stared down at his daughter who remained comatose and backed away from the door. "What's up?"

"I need your help with something."

The baby shifted and Vic rocked from one foot to the other, his eyes wide and horrified. "My sweet Ava," he sang, "Daddy loves you. But if you wake up, I will go fucking crazeeeee."

Both men stayed silent. Lynx might have laughed at his stud friend who feared nothing. Except his baby. Ava found another comfortable position and settled back to sleep. Vic shook his head and focused on the ceiling. A second later, he looked back at Lynx. "Close one."

"I'll say."

"What do you need?"

More rocking from Vic. Back and forth, back and forth, and Lynx found himself swaying along. "Jillian was supposed to call me. We were gonna meet at Starbucks after she took pictures at the warehouse."

"Say what now?"

Ava shifted again, then hiccupped. Vic held his finger to his lips and mouthed "Be right back."

Vic with a baby. That was like the Terminator in a diaper. Bizarre.

Lynx leaned back against the newly installed kitchen counter and folded his arms. Gina had been on a tear recently updating the hundred-year-old house and things were shaping up. Before, the place had that nice lived-in look guys like. Now it was more slick and shiny.

Oddly enough, it was also quiet. Typically the television or the boys yelling at their video games drifted into the kitchen. Maybe, given the Ava situation, Vic and Gina had nixed any noise.

Vic returned. "We're good. I hope she stays down. My wife is so sleep deprived, I'm afraid to go lights out. She might kill me in my sleep for doing this to her. I've got all the knives on lockdown." He scrubbed his hands over his face. "Tell me you're here to save me."

"Actually, I am. I've called her three times."

"Jillian?"

"Yeah. She was supposed to call me as soon as she got out of the warehouse. My guess is she should have called me thirty minutes ago."

"You think something is wrong?"

"Yep. I'm gonna check it out. See if she's there."

"You're just gonna walk in there?"

He shrugged. "Not much choice. If there's anyone there, I'll tell them she was supposed to meet me. Not a lie."

"They'll also think you're some psycho junkie looking for a fix."

The second it came out of his mouth, Vic smacked his lips together. Lynx held up his hands. "It is what it is."

"Yeah, but—"

"No. I can't have everyone around me watching what they say all the time. It's ridiculous and it's unfair."

"Hey, I was being sensitive. Enjoy it while it lasts."

Lynx cracked a smile. "Because you're a stupid fucking redneck?"

"That and you're a paranoid ass-kissing Boy Scout."

Ah, yes. The reset button had been pushed. All things back in balance. "Then nothing has changed in the thirteen years we've known each other. Now, can we wrap up this lovefest and find Jillian?"

"You're on, Boy Scout. Give me two minutes to let Gina know I'm going out."

When they got into Lynx's car—the Mercedes Mike shoved down his throat—Vic held a .38 out to him.

Crap. The big man had done more than tell his wife he was leaving.

Vic inched the weapon closer. "When's the last time you practiced?"

Years. "A while."

"Forget it," he said. "Take the fucking gun and make sure you don't shoot my balls off. When this is over, remind me to drag your ass to the range."

Lynx took the gun and held it in his open hand. Slowly, he wrapped his fingers around the grip and absorbed what used to be the familiar feel of a weapon. Back in the day, he'd preferred a .45 in his grasp. Now the .38 would have to do.

WITH GREAT CARE, JILLIAN SAT UP AND LEANED AGAINST ONE of the stacked boxes. Her head *whooshed* and her stomach instantly rebelled. She closed her eyes and concentrated on not throwing up.

When she opened her eyes again, Cliff stood over her, hands on hips, his eyes slightly narrowed.

"Jillian, what the hell were you doing? We thought you were a thief."

She glanced around. Beside her was her purse. Had she dropped it? And the camera? *Where is it?* She glanced to her other side. Nothing

"Where's my camera?"

"What camera?"

She reached for her purse, hoping the camera might be under it. Nothing.

"I had it with me. It's gone."

Cliff glanced at the other guy, raising his eyebrows in a she's-cooked gesture, then squatted to eye level with her. "No camera. You feel okay? You whacked your head when you fell."

They took her camera. The sons of bitches stole her camera. She resisted pressing her fingers into her chest to check for the SD card tucked into her bra.

"Yes, but I had my camera with me."

Cliff shook his head. "I didn't see any camera. How's your head?"

Despite the throbbing, realization had set in. They took her beloved camera and were now attempting to convince her she never had it. She focused on Cliff, her eyes burning. Hopefully he'd get the point and stop screwing with her. "I feel fine. I know I had my camera. Where is it?"

The other guy stepped closer, way too close. Looming over her. The base of her skull hammered. Along with her cheek and the side of her head. Total mess.

She scooted back an inch and looked up at the man standing over her. "Who are you?"

"This is Ron. He's a part-timer."

She didn't know any Ron. Then again, she didn't know everyone who worked in the warehouse. "Okay, *Ron*. You need to step back and give me room to get up."

He shrugged his massive shoulders. "You need help?"

"No. Thank you." The aisle swayed and she propped a hand against a box to steady herself. Little dizzy.

Cliff tilted his head. "You blacked out for a few seconds."

Blacked out? She didn't remember that. Could have

happened, she supposed. "I'm fine. I need to get home." She swiped a hand over her cheek and came away with a smear of blood. "I'm still bleeding."

"You cut your cheek when you fell," Ron said.

"You mean when you tackled me."

Cliff sighed.

"Yeah. Because I didn't see it was you and I thought you were trying to rob the place."

From the corner of her eye, Jillian spotted someone swing around the corner of the aisle. Ned. Marching toward them. He zeroed in on her and it seemed to register that she was bloody. He shot a look at Cliff and his playmate. "What the hell is going on? Jillian, why are you bleeding?"

"She fell," Ron said.

Jillian ignored him. "Ron *tackled* me."

Ned spun on Cliff, who held his hands in surrender. "I saw someone sneaking around. I thought she was a thief and we chased her down. She fell and hit her cheek on the floor."

Ned pinned his gaze on Cliff, shifted to Ron then back to Cliff. "She's hurt and you're standing around? She could have a concussion."

Finally, someone defending her. Ned took Jillian's arm and squeezed.

"Ow," she said.

"Sorry. Come up to my office and sit." He turned back to Cliff. "You two join us so we can figure this out."

Jillian tried to tug her arm free, but Ned held on. "I need to go home."

"Not yet, you don't. You can't drive with a head injury."

"I don't have a head injury."

Cliff drew up beside her. "She blacked out."

"I did not."

"How would you know?"

Damn.

"Either way," Ned said. "You're coming up to my office while I get to the bottom of this. I'll have to report your injury to HR."

Human Resources. Fantastic. An incident for her file. This wasn't her fault, though. She'd been accosted and wouldn't let them spin it. No, sir.

In Ned's office, she took one of the guest chairs while Cliff and Ron stood to the side. Ned had gone off to grab the first-aid kit. Fine. She'd wait.

She poked a finger at Cliff. "I want my camera back." Somehow she'd managed a firm voice.

Cliff puffed out his cheeks and blew air. "I don't have your fucking camera."

Ned stepped into the office carrying the first-aid kit and a wet cloth. "Watch your language." He handed Jillian the wet cloth. "Put this against your cheek."

She took the cloth. Pressed it against her face, thankful for the shock of cold because—holy cow—her entire skull felt bashed in. "Thank you."

He cruised around the desk, sat in his chair and looked at Cliff. Maybe Ned was on her side? Considering the psychological warfare he'd put her through this past week, it would be a gift.

Finally, he brought his attention to her. "What's this about a camera?"

"I had my camera with me in the warehouse. It's gone. It's worth two thousand dollars. One of them must have taken it."

"I don't think so," Ned said.

Yes. *Here we are.* The warfare again. Making her think she'd imagined it. "Well, I *do* think so."

"And what exactly were you doing with a camera in the warehouse? After hours?"

"I dropped my phone and was looking for it. I had the camera with me. It's too expensive to leave laying around." Jillian held the wet cloth to her cheek again. She wasn't sure what hurt worse, the cheek or cracked skull. "I have a headache. I need to go." She stood, wobbled a bit and steadied herself.

"Jillian," Ned said, "have you been drinking?"

"*What?*"

"Your behavior. It's odd."

She brought one hand to her forehead and closed her eyes. *Don't let him rattle you.* "Of course it's odd. I cracked my head open on a cement floor. I'm bleeding and you're accusing me of being under the influence? Are you insane?"

"I'm quite sane."

And didn't this just push every one of her hot buttons? The daughter of an alcoholic, a woman who spent her life not overindulging so she could never be accused of being irresponsible, was now suspected of being loaded.

The hot, slick ooze of outrage curled around her spine. This bunch had something funky going on with phantom shipments and locked databases and they were accusing her of wrongdoing? The entire place had gone crazy. No other explanation.

She opened her eyes and met his direct stare. "I won't let you do this to me."

Ned held his hands out, all Mr. Calm. "What am I doing?"

"Harassing me. Making me think I blacked out when I didn't. Making me think I didn't have my camera when I did. I won't let you do it."

"I think you need to relax."

She tossed the wet rag toward the desk and it landed on a stack of files. See how he liked that. She wouldn't wait around to find out, but his brick face was enough of an indicator.

"I think you need to go to hell. I'm leaving. If anyone lays a hand on me, I swear to God, I'll call the cops." She glanced at the two men by the window. "Got it?" They nodded. She shifted back to Ned. "Got it?"

"You are free to leave anytime you'd like."

If only that were true.

She left the warehouse, not really running, but not walking either. *Just get out.* On the way to her car in the neighboring lot, she looked behind her and didn't bother to be subtle about it. After tonight, any faux pleasantries would be cast aside.

In short, this was war.

Her phone rang. She glanced down at her purse. How the hell did it get there after she'd thrown it? Cliff must have put it there. She dug it from her purse. Jack calling. "Hi."

"Where have you been?"

"Hold on. Let me get into my car."

She fumbled her keys and her vision blurred, but she managed to hit the button to unlock the doors. Once inside, she locked the door again, and tossed the phone on the seat so she could concentrate on driving. Not an easy task with the road bending and twisting in front of her. Driving with a head injury. She'd be lucky to survive it.

Her Bluetooth connected. "You there?"

"I'm here," he said.

"They caught me taking pictures."

"Dammit! What happened? I knew you shouldn't have done that alone."

Now he's going to lecture me?

"Can you save the nagging? It's been a trying night. Meet me at my house—nope, forget that, can't talk at my house. Meet me at your house and I'll fill you in."

BY THE TIME LYNX ABANDONED HIS TRIP TO STENNAR PHARM, hooked a U-turn to drive Vic home and got to his building, Jillian was in front of the main entrance, probably freezing her ass off in the misty rain blanketing the city.

The ride home enabled him to conjure all sorts of possibilities. None of which were good. Best to let her tell him what happened.

She looked like hell. And something about the way her coat was buttoned up to her neck was off. Toss in the shadows under her eyes and—*whoa*—that had better not be a bruise on her cheek.

A storm raged inside his mind. All those scenarios he'd conjured? One had her strapped to a chair being interrogated. Mr. Paranoid, that's him. Now he wasn't so sure it was paranoia. But before he lost his shit on someone, he'd get the details. "What happened to your face?"

"I fell." She pointed to the side of her head. "Feel that. Gently. Please."

A lump the size of a tennis ball met his fingers and his shit-losing meter ticked up another notch. "What the hell?"

"Hit my head on the warehouse floor when some part-timer tackled me."

He folded his arms. "*Tackled* you?"

"Save it, superhero. Not worth the energy and I don't need you going all alpha on me. I'm tired, I'm cold and I've got the SD card from my camera stuck in my bra, so let's get upstairs and you can give me ice while you download photos."

He punched in his building entry code and held the lobby door open. "And you'll tell me what happened."

"Yes. I'll tell you what happened."

"Do we need to get you to a hospital?"

She started to shake her head, but stopped. Better to not incite a dizzy spell. "No. It just hurts now."

On the elevator, he tried not to stare. Tried. She refused to look at him. Just as well. One thing he hadn't expected—which was saying something for the King of the Paranoids—was Jillian getting physically assaulted. Whatever happened in that warehouse, she'd, as of this evening, thrown herself into the lion's den.

He stepped through his door, flipped on the hall light and gave the room a quick scan.

"Are you okay?" she asked.

She had her head mashed and she was concerned about *him*? He tossed his keys on the end table near the sofa.

"I'm worried about you." He pointed to the sofa. "Sit. I'll get ice and you'll tell me what happened."

Tell him, she did. He sat across from her listening and controlling his temper because—*holy buckets*—his nerve endings were in the red and boiling his skin from inside out. Total overheat. He wanted to goddamned strangle someone. Just wrap his fucking fingers around Cliff's throat and squeeze.

But he needed to stay calm. He'd known it was too much of a risk to let her snoop around that warehouse and—fucking imbecile that he was—he'd let her do it anyway. *Dumbass.*

A few times, he stopped and questioned something in her story, but all in all she'd provided fairly expansive details. "So, they didn't hit you? You got the bump when you fell?"

"Yes. And Ned was careful to make sure I was taken care of."

"He's not gonna risk a lawsuit."

"They stole my camera."

"Of course they did. They don't realize you took the SD card out."

To think she'd stayed dialed in enough to do that. Smart woman.

She closed her eyes. "I love that camera. I worked so hard for it."

He reached over and squeezed her hand. "I know. I'm sorry."

"I want it back. I'm gonna get it back."

He didn't have the heart to tell her that camera was probably already at the bottom of the Chicago River. "I'll download the pictures from the SD card and send them off to a few people. See if anything pops."

"Is that safe?"

He sat back. "Compared to what? We don't know what the hell is going on."

"Good point."

"I'll take care of the pictures."

She held the ice pack to her head and closed her eyes again. He'd have liked to sit next to her and hold her, but she might think of it as babying and he was damned sure that wouldn't fly.

"Jack?"

"Yes?"

"Today is Friday. I have to go to work on Monday and face these people."

Screw it. He moved to the sofa and wedged himself next to her. "Give me that ice." Without an argument, she handed it over and he held it against her head so she could rest her arms. "I wouldn't blame you if you didn't go."

"I can't do that. It's not me."

"I know." He kissed the top of her head. "I'm sorry this happened."

"Yeah. Me too."

For a second, she put her uninjured cheek against his chest and played with one of the buttons on his shirt. Not a bad thing. A very good thing, in fact. One that he'd sorely missed about having a woman in his life.

But then she sat up, leaving him with the ice pack in midair. "Now I'm mad. They've invaded my life and taken every ounce of security I'd managed to build for myself. They stole my damned camera. I can't get past that."

"I'll get you the camera back."

Even if he had to buy her a new one.

"How will you do that?"

"I don't know, but we're not gonna let them do this to you. At least not again."

11

JILLIAN UNLOCKED HER OFFICE AT 8:27 MONDAY MORNING. Three minutes to spare before her official start time. The pounding in her head had ceased, but her face wouldn't let go of the purplish bruise marring the right side. At least she'd had the weekend to rest. She'd even enjoyed going to yoga with Jack. Perhaps she found it odd arriving with him while holding hands, like their rules of engagement when it came to yoga had suddenly changed, but there was comfort in this unchartered territory. A stability she'd never known was missing.

Today, she'd hide in her office—not hard to do. What did it matter? The company had basically cut off her work flow. If she sat up here all day napping nobody would know the difference.

But she'd come into work anyway. To save a job she was no longer doing.

Find the logic.

She sighed and started the morning email ritual. Not that there would be much, but she liked the simplicity of the routine.

Debbie, her friend from HR, swung into her office and halted. Her eyebrows inched up at the sight of the blue-green bruise on Jillian's upper cheekbone. "I just heard. Wow. Your cheek is a mess."

"Gee, thanks, Deb."

"Sorry. I'm just...shocked. I can't believe you're here today."

She wasn't the only one. "I have work to do." Not really, but what else could she say?

Deb finally stepped into the office, her stride quick and purposeful. "You don't look good. You're entitled to a sick day. Particularly after what happened. You should rest."

"I want to work."

"I don't know that I'd be here after that ordeal."

Sister, you have no idea. "The whole thing was insane. I still don't know where my camera is."

Debbie crossed her arms, the fingers of her right hand tapping against her bicep. "You think Cliff took it?"

"I don't know."

Liar, liar. Simple fact: Cliff or his buddy had taken the camera. She had the memory card to prove it. Not wanting to risk *that* disappearing, she'd left it with Jack. Even with the alarm on her house, she wouldn't chance leaving it at home. Bad enough her camera was gone, when Cliff, or whomever, realized the all-important memory card had been snatched out of it, they'd come looking.

Jillian rubbed her forehead. "They said I blacked out when I hit my head. I don't think I did, but I don't remember my purse getting to the floor beside me either."

"So it could have happened?"

She held Deb's gaze. "I *know* I had the camera."

"How do you know?"

Decision time. Did she admit she had the memory card?

Debbie, although her closest work acquaintance, wasn't necessarily what Jillian would call a friend to confide deep dark secrets to. In the end, Debbie was still an HR representative for a company trying to make Jillian look like a nutcase.

She sat forward. "After last week, I'd never leave my camera lying around."

"But you forgot it last week."

"I just said I wouldn't do that again."

Debbie held her hands up. "I want you to have your story straight."

"What does that mean?"

Debbie reached behind her and shut the door. "They know we're friends, so I'm not in the loop on this, but I overheard part of a conversation this morning between Ned and Mr. Ingrams. They want to investigate your erratic behavior. They're sending you for a drug test."

Jillian smacked her palms on the desk. "Oh, come on!"

The second the words left her mouth she checked herself. *Dammit.* A trench opened inside her and a rush of anger—water running over a dam—engulfed her. She sat back, held her breath against the rising flood and focused on the wall behind Debbie's head.

These freaking people. On one side of the trench sat rational Jillian who had lived with emotional trauma her entire life. That Jillian knew not to get emotionally invested in any one person or thing. Emotional investments only brought heartbreak. On the other side of the trench sat the Jillian who feared unfair evaluations. The Jillian who made sure to do a good job because she'd had a childhood of living with a drunk who sometimes scolded her for the slightest infractions.

Over the years she'd learned to balance the two sides of herself. To a certain extent, they'd both served her well, but today? Right now?

Both useless.

She brought her gaze back to Debbie. "This is seriously messed up."

"I shouldn't even be talking to you, but I consider you a friend and if you ask me, they're trying to build a competency case against you. Look at what's gone on around here. The office move, and now this thing Friday night? What did you do to piss them off?"

Million-dollar question. "I don't know."

Another lie. No choice. Debbie could be some kind of corporate spy sent to excavate information. The way things were going, Jillian didn't trust anyone.

"Well, be careful. For whatever reason, Ned has you in his sights."

Lynx sat at his desk scrolling through the pictures from the SD card Jillian had given him. Over the weekend, he'd forwarded them to his buddy at State. He'd find someone who could help.

Sometimes Lynx missed politics.

He'd also given the photos to Gavin in case one of his Bureau contacts knew anything. He finished studying the images, but really, he didn't know what he was looking at. To him, they were photos of labels. Nothing special or out of the ordinary. Only, in this case, he didn't know what ordinary was.

Maybe he'd call Jillian and take her to dinner. If dinner led to something more—uh—intimate, maybe he wouldn't fight it this time. Finally give in and allow himself to feel like a man again. All this thinking and analyzing and planning wasn't doing him much good.

Yet the damned calendar hissed at him.

He should rip the thing off the wall. Not that it would make a difference. The calendar flashing in his mind would assure him he'd failed at the one thing he swore he wouldn't fail at. *Great job, kid.*

Two more days. That's all he had left.

Someone knocked and Lynx glanced up to see Mike stepping in. He shut the door. Not an unusual occurrence, but his stride held urgency.

Nothing good in that body language.

Lynx sat back and waited for Mike to drop into one of the two chairs in front of the desk. "What's up?"

Mike propped one hand on the armrest and tapped his fingers. "I just got a call from our contact at State."

"Edwards?"

"Yeah."

Lynx knew him. Weasel. "Problem?"

"He wanted to remind me—like I'd forget—that our contract will need to be renegotiated this year."

Lynx grabbed his legal pad from the corner of the desk and jotted a note. "I'll take care of it."

Maybe he'd even get them a better deal. Taylor Security provided elite operatives who guarded diplomats and ambassadors all over the world. The continued danger in the Middle East would require more diligence. Translation: more men.

"Not why I'm here." The hard tone in Mike's voice stalled Lynx's note-taking. He dropped the pen and waited for his boss to continue. "Edwards said the contract is in jeopardy."

Lynx's stomach pitched. The current contract's value was three hundred million dollars. Not chump change. Losing it would put hundreds of people at Taylor Security out of work. Most likely, Lynx included since the government contracts were his responsibility. But all those employees and their families... *Bad news.*

"What's the issue? I'll get on it."

"Someone from our office is making noise about a pharmaceutical distributor called Stennar Pharm."

Son of a bitch.

"Mike—"

"Stennar Pharm contributes heavily to a certain democrat on the foreign relations committee."

Clearly, whomever was listening in at Jillian's had checked him out, understood his connections and decided to play hardball. Helping her might cost them the contract. The blame would sit with him. Another spectacular screw-up for the golden boy who'd had a rash of spectacular screw-ups.

"Who's the democrat?"

"Don't know. Don't care." Mike sat forward. "I care about my three-hundred-million-dollar contract. Edwards tells me this greaseball politician doesn't want people fishing on Stennar Pharm. Whatever the fuck they have to do with anything."

First priority: figure out who the greaseball politician was. "Mike, it's me nosing around. One phone call to Watkins on Oversight to see if there was anything on the books about Stennar Pharm. That's it. One call. And I asked him to do it quietly."

"I figured. Doesn't matter. That one call rattled nerves. What's the deal?"

"Jillian—the one I called you about who needed the alarm?—works there and got caught in something. No idea what. All we know is her house is bugged, there are screwed shipments and she's being isolated at work. And her supervisor tossed himself off a building a couple of weeks back."

Mike ran his thumb and forefinger along his eyebrows. "Why can't the people working for me stay out of this crap?"

Lynx wasn't sure he'd heard right. "Come again?"

"Nothing." He dropped his hand and flexed his fingers in and out, in and out, in and out. "You think the pharma company is into something illegal?"

"I don't know. My thought is they're dealing in the black market and keeping the cash. I could be wrong. The drug that comes up most often is a blood thinner. If it was a narcotic, I could see it. A blood thinner? That, I don't get."

Lynx waited. One thing he'd learned in his lifetime was when to speak and when to listen.

"How deep are you in this?"

"Not that deep." *Bullshit.* "I'm helping her get info. Whatever it is, they've got her targeted and I'm not gonna let her get hurt."

Mike's dark stare met his. Sure, he was his boss and they were talking about a three-hundred-million-dollar contract, but Mike was an alpha among world-class alphas. He never ran from problems. Or turned on people in trouble. "Do what you can, but no more fucking calls to D.C. We lose this contract, it's on you. Unless you can come up with three hundred million, that'll piss me off."

Lynx nodded. "No more calls to D.C. I'll find another way. Is that it?"

Mike snorted. "Should there be more?"

"No." He should tell him about Janet. He smacked the

pad against the desk a couple times and Mike drilled him with the death look again.

"Oh, fuck me. What is it?"

More smacking of the notepad. "I asked Janet and Gavin for help on the info gathering."

"Son of a bitch!"

"It was after hours and it was done quietly."

Mike poked his finger. "That's what you said about Watkins."

"I know, but this is Janet and Gavin. They wouldn't compromise us. I wanted to be up-front about it. Only reason I said anything."

A muscle in Mike's jaw flicked. The guy was about to lose his cool. In a big way.

"Understood," he said. "It's not the first time we've used either one of them and I'm having a pisser of a time figuring out why I should kick *your* ass for it. Now that you've blown my day to hell, any other confessions?"

Lynx moved his head side to side. "No."

"Hallelujah. You better pray we don't lose that contract."

JILLIAN STORMED THROUGH HER FRONT DOOR, SLAMMED HER keys on the side table and flipped on the hall light. After the break-in, never again would she feel safe walking into a darkened home.

The alarm's annoying, incessant warning beep counted down sixty seconds until launch. *Stupid beeping.* All she'd wanted was a good job that provided financial security. Now she suddenly had prowlers stealing her stuff, a banged-up face and management accusing her of being a drug user. All day she'd been dealing with this ravaging aggravation and yet, she pasted a smile on her face and pretended all was right in her world.

The idea of quitting floated in her mind. It would be the easy way out. But they'd win. Allowing that to happen would be an injustice she couldn't live with. She was worth more than that.

She spun to the keypad on the wall and punched in her code. Blissful silence filled the house.

Thank you.

She dumped her laptop and now much lighter camera bag on the couch and kicked off her shoes. Everything ached. Feet, arms, legs, head. She felt like someone had taken a wrecking ball to her body.

To her *life.*

All I wanted was a good job.

Someone knocked on the front door and she snapped her head toward it. Had she locked it when she came in?

No.

She dove for the lock and flipped it.

"It's me." Jack's voice.

She slumped against the door, rested her head back and found herself torn between laughing and crying. This is what her life had become. Constant paranoia and angst. The very things from her childhood she'd worked so hard to leave behind.

"Jillian?"

She straightened. No need for drama. *Take control.* Gently, she ran her fingers under her eyes, gave her hair a finger comb and hoped she didn't look like a bombing site.

Too late for that. She swung the door open and slapped on her much-utilized I'm-a-happy-person smile. "Hi."

And yes, the sight of him in his button-down shirt, no tie and dress pants, his blond hair a little rumpled, instantly gave her a lift. He looked lean and fit and handsome, and if he'd give her that Boy Scout smile, she'd be cooked.

"Come on," she said. "Let me have it."

He stared down at his feet a second, shook his head slightly, then brought his gaze back to her, the hint of a smile squeaking from his lips.

"You need some grease on that smile, mister. It's not a lot for a girl to ask."

Finally, he let one loose and it reached right inside her and bloomed. "Thank you." She waved him through the door. "Now get in here."

"You're awfully bossy tonight."

"I'm in a foul mood."

"Hadn't noticed."

She pointed toward the back door and marched in that direction. Jack followed her, sticking close to her heels. He knew where she was heading and why. Her home, the place that had been her sanctuary, her landing pad, her *safe zone*, had someone listening to every noise, every movement, every toilet flush happening on the first floor. Not only had her privacy been invaded, her sense of safety had been obliterated. Thinking about it ignited her barely controlled fury.

Pushing open the sliding glass door, she stepped onto her cement patio and moved into the center of the yard before spinning back to Jack, who'd shut the door behind him.

"They're launching an investigation into my erratic behavior. As if *I'm* the crazy one. They're destroying my life and I don't even know why."

"How do you know this?"

"Deb—my HR friend—told me." She paced the yard, propped one hand on her hip and waved the other one. "They're sending me for testing to make sure I don't have a

substance abuse problem. Can you imagine? Me? A
substance abuse problem. With the way I feel about that?
Unbelievable! These people are insane."

Her whole damned life she'd been battling the shame
and embarrassment of being the daughter of an alcoholic.
All those years she'd come home from school or work to
find her father curled up with his favorite scotch. He'd spent
her childhood in three modes: drunk and pissy Dad, drunk
and affectionate Dad, or unconscious Dad. The simplicity of
her complicated youth never ceased to boggle the mind.
Basically, the only time she wasn't on edge was when he was
asleep. Otherwise, she never knew what mood he'd be in
when she got home.

Now someone dared to accuse her, the woman who
vowed—*vowed*—she'd never take a second drink. How
incredibly ironic.

"Bastards!"

"Hey," Jack said. "Take it easy."

Take it easy?

Did this man not understand there was nothing easy
about this? "I have spent my whole damned life battling this
—and to have someone accuse me of it? That, I won't
accept."

He held his hands wide. "Jillian, please. I don't know
what you're talking about."

She stalked the yard again, all that negative, spewing
energy propelling her. "Years, I've worked to take care of
myself and not be like my mother, stuck in her miserable
life, married to an alcoholic who refused to get help. And
this is what my hard work cost me? An employer determined to destroy my reputation. They could kill my career."
She stopped pacing and jerked her hands toward him. "I've
been running from addiction my whole life. This is why I

refuse to be around alcoholics. I don't want the blowback. And now I have to put up with *this* crap."

LYNX PLANTED HIS FEET, CROSSED HIS ARMS AND ABSORBED the information. His temples throbbed, but he focused on Jillian's words and devising a reaction. After all he'd told her about his addiction, she'd never thought it necessary to share her family history?

"Your father is an alcoholic?" No response. Only a blank stare. "Jillian!"

Her eyes locked on his—those big doe eyes he'd loved from the second he'd seen them—and her lips dipped into a frown. Stalling. Obviously formulating some response he would accept. Because, after all, he'd been the asshole who'd been played this whole time.

Finally, she bobbed her head. "He's a drunk."

At least she'd been honest. Somehow, in the conversations they'd had about his recovery, about trying to stay clean, she'd failed to mention her father was an alcoholic.

That meant only one thing. "Am I blowback?"

"What?"

"You said you don't want the blowback. That you've been running from addiction. If you don't want to be around addicts, what am I? Am I useful in helping you with your problems? Am I a *usable* resource? That's gotta be it, right?"

Her head dipped forward and her mouth slid open. *She* was horrified? Fucking priceless.

She stepped closer. "You think I used you?"

He didn't want to believe that, but the snickering in his head, the one that reminded him he'd eviscerated his life, couldn't be ignored. "Since you won't be around addicts, why not? I've been honest with you. From the beginning, I put my issues out there. I'd say, on some level, we've been intimate. Yet, you never mentioned that your family suffers from addiction issues."

Once again, her eyes locked on his. The corners creased in a way that let him know he wasn't the only one mad. "Forgive me if I'm not comfortable broadcasting it. My father refuses to get help. He's not like you. He won't take responsibility. It's humiliating."

Screw that. She'd had plenty—*plenty*—of opportunities to tell him. "My issues aren't embarrassing? You don't think it takes a piece out of me every time I have to admit it?"

"I know that. That doesn't give you the right to accuse me of using you."

"What the hell am I supposed to think? You came to me with a problem and I helped you. At the very least, you're messing with a guy who hasn't gotten laid in over a year. How's that? That about sum things up?"

She jerked her head. "You think I *manipulated* you?"

"That's what it's looking like."

"Come on, Jack. What am I? Some femme fatale who sways men with my sexual prowess? I barely have friends. I'm inept when it comes to caring about people."

He scoffed and she jumped all over him, got right into his face and—*wow*—the woman could blow her top in an outstanding way.

"Maybe I screwed up by not telling you about my family, but you don't get to accuse me of prostituting myself. The way I see it, you've immersed yourself into this process. All I asked from you was help getting a security system. That's it. You couldn't resist strapping on your cape. Not that I don't appreciate it—" she poked him in the chest, "—but you don't get to call me a whore."

"I didn't call you a whore."

She put her hands up. "I'm done. I've had a truly sucky day and I don't need you accusing me of despicable things. Thanks but no thanks. You can leave now."

When he didn't move, she marched past him toward the door.

"Jillian."

"Let yourself out. Thanks for all you've done."

Lynx stood in the yard, half shell-shocked, half pissed that she'd walked out on him. Damned women. To think he'd gone almost a year without this kind of turmoil.

Sure he missed the familiarity and comfort of climbing into a warm bed with a woman he cared about, but this? Forget it. Who needed the bullshit? This is what all the recovery books warned about. The emotional upheaval, the quakes that rocked a solid base and sent a building crashing to the ground.

This was why he should have waited the goddamned year to get emotionally involved. Too late now. The calendar in his head bitch-slapped him. Again.

A car door slammed from the front of the house and then an engine started. Not only did she walk away, she was leaving her own damned house.

"Great," he yelled, sounding like a sarcastic moron. "I'll lock up for you."

Get to a meeting.

That's what he needed. Routine. If he focused on the end goal, he'd make it. He'd been telling himself that for almost a year. For the most part, he believed it.

Except, right now, between this and possibly blowing Taylor Security's three-hundred-million-dollar contract, he was so aggravated he could see how popping painkillers might even him out. Take the edge off.

Get to a meeting.

He ripped his phone from the front pocket of the pants Mike's tailor had forced on him. Everything was fucking changing. Even his clothes. The closest meeting was on the West Side in sixty-three minutes. He had an hour of dealing with whatever this emotional shit storm breaking him down was. Had he stuck to the one-year plan of staying away from women, he wouldn't be trying to justify Jillian's lie by omission.

Did it matter?

Obviously, she'd been using him for his contacts. For what he could do for her. Too bad he'd deluded himself into thinking it was more. He should have listened to his instincts. The ones that had warned him three months ago that she'd rip his heart out.

Screw that. He marched into the house, locked and bolted the back sliding door then went out the front, making sure to lock that door as well. Good thing the damned lock wasn't a double key lock. Then he'd really be screwed and have to wait for her to come back because he damned sure wasn't leaving the house unlocked.

How did he always get sucked into these messes and then wind up feeling like shit? Because he was an asshole who had to take on everyone's frigging life, that's how.

He stopped in her driveway, breathed in and out a few times and let the cold air douse him. All he needed was to refocus. Get himself back on track.

He drove out of Jillian's neighborhood and headed downtown.

At a red light, he rested his head back and closed his eyes because—*son of a bitch*—what kind of sign was it that had him stopped at a red light in front of an urgent care where he could hobble in on a bullshit knee injury and score some meds?

He closed his eyes and swallowed. All this emotional torture could be gone. After a year of being clean, it wouldn't take much to get him numb again. Just a few pills would let him forget. Then he'd start over. He'd done it once already, he could do it again.

Now, though, he needed something to deaden him.

The red light switched to a green arrow and Lynx snorted. A fucking green arrow. Pointing into the parking lot. Message received.

He pulled into the first spot he saw, the one farthest from the building. Maybe he'd talk himself out of it while schlepping to the door.

That didn't happen. Nope. He marched through those sliding front doors, limping a bit for effect. The antiseptic, closed-in scent brought back memories of rehab. It had been over a year since he'd first experienced that caged sensation, but clearly the feeling would never go away.

The young woman at the reception desk glanced up. "Uh-oh," she said, smiling up at him. "Someone has an injury."

You're not kidding, honey.

"Yeah," he said. "I had knee surgery and I just fell. I think I screwed up the doc's good work."

After ascertaining that he'd never been there before, she handed him a clipboard with paperwork and a pen. "Fill these out and get them back to me."

He turned to the waiting room where a handful of people sat. Terrific. Time to kill.

He took an open seat and started in on the paperwork. The voice in his head hissed at him, but he shut it down, focused on his personal information because he couldn't think about a year of sobriety now. He needed relief and it was at the end of this paperwork.

Sweat beaded on the back of his neck. Was it that hot in there? He glanced around. The woman across from him still had her coat on. Must be him.

Shit.

He went back to the clipboard and checked no in all the boxes asking about everything from heart disease to cancer to diabetes.

Perfectly healthy. That was him.

Except his stomach rolled with nausea and sweat poured down his back and—*goddammit*—this was not the way this should be.

His phone rang and he dug it from his pocket to silence it. Vic's name on the screen. *Can I not get a break tonight?* He pushed the ignore button and shoved the phone back into his jacket.

The voice mail chime sounded.

Jesus Christ.

And then the hissing started. *Get to a meeting.*

He set the clipboard on his lap and leaned his head against the wall. Closing his eyes, he took a few breaths of stale air. Air that reminded him of his days at rehab and windows that wouldn't open.

Get to a meeting.

"Mr. Lynx?" the receptionist asked. "Are you all right?"

No, I'm not.

He opened his eyes, stared at the young woman with the kind brown eyes, and he felt like a lying piece of shit who would deceive anyone for a fix. Exactly who he'd never wanted to be.

He stood, walked to the desk, pulled the sheets off the clipboard and handed it back to her. "I can't stay. I'll have to come back later."

Not waiting for a response, he hauled ass from the room.

A digital clock on the lobby wall told him he had twenty minutes to get to that meeting on the West Side.

Twenty minutes. He shoved the crumpled paperwork into his jacket pocket and once again stepped into the night air.

12

HE ARRIVED AT THE MEETING FIVE MINUTES LATE. BUT HEY, HE was here rather than in some clinic faking an injury to score pain meds. That nasty seed still had some life to it, but one thing about him, he knew how to surround himself with people who got shit done.

Which is what he had to do now. DEFCON 1. He'd almost blown it. How many days had he craved the numbness that drugs brought him? After the first six months of recovery, he'd stopped counting the nights he dreamed about using. The counting did him no good. It only reminded him of the battle.

Probably always would. It had taken months to intellectually wrap himself around the idea that he liked being high. As with anything in life, just because he enjoyed it, didn't mean it was a good idea.

Sort of like Jillian.

The responsible Lynx knew that, but for the past three hundred sixty-three days, his life had been about battling the cravings. Christ, he wanted to give in. Forget all this thinking and fighting and yearning.

The meeting moderator saved him, the latecomer, for last and asked if he had anything he'd like to share.

Not particularly, but he knew this was an integral part of staying on the right path. He introduced himself and went through his spiel, offering only the basics on how he'd wound up addicted to pain meds. Getting oriented to new meetings would never be his favorite activity. He liked his regular meeting with the familiar narcotic addicts who shared the same issues. There was peace there. A common bond that connected them.

But, sometimes, when he felt unsteady and panicked and about to wreck all his good work, any meeting would do.

By 7:55 he was back on Lake Shore. His mind may have been rescued from the immediate urge to swallow a few pills, but the idea of going home to his empty apartment—and cold bed—wouldn't do him an ounce of good.

Detour.

He turned onto Ashland just as his phone rang. Jillian.

Third time.

He couldn't talk now. Not to her, anyway. What he needed was to get his head together. Talking to her when he was still teetering on that critical ledge would screw him over.

At the very least, he should make sure she was okay. He pulled into a pharmacy parking lot—how appropriate—and shot her a text. When she responded that she was fine, he told her he'd call later.

After he got through his fucked-up crisis and figured out what the hell he was supposed to do.

He pulled back into traffic and punched the radio on. Sammy Hagar asking why it couldn't be love.

"Oh, hell no."

He silenced the radio. Everything was a frigging trigger.

Five minutes later, he pulled into the open spot in Vic's driveway. The Tahoe was there, the minivan not. Someone was gone. Most likely Gina, because the big man would rather bludgeon himself than drive a minivan.

The curtain on the back door swept open and Gina looked out. Lynx sighed. His entire rebuilt world was coming apart at record speed and Vic driving a minivan only added to the insanity.

She waved him in. No choice now. He pushed the car door open and trudged up the steps.

"Hey," he said when Gina opened the door.

By the looks of the dark rings around her eyes, the twins were exhausting her. As usual, she offered him that welcoming smile—a mother's smile—that instantly put him at ease. "Hey, yourself. This is a nice surprise."

He stepped through the doorway. "Am I interrupting?"

"Nope. I'm guessing you're looking for Vic. He's not here. He'll be back in a few. Ava won't sleep so he's driving her around. Which we'll pay for later when she can't fall asleep without movement, but right now, we're desperate."

"I'm sorry."

"Yeah, me too. All I keep hearing is that Justin is a good sleeper and we females are a pain in my husband's ass."

Lynx forced himself not to laugh. "Tell me Vic did not say that to you."

"Of course he did. He's an idiot. But he's also an idiot who's been up since four, worked all day and is now driving our crabby daughter around so I can get a few minutes of peace." She pushed Lynx to a chair. "Have you eaten?"

"It's okay. I'll grab something."

"Don't be a jerk. I have leftovers from dinner. Meatloaf."

"Not the meatloaf. Vic loves the meatloaf. He'll crucify me if I eat the last of it."

Already, she was in the fridge, pulling containers and stacking them on the counter. "He'll moan about it and I'll make him another meatloaf. He just needs to be heard."

"Most of us do, I guess."

"I'd like him to be heard a little less often."

Now he laughed and it was a good, honest one that hit him square in the chest. "You guys are nuts."

She closed the fridge and faced him. "That's for sure. I look at him and, after knowing him all those years, the bachelor, the loner, the *player*, I can't believe he's so good—in his own perverse way—at being a father to my children. Even the ones who aren't technically his."

"Some truth there."

On cue, the back door opened. Vic stepped in carrying Ava in one of those car seats with the handle. A pink fuzzy blanket had been tucked around her little body, and she looked sweet and innocent and peaceful. Lynx took another blast to the chest. *Tough night.* Vic held his finger to his lips.

"Thank God," Gina said.

Ava's cute baby eyes opened and she looked straight up at Vic, who said, "Oh, shit."

Then her sweet bow lips parted and the sound that came out defied human possibilities. The high-strung wail hit Lynx's ears like a pick ax. "Yikes."

"Christ sakes, Gina," Vic hollered, and Ava screamed louder. "She was out. *Was* being the key word."

Gina rushed over and grabbed the car seat. "I'm sorry. I'm so sorry." She went up on tiptoes and kissed him smack on the mouth. "Thank you for trying."

"All the good it did us."

"I'll take her upstairs. She's overtired. She may just need to cry it out."

"She'll wake up Justin."

"I'll move him to our room until Ava goes out." She turned to Lynx. "Welcome to the chaos of twins. Heat up that meatloaf for yourself."

"Hold on," Vic said. "First you wake up the baby, now you give him my meatloaf? What's next?"

Gina grinned. "You know I love you."

"Besides," Lynx added, "she said she'd make you more."

Ava continued to scream and Gina hustled her upstairs. Damn, the kid had a set of lungs. Definitely inherited from her father. Lynx piled the last of the meatloaf on the plate—might as well polish it off—and shoved it into the micro.

"You know you're giving me a hunk of that," Vic said. "My ass if you're gonna come into my house and eat my meatloaf without sharing."

The microwave dinged. Lynx grabbed an extra plate and fork out of the drain and handed them to Vic.

"Give me some of that corn too."

"What the hell? I thought you ate."

"I did. All that baby crying makes me hungry."

Lynx dumped most of the corn on his plate and gave the rest to Vic, who said, "I called you before."

"Yeah. I had a meeting. Stopped on the way back."

Vic eyed him. "It's not a meeting night."

He dove into his meal. "Needed a meeting."

"What happened? You're as predictable as my dumps and, once again, you're out of your routine. Not a good sign."

More food shoveling. "I needed a damned meeting is all."

"And you hate strange meetings." Vic dropped his fork and it clattered against the table. "You got laid." Lynx shook his head when Vic dabbed at his eyes with his napkin. "Oh, Boy Scout. I'm so proud."

It appeared assholes really did come in six-foot-five packages. "I didn't get laid. Eat your meatloaf and stay out of my nonexistent sex life."

"What happened then?"

Lynx swallowed another bite of his dinner and realized, yes, this is why he'd come here. To talk it out. God help him. Not the talking part so much, but the talking with Vic, a guy violently lacking the sensitivity gene.

But, hell, he might as well admit it. He set his fork down and settled in. "Jillian's father is an alcoholic. Won't get treatment."

"Whoosh."

"Maybe she could have mentioned it? I mean, I've been straight with her from the beginning. At any time, she could have said, 'Hey, I get it. My dad's a drunk.' She didn't say that. She didn't say squat. About anything. So why am I playing the honesty card and she's not?"

After bullying a hunk of meatloaf down his throat, Vic shook his head. "You think too much. You're a goddamned girl."

Lynx's phone rang. Jillian again. He silenced it. "I'm just saying. At some point in all this mess, she could have opened up."

"You don't think that maybe you're overreacting because you want to blow your one-year plan and that scares the crap out of you?"

"Shut the fuck up. Okay?" Even if Vic did have a point, who needed it?

"When has that approach worked on me? Maybe, dickweed, she was embarrassed. Maybe she was thinking if you knew she was a magnet for addicts you'd take off. How 'bout that theory?"

"No."

"Why?"

"I don't know."

Vic laughed. "So, what? You found this out and left? Walked out? You two are a fucking disaster. She's afraid of you because you're an addict and you're afraid of her because you think she'll make you blow your recovery. Twisted."

The phone rang again. Vic pushed out of his chair, grabbed the phone and tossed it out the back door.

Lunatic. "Uh, that was my company phone."

"You'll get a new one."

"Yeah. After Mike screams at me."

"He won't care. I broke his plane once. It's all relative."

"You broke his *plane*? How the hell?"

"Let's focus here. We gotta clean up this Jillian mess before you wind up back in rehab." Lynx threw his hands in the air, but Vic wanted no part of that. "You want sensitive, hire a shrink. Besides, *you* came *here*." He picked up the empty plates and took them to the sink, where he rinsed them and loaded the dishwasher. "You need to talk to her."

"Not tonight. I'm still pissed."

"Fine. Then tomorrow. You gotta call her or do something to initiate the conversation. You need to calmly—calmly, asshole—tell her how you feel. Christ knows I suck at that, but you're basically screwed here. Suck it up, Boy Scout."

Unfortunately, it made sense. He'd been so pissed off that she'd never admitted her father's addiction to him that he'd forgotten to ask her why. Talk about a missing sensitivity chip.

"For the record, *she* walked out on *me*."

"Wah, wah."

"I did go at her hard. And look at you giving me relationship advice. Maybe we'll give you your own daytime talk show to go with the minivan you're driving."

Vic cracked a smile while he added soap to the dishwasher. What Lynx would do for a photo of this. Considering his phone was probably in pieces on the driveway.

"Boy Scout, I could still end your life a thousand ways. And, by the way, you're sleeping on my couch tonight."

"No, I'm not."

Vic assumed the arms-crossed, I-will-bring-pain-to-your-life stance. "Yeah, you are. You came here for a reason. My guess is you're thinking about popping some pills. You're a pain in the ass, but I like you and I'm not gonna let you do it. Are we clear?"

Crystal. This was absolutely why Lynx had come here. To Chicago in general. Down deep, he'd known, despite the crap Vic would give him day in and day out, he'd find a safe place to land.

In his go-for-broke way, Vic brought him out of his sudden turmoil.

Lynx nodded. "We're clear. And thank you. Maybe I'll take you up on the couch offer. I need to talk to Jillian first. This will bug me all night if I don't."

"Take care of it and come back. We'll watch SportsCenter until Matt gets home late for curfew and I have to blow a gasket. Goddamned school night and I know he's gonna jerk my chain."

Lynx stood, looked around the homey kitchen as Vic strode past him to the living room. Even with the crying babies, the aggravation of a teenager and the total lack of sleep, Vic's life didn't seem so bad.

At least he had something to come home to.

JILLIAN PULLED INTO HER DRIVEWAY AND SHOVED THE CAR into park. The motion-controlled overhead light on the garage lit up and she closed her eyes against the glare. She could nap right here. In the two hours she'd been driving around trying to clear her mind after what could only be categorized as her and Jack's first grand-mal argument, she hadn't accomplished much. Sitting in the dark, at least, gave her a moment of peace from worrying about her attachment to him and whether or not their fight had him running off to get high. Or maybe she was giving herself too much credit about *his* level of attachment.

Regardless, she'd called him three times and each time he'd ignored her. Three times he'd refused to pick up.

What was that about? Sure, he'd texted her, but she wanted a *conversation*. That thing people did to resolve their differences. Not a lot to ask. Except he was being a child.

For her part, she wanted to apologize for walking out on him. Terrible blunder. At the time, she'd felt attacked. Violated even. She'd been keeping her family's issues to herself, opting not to share their nasty secrets. She'd been living this way for years and suddenly, the pressure of carrying all that pain and angst burst free, her wounds gaping open, bleeding and vulnerable.

Her immediate instinct had been to self-protect. To hide.

So she ran. And now, Jack had decided to torture her by not taking her calls.

Or he was on a bender somewhere.

She slammed the car door. She couldn't do this to herself. This man was not her responsibility. Nor was he her father, who took every available opportunity to get up close and personal with a bottle. This was the life she'd worked so hard to leave behind.

A life without worry, obsession and codependence.

She jammed her key into the lock. At least he'd done her the favor of locking up. Stupid of her to walk out of her own house. Dumb girl giving into the flight instinct because things had gotten rough. She flipped the key and gave the door a push.

From behind her, someone clamped a hand on her shoulder.

Jack.

A shove sent her flying through the doorway to her elbows. Panic exploded, making her arms and legs, her entire body, itch. She had to move.

Get out. Back door. She scrambled to her feet and bolted.

"She's quick," came a gruff male voice from behind her. "This will be fun."

"Right." A second voice. Not as deep. "Better challenge."

One person she might be able to evade. Two wouldn't work. She reached the kitchen, had the door in her sights, her gaze on the lock and then the inside of the doorframe.

A chunk of her already faltering control slipped. Mr. Responsibility had bolted the damned door. She'd never get free if she had to stop and unbolt it.

The alarm keypad. Next to the door. Panic button.

A thick arm circled her waist and tightened. She kicked backward, landing somewhere in the region of his shin. In one giant swoop, the beefy arm lifted her and slammed her on top of the breakfast bar. Her hip took the full blow and a shock of paralyzing energy careened down her leg. She slid across the counter, ricocheted off the other side to the floor and bounced off her tailbone. Breath-trapping agony brought tears to her eyes.

So much pain. The room spun in a dizzying circle.

No time for pain. One of the men came into focus. A hulking man. His arms were the size of her thighs.

He'll hurt me.

She rolled left, jumped from the floor and dove over the counter, her palms skidding across the cold surface.

The heavyweight's eyes widened. He reached for her again, but his hands slid down her legs. No grip. She spun, threw a side kick and caught him under the armpit.

"Umph," he gasped. "Grab her!"

The second man was shorter but just as big around. Fleshy. He lunged for her and, using the only weapon she had, she smashed an elbow across his face. She connected with his cheek and he stumbled back.

"Bitch," the guy shouted.

He shook his head and his face split into a grin. *He's not done yet.* Her attacker squatted and readied for the fight.

From the corner of her eye, she saw the alarm keypad. A few feet. If she could press the two keys that initiated the alarm, she might get out of this. Five seconds to initiate the alarm. That's all she needed.

She sidestepped, but behind her, the bigger man wrenched a fistful of her hair and yanked. A ripping sensation burned her scalp.

"Ow-owwww."

"Shut up," he said, while his friend crowded her.

"You want to play rough?" The shorter guy backhanded her—hard—on the unmarred side of her face and his ring split her cheek just below her eye. The other man tightened his grip on her hair. More ripping.

Think. "I'm sorry," she said. "You scared me."

"That's the point, you stupid bitch." The bigger guy

tugged her hair again and wrenched her neck. "You need to learn to mind your business."

Finally, he released her, shoved her forward and smacked her on the back of her head. By now, her aching skull stopped absorbing the blows.

She blinked once and steadied her gaze. *Keypad...just a few more feet.*

The beefy guy slapped her on the back of the head again and momentum carried her a step closer to the keypad. She faced the other man. "Wh—who are you?"

"Shut up!" He smacked her again. Same cheek. She sucked air as the burst of pain flashed white and blinded her. She fell toward the wall, her vision floating. Why were they doing this? She closed her eyes and the blissful tug of unconsciousness teased her.

After that last slug, the keypad was almost within reach. Fuzzy...yes, but the panic button was so close. All she needed was to stay conscious and take another step. Or maybe one last smack would get her there.

How much more could she take, though? She had to try. She turned toward them. "You scumbags. What do you want?"

The shorter man stared, his mouth agape. He glanced at his friend. "Can she be this stupid?"

"I'll shut her up."

He raised his fist and Jillian held her breath, waiting for the blow that would either launch her to the keypad or knock her out. A sob caught in her chest and she burrowed into the wall as she inched her way to the keypad.

Right there.

But the huge guy was on her, his big fist knotted, ready to strike. She spun to the keypad and jammed two fingers against the panic button.

Four, three, two, one.

A piercing siren filled the house. Through the door she heard the wail from the outside speaker. Help would come. Someone. Anyone. *Please.*

The man grabbed her hair again, wadded it into a knot and slammed her face into the wall. "Bitch!"

What was left of her cheek succumbed to the attack and nausea took hold, seizing her, making her vision swim. She swallowed once, then again. Her knees gave out and she buckled for a second, but forced herself upright.

Help me.

"Turn it off," the shorter guy screamed.

Not a chance. The only thing that might save her was that screaming alarm. The house phone rang. Alarm company. If she didn't answer, they'd send the police.

The shorter man clasped her hair again and shoved her toward the keypad. "I said turn it off. Don't make me carve you up."

Jillian remained silent, her hands trembling at her side. *They'll kill me.*

He gritted his teeth, set his jaw and his flat, dead eyes told her the next blow would be the worst. She raised her arms in front of her face again.

"Turn it off!"

"My neighbor is a cop. You've got thirty seconds before he comes." A lie, but they didn't know that.

The big guy tried to snake his hand between her arms, but she slapped it away. The shorter one shoved her, grabbed her wrists and pinned them against the wall above her head. Then the other man slid his hand up, hooking her throat and squeezing. She gagged, then swallowed against the fingers digging into her neck.

No air.

A loud banging and yelling started at the front door, but he squeezed harder, cutting off more air. Her chest ached and she gagged. More banging from the front. Hazy now. Distant. Her attacker glanced over his shoulder, seemed to calculate the odds, then came back to Jillian and stared her straight in the eyes. "Got plenty in store for you. Meantime, stop messing with our shipments."

He released his grip and the second guy slid the bolt on the door. "Let's get out of here."

Once again, her knees buckled, but the banging on the front door called to her. Pushing against the wall, Jillian leaped to the slider and engaged the bolt while the shrill, piercing wail of the alarm battered her already maimed head. She ran to the front door, checked the peep hole and saw her neighbor, elderly Mr. Krohl—as if he could help her?—standing on the other side. She swung the door open and Mr. Krohl's gaze widened.

"Good Lord," he said.

She must look a fright. She reached for the keypad, punched in the code and the house descended into silence. The phone rang again and she grabbed it from the end table. The alarm company.

After she gave them the all-clear code, they informed her the police were on the way. What would she even tell them? She'd have to come up with something that didn't sound half-baked. Two break-ins in nine days wasn't a coincidence.

Mr. Krohl peered inside. "What happened?"

Against her good judgment, not to mention every survivor instinct she possessed, she burst into tears. Mr. Krohl wrapped his boney arms around her. "There, there. It's okay now. Let's get you inside."

"Jillian?"

Jack.

His voice forced her upright. He stood behind Mr. Krohl, the porch light illuminating his baby face that had somehow morphed into steel.

"What the hell?" he hollered, shooting a vicious glare at Mr. Krohl.

Her arms came up in a flash. "No! This is my neighbor. Mr. Krohl."

In the distance a siren blared. *On their way.* Time to think. But her mind and body were sludge, everything ached. She glanced at Jack and, as usual with him, an immediate stillness settled her. Somehow, he always managed to help her.

"Who are *you*?" Mr. Krohl asked him.

"Mr. Krohl, this is my friend, Jack." She touched the man's arm. "He'll help me now. I'm sorry I disturbed you."

He glanced at Jack, then back to her, clearly wondering. "Are you sure you're all right?"

She nodded. "Yes. Jack will help me. I promise you."

The sirens drew closer and a flash of red bounced off the street and adjacent houses.

"I've got it from here, sir," Jack said in that officer's voice that made the request sound more like an order.

Mr. Krohl took one last look at Jillian and shuffled back to his adjoining home.

Jack stepped closer, brought his hands up to touch her face, but stopped. "Baby, what happened to you?"

13

LYNX'S THOUGHTS SCATTERED INTO A MESS OF FURY. JILLIAN stood before him, her left cheek busted open, turning purple and oozing blood. The other side didn't look much better. What the fuck had happened?

He brought her close and hugged her and her shoulders heaved. Crying. Behind him, the police cruiser came to a stop and the piercing siren went quiet. Jillian started screaming, howling in his ear about two men who went out the back door.

Chaos. His mind drifted. Gunfire. Bombs. Wounded soldiers. Officer in charge. All of it came back to him. He gathered her closer and held her, making sure not to press her face against him and cause further injury. "Sshhhh. Take it easy. You're safe now."

If he could get her to calm down, to tell him what happened, he could help. From what he gathered, two men had broken in. How, though? He'd locked up. He glanced at the intact doorframe.

She must have let them in. After all she'd been through, she'd never open that door.

The house grew quiet. No more screaming. She hiccupped and gripped his shirt at his waist. Tighter and tighter she twisted the material, clinging.

"I've got you," he whispered. "I've got you. The police are here. Okay?"

She took a huge step backward, her watery eyes on him as she reached to swipe the blood from her cheek.

Two car doors slammed. Any second they'd be walking up to this door thinking Lynx had beat her. Potential shit storm considering he didn't even know what happened.

Throughout his career, he'd learned there was a certain deranged order to a crisis. Once she settled down, she'd tell him everything. First, they'd have to get through the police interview. Not knowing the story, he wouldn't be able to help.

She was on her own.

"What do I tell them?"

"Honey, you have to tell them the truth. We don't have time for anything else."

THIRTY MINUTES LATER, AFTER LYNX AND JILLIAN HAD BEEN separated by the cops, the officers were persuaded that he hadn't been the madman who'd pummeled her and let him back in the house. He still didn't know what the hell had happened. All he knew was that when he came in the door, the cops were walking out to call the crime scene people.

Jillian sat on the sofa and he squatted in front of her. "You okay?"

She nodded. "I had to tell them something. They wouldn't leave."

"That's okay. What did you say?"

"That I saw a weird shipment at work and then my house got broken into."

He rubbed her leg. "That's it?"

"I didn't know what to say. It all sounds so crazy. Tell me I did the right thing."

Lynx moved beside her on the sofa. "You had to give them something. And, hey, if this puts pressure on Stennar Pharm and gets them to back off, then it'll be worth it. I'm getting you protection, though. You can't stay here alone."

She raised her hand to her cheek, but he grabbed it before she touched her face. "Don't."

He took her hand and dragged her upstairs—away from the bugs—to the bathroom, where he settled her on the toilet seat, soaked a towel and gently cleaned the wound.

"Hold it there," he said. "You're gonna need a few stitches. How'd they get in?"

"I was coming home. I had just opened the door and someone touched my shoulder. I thought it was you."

She thought it was him. Sickness filled his gut. "I'm sorry."

"I ran to the back door."

The door he'd bolted. *Oh, Jesus.* His good intentions trapped her in the house. "Did you recognize them?"

"No. They said I needed to learn to mind my own business." She leaned forward and rested her head on his shoulder. "Why are they doing this to me?"

Slowly, he ran his hand over her back. "I don't know, baby. We'll find out, though. I promise you, we'll find out."

After getting the name of the doctor Vic kept on retainer, as he put it, to deal with minor injuries their operatives got while playing with weapons they shouldn't necessarily be playing with, Lynx made sure Jillian was taken care of, got a couple of guys to stand guard outside her house and then, running on pure instinct, had Janet track down Ned Dillard's address.

He now stood in front of Dillard's two-story colonial with the wide front porch and covered chairs. In the dark, the house looked white. A typical middle-upper-class suburban home that may or may not have been paid for with illegal funds. Lynx didn't know. Not yet.

He propped his hands on his hips, fingers tapping and catching on the pockets of his slacks. The March chill pricked the back of his neck.

Don't do this. There were a million reasons he shouldn't walk up to that house. Out of the million, not one, including Mike's three-hundred-million-dollar contract could convince him. This whole goddamned sitch needed to be nuked. And Lynx was the guy to do it.

He climbed the three brick steps, rang the bell and slowly drew a few breaths of night air.

Then he heard voices. One distant and one coming closer. A man's voice—Ned probably—saying he'd get it.

Lynx kept his hands loose at his sides. He might need them. Might not. All depended.

The door opened and revealed a guy dressed in track pants and a T-shirt. His hair was dark with specks of gray and he was an inch taller than Lynx. He looked fit, but if it came down to it, he'd be no match.

"Can I help you?" he asked.

"Ned Dillard?"

"Yes."

Lynx focused the energy consuming him. "My name is Jack Lynx. You know who I am. You've heard my name on the bug you planted in Jillian Murdoch's house. What you

don't understand is the shit storm I'm about to bring you."
He thought about Jillian's battered face, let the spewing rage
build another layer while Ned's gaze darted side to side.
"Lay off Jillian. If she breaks a nail, if she trips on a curb, if
she gets a paper cut from a report you gave her, the shit
storm doubles."

Ned stared at him, his brows drawn together. "What are
you talking about?"

"Tell me you understand."

"I don't—"

Blood barreled into Lynx's brain, a literal onslaught of
anger squeezing through his neck and rising. *Don't lose it.* He
got quiet, relaxed his shoulders and folded his arms. His
years as a military officer taught him how to get people in
line. "This is not a conversation. I'm telling you how this will
go. I know what you had done to her tonight. Tell me you
understand. Either way, you're going down."

"Who is it?" a woman yelled from the top of the stairs.

Ned kept his eyes on Lynx. "A work thing. Be right in."
He came out of the house and closed the door behind him.
Lynx didn't move. Let the fucker work around him. Ned
shifted two feet to the right. "What happened to Jillian?"

"In three seconds I can have you on the ground begging
for your life. Do not fuck with me. Do not fuck with Jillian.
Tell me you understand."

Silence passed between them. Lynx stood still—not
even a flinch. Ned opened his mouth but shut it again.

"Don't make this hard," Lynx said. "The stitches on her
face are enough for me to fuck your world up good. I'll
probably do that anyway, but you help your own cause by
telling me you understand."

Ned shook his head, actually looked sincere. "What
stitches?"

This guy was good. Not that good, though. Lynx grabbed him by the shirt, shoved him against the house and clawed his fingers at his throat.

Ned gagged once and Lynx released the pressure. "That's what you put her through tonight. You like how it feels?"

No answer.

"Any of your men put their hands on Jillian again, I'll rip your throat out. Do you *understand*?"

Finally, Ned nodded, but his dark gaze bounced around again. Confusion. Either this guy was totally playing him or he had no clue what the hell was going on.

Lynx let go and Ned leaned against the house, gasping for precious air.

"One paper cut," Lynx said, "and I come back here."

He turned and left Ned Dillard standing on his pristine white porch, the two-story columns gleaming against the overhead light. Lynx didn't look back. He'd done what he'd set out to. To let this asshole know the game was on.

Only, after this power play, Lynx wasn't sure who exactly the players were.

JILLIAN SAT ON HER SOFA STUDYING THE ANCIENT PORCELAIN lamp on the end table. The one with the bug hidden under it.

Sons of bitches.

She'd loved that lamp the second she'd seen it in the consignment shop. Sure it was yellow, but she liked the splash of color it gave the room. Such care had been taken with this room, right down to the silk drapes she'd found on eBay. So what if the drapes were too short and she had to build a cornice to go over the top of the windows? The cornice had cost her twenty dollars in material and she'd been able to hang the drapes two inches lower to hide the length issue. Stretching a buck had never been a problem for her and it enabled her to make a home. One that provided warmth and comfort and peace of mind.

Except for the illegal listening devices.

Sons of bitches.

Someone tapped on the front door and she spun to it. Must be Jack. Otherwise, Bobby, the heck of a nice guy standing guard in her driveway, would have alerted her. His presence, although a welcome sight, would never make her comfortable. Who could be comfortable knowing their situation had grown so tenuous they needed a guard?

She rose from the sofa inch by tiny inch. Her aching body couldn't move much faster. "Jack?"

"It's me."

"I'm coming," she hollered. "A little banged up here. Moving slow."

I should give him a key.

That was something that had never entered her mind. With anyone. Even the thought of it sent the not-so-dull drumming in her head to a full cymbal crash.

Reading too much into the idea that she liked Jack being here would be a mistake. She never denied her self-imposed loneliness. What was the point? She'd chosen her lifestyle for her own protection. This mess of emotions she was feeling now? That could only be attributed to the torment that had taken over her life. To the vulnerability of having her home invaded not just once, but twice.

She checked the peephole and saw Jack on the other side of the door. The cymbals mellowed. *Thank you.*

She cracked the door and he slipped in. "Sorry you had to get up."

"Me too. I'll give you a key before you leave."

So much for self-protecting.

She shuffled toward the sofa and levered herself into it, wincing as her joints creaked and popped. "They beat the crap out of me."

Immediately, she glanced at the stupid lamp with the stupid bug. They could hear everything.

Jack followed her gaze and wandered to the lamp. "You should soak in the tub."

"My tub stopper doesn't work. One more thing that needs attention."

He picked up the lamp, pulled it apart as he had the night he found the bugs and stared at the tiny listening device.

Then he ripped it out.

A zing of power, or maybe relief, she wasn't sure and certainly didn't care, buzzed up her arms. Maybe Jack had the right idea here. She'd been the target of these maniacs while they invaded her home, her sense of safety, her work environment. Her entire life, up to this point, had been at their mercy.

Until Jack ripped out that bug.

"Jack Lynx, I adore you." Gently, she levered off the sofa.

He put the lamp back together, set it in place and went to work on the device hidden in the dining room air vent.

She walked to the kitchen, waving him to follow. "Quit staring at my face. It's a bruise." *And stitches and a load of swelling.* "It'll go away."

When she reached the kitchen, she scooped up the decorative vase, flipped it over and ripped out the listening device. Jack grinned at her.

"I hope these *scumbags*," she said, getting a little loud on the word *scumbags*, "hear us tearing out these listening devices.

Maybe then they'll realize I'm done with them terrorizing me. They should get out of my life!" She squatted to the floor, lifted the vent cover and, for kicks, banged the metal against the opening a few times. *That'll hurt their ears.* "Bastards."

She ripped the bug out of the vent and slapped it into Jack's hand. "Good work," he said, shoving the bugs into the sink drain. "Hit that switch."

"On it." Marching to the wall switch, she flipped it up. The disposal churned and coughed and, after this nightmare of an evening, she burst out laughing.

They'd tossed the bugs down the disposal. She imagined there was a powerful statement there somewhere, but she wouldn't analyze it.

She followed Jack back into the living room, where he settled himself on the arm of the sofa and she lowered herself into the cushions. "Do you need anything?"

You.

"I need my employer to stop harassing me."

He brushed his hand over the side of her head. Warm hands. Always. Another thing to like about him. "Working on it, babe."

What she didn't trust about that simple statement, she wasn't sure. But there was something in his inflection. Not quite confidence, but not doubt either. *He's up to something.* "Where did you go?"

He shrugged.

"Jack Lynx, you tell me what you did."

He studied the room then jerked his head. "I paid your boss a visit."

"Oh, damn you."

"Damn me, nothing. He needed to make my acquaintance and understand the kind of turmoil I can create with a few phone calls. Now that he's aware, I decided the bugs were no longer necessary."

She closed her eyes for a quick second. "Why would you go there?"

"A look in the mirror will tell you why. I went to plan B."

"One you never discussed with me."

"Here we go." He shook his head. "It was spontaneous, and you'd had enough for one night."

According to him anyway. What gave him the right to decide when she'd had enough?

Or was she being too hard on him? Being alone for so long had deadened her to the complexities of a relationship. "All I'm saying is you could have waited. You chose to disregard any opinion I might have. Reminder, Superman, this is my life."

His stare went rock hard. Pulverizing intensity. She pulled the throw pillow closer. As if that would help her.

"I know it's your life. Exactly why I went to see your boss. What happened tonight will never happen again. I'm not gonna sit around and let some asshole pound you bloody. I have an arsenal I can use against these people. Now they'll see that."

"And you don't think you made it worse by threatening them? They know who you are. They definitely know who I am. If they went to the lengths they did tonight, what else will they do?"

He stood, wandered to the window and peeped out the blinds. Stalling. Eventually, he turned back to her. "If something happens to one of us, I've made sure enough people are aware of my suspicions that the feds will know exactly where to look. Stennar is going down. It's just a matter of when and how. I'm praying I'm the one to do it."

"And where do I fit? Does what I want matter?"

"Of course it matters. My assumption has been that you'd like to bring these people down. Am I wrong?"

This man had an answer for everything and it was starting to make her head hurt. Either that or the painkillers the doctor gave her had worn off. Suddenly, she understood how people got hooked on those things. It would be easy to swallow a pill and let her worries go with it. "No," she said. "But I don't want you getting killed doing it. Whatever they're doing, it's not worth that. For either of us."

"Jillian, I've just showed them my hand. *My* hand is unbeatable. They know that. There are a million ways this could play out. It starts, at the very least, with an investigation by the Oversight committee. If they get through that, there's the FDA and the IRS. There will be so much pressure on these guys, whatever they're doing will have to stop. And, hopefully, these assholes go to prison."

"I agree that's the end goal. You're missing the point, though."

He boosted off the window frame and smacked his hands on top of his head. "What's the goddamn point?"

Oh, no, sir. He was not going to raise his voice to her. "Watch your tone. The point is I need to trust you. I need to know you're not doing crazy stunts like you just pulled. These people are lining me up to look like a nutcase so they can fire me. They want me gone, but I'm too far into this thing to walk away now. It's not about keeping my job anymore. This is about stopping them. I don't know what they're doing, but based on the condition I'm in, it's nothing they want made public. As dangerous as this has become, I want them to burn. So, yes, I'm going into that hellhole tomorrow and I have to face the boss you just threatened."

He propped his hands on his hips and grunted. If he thought she was being a hysterical female, too bad. He'd have to live with it "We're partners in this, Jack, and you disregarded me. I will not be disregarded."

"Hang on. Is this about Stennar Pharm or us?"

Prior to this conversation, she hadn't pondered that. Either way, it terrified her. "I suppose both. One has everything to do with the other. I need to trust you. I don't want to wonder what you're doing and when."

"Meaning if I'm popping pills?"

"That's not what I meant."

"Yeah, it is."

AND DIDN'T THAT JUST SUCK THE MUD? AFTER ALL THIS, HIS hard work, his dedication to his recovery, his self-loathing and subsequent attempts to heal himself, somewhere in the back of her mind, she was afraid he'd relapse.

It could happen. He didn't know any way around that. Every morning he woke up and told himself he'd stay clean. There were also mornings he missed the numbing bliss and had to work harder to convince himself that staying clean was the more important battle.

None of it mattered if Jillian couldn't trust him. Years of dealing with her father's addiction left her jaded. "The addiction is part of me. Love me, love my disease."

"There's nothing simple about it. I *want* to trust you and that means you not throwing your addiction in my face every chance you get. You assume I was talking about you relapsing. I wasn't. I'm talking about trust in general. But you're as scared as I am, so you figure you'll keep reminding me and I'll make a run for it, right?"

"Well, Christ, Jillian, don't hold back."

"Now you're going to spin this? Like it's my fault?"

Whoa, Nellie. He held his hands out. "None of this is your fault."

That, he believed. Bad circumstances, rotten timing, he could come up with at least a dozen reasons why none of this was her fault.

Including him being scared.

She tossed aside the pillow she'd been mangling. "I hate fighting with you."

She slouched back, then winced. If he hadn't forgotten to set the alarm before he left, she might not be dealing with this. "You okay?"

"No. I'm not okay. I need you to...nothing."

"What?"

"Stop being a superhero. I love that you care enough to help me, but what you did tonight? Not acceptable. We're a team in this. All of it. You confuse me. I don't want to care about you. I really don't. But there are complications in every relationship. I at least owe it to myself to try, because I'm crazy about you. Maybe I'm deluding myself, but I could love you. A recovering addict. Do you know how hard that is for me?"

He sat next to her, shifted and stretched his arm across the back of the sofa, close enough that his fingers skimmed her shoulder. "I do know."

"Then let's work together. Earlier tonight you avoided my calls. Don't do that. When you're upset with me, talk. Don't make a plan without discussing it. And please, please, tell me when you're feeling vulnerable. It's the only way we'll survive."

Shit. The woman knew how to set a guy straight. "Uh...okay."

"Are you agreeing or humoring me?"

He laughed. "Maybe both."

That response might get him another ass whupping, but hey—she smiled. Nice to see. Even if her face looked like something out of a horror flick.

"Are you *mostly* agreeing with me?"

"Yes. I won't avoid your calls anymore and I'll discuss plans with you. I don't know that I'll always admit when I'm feeling vulnerable. That's not me. I won't be a whiny pansy-ass. Some things I need to work out on my own."

"I can respect that."

"Thank you. Tell me what I can do for you now?"

She rested her head back and closed her eyes. "Can you find me a bathtub? Please. My body feels bulldozed."

He leaned forward and ran his fingers along her jaw. Just about the only uninjured part of her face. "Baby, your body *is* bulldozed. I'll take you to my place. You can soak and crawl into bed. I'll take care of you."

"I know you will."

14

Jack's tub was better than hers. Deeper and bigger. Not cheap and plastic. She needed this tub. *Add it to the list.*

She also needed to figure out a way to get her battered body *out* of this tub. Slowly, she eased forward and flipped the lever to open the drain. The water had gone tepid anyway. Jack had checked on her a couple of times, making sure she hadn't passed out from the pain meds, but left her be.

Obviously, he'd learned she needed alone time.

You're in trouble, Jillian.

Understatement. She sighed and rolled her body so she could lever out of the bathtub. One thing at a time. After three tries, she'd managed to push herself to her feet without taking a header and splitting her skull open.

That would be the topper.

Jack knocked on the door. "I hear movement. Do you need help?"

I need a lot of help. "I'm good. Thanks. I'll be out in a sec."

"I'll be in the living room. Holler if you need something."

She grabbed the towel and started patting herself down. Oh, the things she needed. Like his hands working this towel instead of hers. She snorted. The stress must have fried her common sense.

"Right, got it." More patting. She'd get good and dry. That's what she'd do.

This whole thing was a little weird. Taking a bath in a man's home had an intimacy to it. Maybe if they weren't alone or maybe if he were her brother—if she had a brother—it would be okay. This, though?

This was weird.

And she had to act like it wasn't. She scooped her underwear, T-shirt and yoga pants off the vanity and began dressing. Creaky bones and all.

She stood in front of the mirror, combing her hair and studying what used to be her face. Now she didn't know what to call that mess. Still, she smacked a smile on and opened the door.

None of this had to be awkward. They were adults. He was just a guy helping her out.

A good-looking, take-charge guy who she'd just told she could love, but still had a couple of days of celibacy to complete.

Lynx heard the bathroom door open and turned toward the hallway where Jillian appeared. She wore a light green yoga top and black pants. He'd seen them on her in class. Comfortable. Unconfining.

"How was the tub?"

"I want that tub. Big enough for two people."

The comment was casual, but a sudden charge filled the room. "Uh."

She closed her eyes. "Mind-boggling how I just said that."

"You're right. It's built for two. Not that I've...uh...ah, shit." Yeah, the wheels were coming off.

Jillian opened her eyes and their gazes locked for a brief second that made him nearly piss himself. *Not ready for this.*

"We'll try it sometime," she said.

He took a step back. What was he supposed to do with that when he still had two more days until he hit a year of celibacy? Technically, at 12:01 the following night it would be a year. Twenty-six hours and he'd be close enough. This year-of-celibacy bullshit was starting to get on his nerves. Starting to? Hell, it had been on his nerves for a year now. Always thinking and not thinking about thinking about women. Avoiding them because he was too terrified to blow his recovery. All because he was Mr. Responsibility, who fucked up and had to prove to everyone he wasn't a total loss.

At this point? Who cared? He was a man, for Christ's sake, and men needed sex every once in a while. Why did getting laid mean he'd blow his recovery?

Again with the thinking. He was tired of thinking.

And avoiding Jillian.

Not until he marched up her walkway and saw her bloody did he realize how much of himself he'd been holding back the past year.

Jillian held her hands in front of her. "No, no, no. Don't freak out on me. I'm just saying it would be fun. Extremely. And now I have this vision of you naked wearing a cape. And, wow, I can't believe I just said that."

She laughed at herself.

He should probably say something. Thanks?

Nah.

Got a helmet handy?

It was his turn to laugh. Although, the tightening at his crotch was absolutely no laughing matter.

She continued to stare at him. "What?"

"I was thinking about whether you had a helmet handy."

A wicked grin slid across her face. "Oh, my."

"Seriously, I'd like to have at you right now. It's all I think about sometimes. For three months I've been thinking about the things I'd do to you."

She opened her mouth and a breathy sound reached him. "Fun things?"

"I'll say this, it always ends with you screaming. And not in a bad way."

"Screaming?"

"Howling."

"I see."

"No, honey, you don't. There are things I'm good at—at least I've been told I'm good at them—and sex is in the top three. Which makes this self-imposed sexual imprisonment even more torturous. I would love to strip you and find one hundred different ways to give you an orgasm. Particularly tonight when all I want is to make you feel better."

Given that she had sworn off men with any sort of addiction issues, he wasn't sure what he expected her to say. He wanted to think they could work on those issues and put all her preconceived notions about life with an addict aside.

She knew better than to let herself love an addict. She knew the risks. She knew the disappointment waiting for her when he relapsed. Everyone relapsed, didn't they?

And yet, she stepped closer and ran one finger down the center of his chest. "What if I wanted that too?"

"Wrong thing to say. I'm trying to hang on here. I got twenty-six hours and I hit that one-year mark."

"Is that what you want? To hang on?"

"I've spent all year working toward it. Plus, what kind of shithead expects a woman to have sex with him after what you've been through? It's barbaric."

"Barbaric? I think you're barbaric to yourself."

She stepped a little closer. He backed up an inch. "I like to think I hold myself to honorable standards."

She rolled her eyes. "But if I say it's okay, why would it be barbaric?"

THE SUPERHERO STAYED QUIET. HAD SHE EVER MET ANYONE SO tough on himself? She didn't think so. Typically, in her world, it was the other way around. *She* took the brunt of her loved ones' emotional deficiencies.

"I don't know," he said.

Finally, they were getting somewhere. Him not knowing, that little bit of doubt, was a whole lot better than his insistence that he was a creep. "Good answer."

Two inches closer and she was right in his space. Barely half an arm length away. Her mind ticked off all the reasons she should walk away. At the very least, this would get messy for her. With her history, her aversion to people with addictions, she wasn't sure she had it in her to give a recovering addict a fair shot. What she didn't want was to take out her emotional issues on him.

But she loved the way life seemed easier with him around.

"I've got almost ten years on you."

She smirked. "Very good. It only took you a minute and a half to come up with another reason why I should run from you."

"It's true."

"So what? You look like a Boy Scout, remember? No one will know. And just imagine, you can be the dirty old man with a young squeeze."

He rolled his eyes.

Then she curled her hand into his shirt and pulled him toward her. "Don't find a reason. Just this once, don't think."

"I have to."

Moving even closer, her lips hovering just below his, his breath wisped over her cheek. So close. "No, Jack, you don't. We're adults. We're responsible. We, I think, care about each other. Stop thinking."

Slowly, he ran his hand down the side of her head, then along her cheek and neck, his touch so soft in contrast to the sensations electrifying her skin.

"I'm scared."

His lips were right there, teasing her, making her want all the things she'd been telling herself she shouldn't have with an addict. All she had to do was lift her chin a bit. "Me too." She inched closer.

Then she kissed him.

"Wait." The word was barely out of his mouth, but she shoved him backward onto the couch and slowly straddled him. She kissed him again. Hard and wet and long and—*son of a bitch*—this was confusing.

"Let's just do it. I can't take the tension anymore. Please?"

One thing he hadn't fantasized about was her saying please and it was definitely something he shouldn't have overlooked. The caged animal inside him busted loose. He cupped his hands over her backside and pulled her closer while their tongues had a party.

So close to a year, it shouldn't matter. Not when every

fiber and nerve ending came alive and made him feel like himself again. Like the guy who wasn't a screw-up. The emotionally healthy guy he'd been before his life derailed. Wasn't that the point? To be healthy again.

To feel alive without the use of drugs.

Gently, he rolled her to her back, let his weight sink mostly into his arm so he didn't hurt her. Damn, he'd missed having a woman under him. Missed the sliding of legs and the heat of skin against skin.

Yep, old Lynx was back.

Jillian broke the kiss, but dragged his shirt from his jeans. "Are you okay with this?"

He cracked up. Her legs must have gone numb, because his hard-on should be telling her exactly how okay he was with this.

"Don't laugh," she said. "I can feel that your body is okay with this. But I shouldn't be pressuring you."

He slid his hand over her chest and took a minute to enjoy holding Jillian's breast in his hand. After all those fantasies. Finally. He gave it a squeeze. "Does it seem like you're pressuring me?"

"A little bit, I think."

"With me pawing at your tits, you think *you're* pressuring *me*?"

That made her laugh. "But the pawing feels so good."

"Then shut up about it. Chances are I'll beat myself up over it tomorrow."

"So, we should wait."

"No. I may drive myself crazy, but I won't regret it. That I know for sure. Now quit talking and let me get laid."

"Okay. But let's do this right."

"Is there a wrong way?"

She wiggled out from under him. "Yes. First of all, my

whole body hurts and the couch will do me in. More importantly, our first time together shouldn't be on a couch like a couple of horny, fumbling teenagers."

"But I'm definitely horny. And fumbling."

"And a comedian to boot." She elbowed her way off the couch, wincing only a little, and reached for his hand. "Take me to bed, young man."

"Ooh," he said. "She's going into schoolmarm mode."

She led him into his own bedroom and his gaze went to the bed. Helluva way to break it in.

"Um, hello?"

"I was thinking about the bed."

She tugged on his shirt. "And all the things you said you'd do to me in it?"

"Oh, yeah."

When she kissed the back of his shoulder, his mind was definitely not on anything other than getting her naked.

Fast.

He spun toward her and kissed her. He'd been thinking about getting this woman into bed for three months. He didn't want to rush it, but his body had other ideas.

Apparently so did hers, because she grabbed the hem of his shirt and pulled it over his head.

Her gaze landed on his upper right biceps and the tribal tat of claw marks and a roaring tiger. "Oh, that is *hot*."

She trailed her fingertips over the claw marks and then outlined the tiger. "You've had it awhile."

"Twelve years. Chalk it up to a bachelor party and a bottle of scotch. Some asshole thought a guy named Lynx would look cool with a tiger and claw marks on his arm."

"It's so you, though."

She kissed the spot where the tattoo sat and his body went berserk. Completely hyperactive.

He tilted his head back and enjoyed her lips traveling up over his shoulder to his neck. "Damn, I've been thinking about this a long time. All I want is to love you." He laughed. "For a very long time."

"Well, tiger, don't let me stop you."

He dragged his fingers over her stomach. Up. Down. Sideways. This was it. All those fantasies and she was right here.

What's the holdup, boss?

He hadn't gotten laid in almost a year. The whole thing might be over in seconds, which, he was quite sure, would obliterate any ideas Jillian might have about a round two with him. That might be the holdup.

He wrapped his hand around her waist and kissed her. Slowly this time. No rush. He pulled back and stared into those big doe eyes and wanted nothing more than to give her the best damned sex she'd ever had.

Except, yeah, it might have to happen in zero-point-two seconds.

Jesus.

She stepped back and held up her hands. "What's going on? You're thinking way too much about this. I can smell the smoke. Are you not ready?"

"I am. So ready."

"And what?"

Here she was, ready and willing, and he was paralyzed. By an erection. That had to be one for the record books.

"I'm concerned."

"Of course you are. When aren't you? Forget it. I'm gonna get naked and we'll have a throwdown. You and me. Cage match rules. Well, maybe not cage match, considering the shape I'm in, but you get the idea."

Cage match? *Gulp.*

"What if the match ends fast?" he blurted. *Way to go, Ace.* She cocked her head.

"It's...uh...been a while. For me." He rolled his hand. "Don't make me say it."

Her eyebrows went up. The big "aha" moment. "You're worried our throwdown will be over fast because you can't—"

He waved his hands. "Zzzzpppp. No need to expand. Please!"

But she went for the button on his pants. "You're a head case. If the first time ends quick, there's always a second. Or perhaps a third. The night is far from over." She drew his fly down, then looked back at him, her gaze right on his. "Shall we?"

That was all the insanity his mind needed. "You're on, babe."

Simultaneously, she was shoving his pants down while he lifted her shirt off. Then she kicked out of her pants, lowering herself sideways on the bed when her feet got tied up in the legs. "Ow," she said. "Crap. That hurts."

He knelt down next to her and grabbed her feet. "Stop. I'll do this."

And he did. Slowly, he eased one foot then the other out of her pants and tossed them aside. Propped on her elbows, she watched him, her eyes focused on his every move while he glided his fingers up her legs. Strong legs. Not skinny, but toned from yoga. Solid.

Everything about her was solid.

His lips followed the path his fingers took and Jillian watched him. "You're not such a Boy Scout after all."

He circled his tongue over her thigh and laughed when she flopped back on the bed. "Boy Scouts have many talents, you know."

"I'm hoping I will see all of them. Tonight. When I'm not sleeping because I'm having so many orgasms."

"Way to pressure a guy."

"Hey, you're the one who said you were good in bed."

He tucked two fingers into her underwear. "Prepare to scream."

"I'm prepared."

"How fond of these underwear are you?"

"Not very."

He reached up, gripped them with both hands and tore. "That way you don't have to move. I can just help myself."

"I like it."

"Somehow, I thought you would." He ran his hand up her belly and cupped her breast. "This bra needs to go."

"Front closure."

"I love when things are easy."

He straddled her and his erection pressed into her thigh, causing her to groan. "Wow."

He undid the bra and pushed it to the side, trailing kisses over each spot his hands touched. She grabbed his face with one hand and brought him up for a mind-bending kiss. And, damn, he was ready. His ravenous, neglected body needed sex. Pure and simple, he needed to satisfy that primal urge that had tested him all these months.

If he didn't think she'd run screaming, he'd enter her and get rid of the chaotic overload in his brain. Then they could get down to the business of making love.

He needed fast, hot sex. Right now. With her body beat to hell, he couldn't risk hurting her.

She knocked on his head. "Hey, fella."

He grinned down at her. "My brain. It's crashing."

"I can tell."

"How about I screw you blind this first time and I'll

make it up to you the second time? I'll be gentle." He nuzzled her neck. "Promise."

She sucked in a breath, but opened her legs. "I say, what are you waiting for, Boy Scout?"

His mind got quiet, yet his head pounded. Using extreme care, he pushed her legs up and entered her in one smooth motion that left them both gasping.

Months he'd denied himself, and his body took a second to adjust to the fierce pleasure of being inside a woman.

Inside Jillian.

And then he began to move, hoping he wasn't hurting her, but the way she urged him on and gripped the bedspread, she just might like her sex a little on the adventurous side.

She shoved his hands off her legs. "I want on top. Now."

Together they rolled and no sooner had he hit his back than she started rolling her hips. He grabbed her hands and squeezed and she grinned down at him.

He pumped his hips and the roaring in his head started. "Oh, shit."

"What?"

"It's gonna be over quick."

She pumped harder. "It's okay. We'll go slow next time. And then the next time."

Groaning, she pressed herself down onto him. "Jillian, you're killing me. I can't take it."

He rolled her back over, shoved her legs up again and went to town, his mind reeling and demanding he be gentle, but his body needed the release that twelve months of celibacy had denied him.

The orgasm hit him hard, searing through him until his body couldn't take it anymore. He caught himself before he completely collapsed on top of her. His breaths came in short, painful gasps and from somewhere, he realized Jillian was running her hands over his back and ass. Just a light touch of fingertips while his dead weight pressed her into the mattress.

"Did I hurt you?" he asked.

"Nope. Kind of wild. And totally fun."

"I'll say."

He slid out of her and rolled to his side, taking her with him. He wouldn't let go. Not for even a few seconds. He'd never been a huge cuddler but after that, it seemed criminal to let her go.

She tickled her fingers over his belly. "Remember when I said I didn't want to love you?"

"Yep."

"I lied."

15

By 9:00 a.m., Lynx was in his office humming "Back in the Saddle Again" while scrolling through his emails.

"Hey, Boy Scout." Vic stood in the doorway and Lynx stopped humming.

"Go away."

Vic stepped into the office. "You missed pancakes and eggs at my house this morning."

"Now I see why you're losing your girlish figure."

"My ass, dickweed. My weight hasn't budged. The agony of teenagers keeps me trim."

Lynx went back to his emails. "You get to do it again in fourteen years."

"Kill me now."

Clearly, Vic was not leaving. Lynx sighed and rocked back in his chair. "Thanks for babysitting me last night."

"I didn't babysit. You had a bad night."

Massive understatement. He wouldn't tell Vic the night ended on a high—very high—note. Right now, he was attempting to not psychoanalyze blowing his one-year mark. As much as he could obsess over it, he wanted to focus on the positives of feeling like himself again, not some tortured pansy-ass who'd thrown his life away. Addiction recovery didn't have to mean he couldn't care about someone. Beyond that, he refused to let himself believe he and Jillian had made a mistake.

Later, they'd have to face the fact that, aside from the outstanding sex, they'd had a major blowout last night and had yet to discuss it. Without question, the sex proved a nice distraction, but they needed to decide what the hell they should do about each other. For now, he didn't want to think too hard on it. Thinking too hard, in his world, meant obsessing. And obsessing was never good for a man in recovery.

For once, he'd give himself a break and not think.

Gavin stuck his head through the doorway and saved Lynx from Vic's curious stare. *I'm popular this morning.* "Hey," Lynx said, "what's up?"

"Got some intel for you on Stennar Pharm."

"The headshrinker is on the case," Vic said.

Vic, being a tactical guy, couldn't quite grasp Gavin's nonviolent approach to matters. From day one at Taylor, he and Vic had clashed. In a big way. They respected each other, but their opinions stretched far and wide. At the moment, all Lynx cared about was what Gavin's FBI contacts had on Stennar Pharm.

"Don't dog him."

Vic slapped his hands over his chest. "Me?"

"Yes, you. I need him. Getting under his skin isn't gonna help."

"How's this?" Vic made a show of clearing his throat. "Good morning, Headshrinker."

"Knuckle dragger," Gavin shot back. "Good morning to you."

"See," Vic said, "it's all good."

Lynx looked at Gavin. "It's difficult, but try to ignore the asshole in the room. What have you got?"

Shoving a legal pad at him, Gavin said, "Stennar Pharm is run by Ted Ingrams."

"Got that."

"He's the CEO of several pharmaceutical distributorships in the U.S. and possibly some overseas. The FBI hasn't been able to tie him to any fraud—yet—but they're not convinced he's squeaky clean."

Lynx perused Gavin's notes. "Is he shipping drugs to the U.S.? I thought it was illegal for overseas third-parties to ship prescription drugs here."

"It is. Only FDA approved drugs that have been manufactured at FDA inspected facilities are legal. Your guy hasn't been caught doing anything illegal, but they know who he is. With the privacy laws overseas, they haven't been able to get any info on the foreign companies."

Vic let out a low whistle and propped a hip on the desk.

"What do they suspect?" Lynx asked.

"Like we talked about the other night, the task force thinks he's selling hard to get drugs at an inflated cost. Supply and demand. They're not sure where he's getting the drugs and suspect they're coming from overseas. Janet is digging into his U.S. companies. She'll see what she can find on the owners."

"Ingrams isn't the owner?"

"Don't know yet. Stennar Pharm is owned by Visionary Pharmaceutical Distribution. It's incorporated overseas."

Lynx jotted the name. "I'll make some calls. See what I can find."

Except Mike had told him to lie low. He'd have to do this without rattling any cages.

The first call would be to Jillian to see if she knew anything about Ingrams running foreign companies.

THAT EVENING, JILLIAN OPENED HER FRONT DOOR AND THE look on her face, that half smile and closed eyes—not quite relief, but close—stabbed Lynx in the gut. He'd called to let her know he'd be coming by with intel he'd received on Stennar Pharm and didn't argue when she offered dinner.

She opened her eyes and stared at him for a long second. He knew what she was looking for. It was what people did with addicts. *I'm clean.* Inside and out.

He couldn't be angry. Not much anyway. Hadn't he admitted he'd thought about relapsing the night before? What did he expect from someone predisposed to expecting the worst from people?

She walked through the house to the kitchen, where she'd set out cheese and crackers and was putting together a meal.

He followed behind. Her ass looked exceptional in jeans. Hey, he was still a man and men noticed those things. "We should talk about our argument last night."

"I don't want to fight."

She wasn't the only one. He shoved his hands into his pockets. "Let's not fight, then."

She picked up the salt and sprinkled the rib eye sitting on a plate. "I was worried about you today. Last night was big for both of us. We had a killer argument, then the thing about not hitting your one-year goal. It freaked me out a little."

"I know, but I'm good. I went to a meeting at lunch just to make sure."

She set the shaker down, but kept her hand on it, her fingers tapping the sides. "I'm glad."

"What I'm stuck on is why you never mentioned your father's addiction. Of all people, I'd be the one who'd understand."

She shoved the salt shaker aside, walked around the counter and stood next to him. "I don't know. I've spent years covering for him. I think it's part of me now. I don't talk about my family. Never have. So when people ask me about my parents, it's awkward. If I say he's an alcoholic, I get the face."

He smirked. "I know that face."

"The pity face. Or, worse, the get-me-the-hell-out-of-here face."

Her shoulders dropped and the tightness in her cheeks eased. Her defense mechanism had finally given him a goddamned break and took a hiatus. Breaking through her barriers was like chipping away at cement with a butter knife.

She grabbed his shirt, pulled him close and kissed him. Just a soft peck on the lips. "I hate fighting with you."

And damn if that wasn't good news. "Me too. It's...draining. But I'm not easy, Jillian. I've got issues and I'm still figuring them out. Combine that with your history and you and I may be a disaster. We'll probably demolish each other before we're done."

"I know."

"So what are we doing?"

She shrugged. "That, I don't know. I like it, though. I like being with you. It makes me want to trust someone."

"You kept calling me last night. You thought I'd blow my recovery."

She stayed silent.

"Jillian, I'd rather you admit it than lie to me."

She finally looked at him and nodded. A solid jerk of her head. "You're right, but it has nothing to do with you."

Ho-kay. This should be good. "Come again?"

"I've spent my life dealing with disappointment. Not just my dad, but my mom too. I love her, but I always wonder why she never had the strength to get us out. Even at eleven years old, I knew she'd never leave him."

A drunk for a father and a confused mother. No wonder. "Has he ever gotten sober?"

"A couple times. It never sticks. I've learned to roll through things not sticking. I still love him, though."

"He's your father. Why wouldn't you? *That* makes sense to me. What I'm worried about is you think everyone who comes into your life will disappoint you."

"I—" She stopped and drew her eyebrows together. From beside her, she grabbed a small plate from a stack, loaded it with cheese and crackers and handed it to him. "I never thought of it that way, but, yeah, I guess I do."

He set the plate down. "Every time I don't answer my phone, are you gonna wonder if I'm using?"

"No."

"You did last night."

"We had a fight."

"Assuming whatever this is between us turns into something, we'll have more fights. I can't promise I won't ever use again. I fight this battle a day at a time. Part of me will always want to use. It's the disease. All I can do each day is decide not to. Bottom line, my demons come with me. I'm good at shutting them down, but I can't promise I won't ever give in. It's a lot to ask, but the woman in my life has to trust me."

· · ·

Trust him. He made it sound so simple. In theory, it should have been. Hadn't he been there for her when she needed a friend? Hadn't he gone above and beyond in this convoluted mess that had become her existence? Hadn't he loved her, even if only physically, when she needed comfort?

In Jillian's world, she couldn't say *that* had happened much.

She grabbed his hand. "I want to. My heart trusts you. You've been amazing to me. My brain is the troublemaker. I look at you and I know you're a good man. You're so diligent about doing the right thing. I appreciate that. And I love being with you. I'm terrified, though, and that's *my* battle. Your addiction is pain medicine. You wake up every day hoping to stay clean. I wake up hoping someone I care about won't disappoint me."

"I don't think there's a twelve-step for that."

She snorted. "I'm guessing not. And I don't want it to be an excuse. I'm trying to explain it to you. This thing with my job? This is a nightmare scenario for me. I've worked so hard to be self-sufficient. To have my employers see me as a model employee. Then they accuse me of substance abuse. I'd rather be labeled a thief than an addict."

"Wow."

"Exactly. We both have demons. Maybe what we need is a little patience with each other. I won't get crazy on you if you don't get crazy on me. If there are times I'm feeling scared about you, about my feelings, whatever, I want to be able to say it to you without either of us getting defensive. It won't be pretty, but that's the chance we take."

The honesty he'd wanted is what he received. In fact, she'd given him a boatload. "I'm open to it. I've done more talking in the last year than I have my entire life. Which, ask any guy and he'll tell you, completely sucks."

She laughed. "I know. I'm not a huge talker either, but, heck, maybe we'll teach each other a few things."

"I'd like that. Let's face it—" he smiled the Boy Scout smile, "—the sex rocks."

She smacked his arm.

He stepped toward her, hooked a hand around her shoulder and kissed her. At first gently, then she slung her arms around his waist and something sparked. He pulled her close and splayed his hand on her lower back. They stood, thigh to thigh, torso to torso, close enough to be a single unit.

To be able to stay this way.

She backed away from the kiss. "I think we understand each other perfectly in *this* area. Now, before I take you to my bed, tell me your new news about Stennar Pharm."

"Such a tease, but I'll make this quick. Ted Ingrams also runs other overseas pharma distributors. The FBI thinks he's shipping drugs into the States and selling them at inflated prices, but they can't prove it."

Jillian pursed her lips. "I've never heard anything around the office about foreign companies. Are they under a different name?"

"Don't know. Janet is getting us some financials on the other U.S. companies. Maybe something will come up on the foreign ones."

"Do you think the delivery I saw last week was an illegal one? And maybe the shipment from the other night?"

"Could be. We need to track where those crates came from. Is that in the database?"

Jillian snapped her fingers. "We can probably get that using Mary's password. Assuming they've logged the shipment."

She walked to the living room, scooped her briefcase off

the floor and dug out her laptop. Using Mary's password from her home was a huge risk, but given what had gone on in the last twenty-four hours, she couldn't worry about it.

War had been waged by her employers and she was ready to fight back.

Upon her return, Jack had added more cheese and crackers to his plate and set it on the table where they could snack. He'd also grabbed a notepad and pen from the drawer by the phone. Always a step ahead. A man who didn't need to be yelled at to get him into action.

Before this, she hadn't known men like him existed.

I could love him.

Whoa, girlfriend. *Let's not get crazy over cheese and a notepad.* Still, he was there with her, taking on her problems, accepting her family issues and not judging her for it. More or less a matched set.

But that way of thinking could leave her with a ruptured heart.

She needed to alter her mindset. She'd known that for a long time, but hadn't wanted to recognize it. Recognizing it meant reacting and reacting meant taking a chance. On him. Last she checked, she had an aversion to such things.

Except, here was Jack with his cutie-pie face and can-do attitude and suddenly, she wanted all he had to offer. That slamming in her chest started. She loved that feeling. A beautiful *whooshing* that let her hope she just might be able to pull off a healthy relationship.

It took Jillian three minutes to log in to the Stennar Pharm system, then another minute and a half to get to the database she needed. She leaned closer to the monitor as she scrolled through the various shipments. Lynx moved his chair next to hers and glanced at the screen. A not so basic spreadsheet contained dates, shipment numbers, locations and various other data. Most of it made no sense to him.

"It's not here," she said.

"The shipment from the other night?"

"Yep. Not here."

"Can you go back to the first shipment? The one from last Friday?"

She tapped the arrow button, held it down for a split second, stopped and then hit it three more times.

"Here it is. That shipment came from Missouri. Mainland is the distributor. I've seen their name, but we don't do a ton with them."

"Anything else?"

"Nothing about where it originally came from. Which is unusual for Stennar Pharm. Well, the Stennar Pharm I used to love. They're strict about documentation. We can typically track a shipment right to the manufacturer. Even if it goes through several distributors."

"Maybe for the regular shipments they're strict, but we already know something is screwed with these other ones."

Jillian sat back. "Do you think Janet can get into those private files again? Maybe there's more information about the origin of the second shipment in there."

He dug his cell from his back pocket and put it on speaker. "Let's ask her."

Two rings and Janet picked up. "This better be good."

Lynx jerked away from the phone. What the hell? "Janet?"

"Yes. Speak quickly. Hang on, you," she said to someone on the other end.

Jillian pulled a fake horror face. "I think we interrupted something."

"Is this a bad time?" Lynx asked.

"Of course it's a bad time. What do you need?"

One thing about the team he'd inherited from Vic: they weren't afraid to speak openly to their bosses.

"Can you get into that Stennar drive you found the other night?"

"Now?"

He glanced at Jillian and shrugged. "If possible, yes."

A long breath drifted across the phone line. "Fine. But just so you know, I'm doing this naked."

Oh, holy shit. "Did I need to hear that?"

"Actually, you did. Gavin just got called out. He needs to leave and your timing sucks."

Gavin getting called out meant someone, somewhere had been taken hostage and Taylor Security would be negotiating the terms of release.

The sound of keys tapping came from Janet's end. "I'm into the database. What do you need?"

Jillian leaned closer to the phone and Lynx caught the scent of her soap. Something flowery again. "Where did the shipment from the other night originate from?"

"Missouri."

"Any other locations?"

"Yes. New York. Mills Distribution."

Lynx made a note of it. "Thank you. That's all I needed. I'm sorry I bothered you. Tell Gavin I'm sorry."

"Yada, yada. Goodbye."

The line went dead and Jillian giggled. "She's funny."

Lynx tossed the phone on the table. "Every person on my staff is nuts like that. Sometimes it drives me crazy. I'm used to being in charge and then I get this bunch. I've learned to be patient and listen because when there's a problem, they come up with a dozen different ways to fix it.

And they all want it done their way. They're a troop of alpha personalities. Even the lone woman."

His phone buzzed and he glanced at the screen. Jessup. From Afghanistan, where a team of Taylor Security operatives guarded a diplomat touring the region. This couldn't be good. He hit the button. "Hey."

"We got a problem."

Lynx shifted his focus to only Jessup. "Go ahead."

"Civilian shooting. The guy came at us with an MP5. Duck took him out."

"Goddammit!"

"The civilian fired first. The shot whizzed past my head. Terrible fucking shot."

That was good news at least. *Jesus.* Another crisis. This one would involve several branches of the U.S. government at a time when their three-hundred-million-dollar contract was on the block. Lynx scrubbed his hand over his face. Time to do what he did best and control the spin. "I'm gonna free up manpower and send them your way. I need you to get me intel on the civilian shooter. Only you. You're the one I trust to schmooze the locals enough to get what we need. And take off the do-rag I know you're wearing. People won't talk to a guy who looks like a warrior."

A short pause. "On it."

"Find out anything you can on the shooter. Innocent civilians don't randomly walk around with submachine guns. There's a reason he came at you. He's either a terrorist or some kind of twisted activist. Find out. We need to head off the PR nightmare."

"Roger that."

Lynx clicked off and immediately started dialing. He needed to reach out to anyone and everyone who could help him contain this story.

"You okay?" Jillian asked.

At the sound of her voice, he jumped. "Yeah. Sorry. I gotta make a few calls."

"Do you need privacy?"

"Only if you're a reporter." He went back to his phone. "Mike? It's Lynx. Can you talk?"

Twenty minutes later he'd spoken to Mike, Vic, two members of congress and the chief of staff for the secretary of state. The shit storm would come, but he'd contained it as well as he could for the moment.

The adrenaline high that came from springing into immediate action began to fizzle and he slumped in his chair. Throughout his life he'd learned to ride out the highs and sudden crashes. During his using days, the highs were mostly smothered, wrestled into submission by the potency of pain meds. Wasn't that what he had craved, though? The lack of highs and lows. Just a steady numbness so he didn't have to think about his screw-ups.

"Holy cow," Jillian said. "You are good at what you do."

He propped his elbows on the table and leaned in. "This used to be my life 24/7. Always a crisis, always a diplomatic situation, always problem solving. For years I loved it."

"And then you didn't?"

He shrugged. "I got tired. It's hard to keep that pace going and still be good at the job."

"You probably didn't realize that Superman sometimes needs rest too."

"Ha-ha."

"I'm right, though."

He spun his phone on the table. "I guess. When I started to break down, the drugs took away that feeling of failure."

"I don't think you've ever failed at anything. You may not have gotten it right, but at least you stepped up."

"That's one viewpoint." One that he should probably think more about.

Later.

When he wasn't dwelling on the idea that he was thirty-six years old and just learning how to accept failure.

16

LYNX OPENED HIS EYES AND SPOTTED A HINT OF MORNING light squeaking through the edge of the window blind. The sun wasn't up yet, but daylight had broken. Jillian's hand rested against his back and he willed himself not to move. To just enjoy the easy warmth of a woman's—this woman's —hand on his back. After a year without it, he realized how much he'd missed the comfort, the familiarity of waking up with someone next to him.

After the taming of the international incident, he'd convinced Jillian to come to his place so they'd both get decent sleep. Bottom line, she wasn't safe in her home. If she'd refused, he would have stayed with her, but he wouldn't have slept. Not with all the dangerous possibilities butchering his mind.

Jillian sighed and he had to move, if only to see her face when she slept. Slowly, he rolled and there she was, her short hair jabbing in all directions and her features softened from sleep. Damn, she was cute in the morning.

Would she get mad if he nudged her awake the old-fashioned way? His mind said possibly, but his body was extremely willing to risk her wrath.

His doorbell rang and any illicit thoughts disappeared. Could a guy not get a break?

He sat up and glanced at the clock. 6:05 a.m. *Hell.*

"What's wrong?" Jillian asked in her froggy morning voice.

Too cute. "Someone's at the door."

He threw on shorts and a T-shirt and made his way to the door. *Better be fucking important.* Ready to rip someone a new one, he checked the peep and found a guy wearing a centuries-old Yankees sweatshirt. The guy assumed someone was on the other side of the door, flipped up a badge and held it to the peephole.

Hello, Mr. DEA agent.

Lynx opened the door and took in the guy's appearance. Late thirties, short dark hair, and a pair of ripped Chuck Taylors on his feet. *This* guy was DEA? Lynx resisted another look at the guy's attire. Nothing short of astonishing for a federal agent. Could be undercover.

"Jack Lynx?" The man's voice had a nasal quality to it. Like he had a cold that had lasted ten years. Odd.

"That's me."

Dude snapped his credentials again and Lynx studied them. Why would Special Agent Kurt Boller of the Drug Enforcement Administration be at his door at the crack of dawn? Probably not a coincidence. He stepped back and waved the agent in. "Come in."

"Thank you."

Boller stepped through the doorway and surveyed from wall to wall. Boxes from Lynx's move still sat in one corner. He'd managed to hang a few pictures, but that was the extent of his decorating on the drab white walls.

He waved Boller to the sofa. "Have a seat."

Boller slumped on the edge of the cushion and glanced around. Nothing about his appearance telegraphed the command a federal agent, in Lynx's mind anyway, should possess. Nope. This guy and his homeless man clothes looked like a three-year-old could take him. Then again, maybe that was what he wanted people to think.

Lynx took the chair across from him. "What can I do for you?"

"What's your interest in Visionary Pharmaceuticals?"

Game on. Boller wanted to catch him off guard and maybe asking about Visionary did that, but he wouldn't think too long or Boller would get suspicious. "Why?"

Boller sat straighter. "Obviously, I've looked into your background. I know you were a decorated army officer who went on to be an aide to the secretary of state. I know twelve months ago you did a stint in rehab for a prescription drug addiction and six months into your recovery left State for the private sector."

"Information that is all readily available. Why are you here?"

Boller didn't flinch. "What I don't know about you is why you're bumping up against one of my cases."

One of his cases? In the words of a very wise man Lynx once knew, holy shit. Visionary was not only on the FBI's radar, they were on the DEA's.

"Visionary Pharmaceuticals is the subject of one of your investigations?"

Boller sighed.

Sighing? From a DEA agent. What the hell was happening in this world? Lynx sat back and contemplated the man across from him. He didn't know squat about this guy. Typically he'd be on the phone with half a dozen people getting background. At this hour? Forget it.

"Mr. Lynx?"

"I'm trying to figure out how much I should tell you. No offense here, guy, but I don't know shit about you." He rose and walked to the breakfast bar where the phone sat. "What's your office number?"

Boller smiled and rattled off a New York City number. The call went to an automated message at the New York field office.

"Extension?"

"Five four two four."

Lynx pressed the buttons. Straight to voice mail. Kurt Boller's voice mail and—yep—no doubt about it, that voice belonged to the guy sitting in his apartment.

A DEA case. *Son of a bitch.*

From the hallway, Lynx heard the bedroom door open. Boller's head swung in the direction of the noise. "I've got company," Lynx said. "Hang on."

"I'm right here," Jillian said.

Her gaze shot from Lynx to Boller then back again. Boller stood. For a second, he paused at the stitches and bruises marring her face. Yeah, she looked rough.

He inclined his head. "Ma'am."

"Agent Boller, this is Jillian Murdoch." Jillian grabbed hold of Lynx's hand. "Agent Boller is DEA." Her shoulders flew back. He turned back to Boller. "Excuse us one minute."

He led Jillian back to the bedroom, closed the door and pulled her to the far side of the room in case the Special Agent decided to listen in. By the window, Lynx leaned forward, right up against Jillian's ear. "I've made calls about Stennar and now I've got a DEA agent sitting in my living room asking why I'm bumping uglies with his case. I shook something loose. And notice he wasn't surprised at the condition of your face. That should have been his first question."

As he'd done, she put her lips right to his ear. "You think he knows about the break-in?"

"Yeah. My guess is he went to the P.D. and told them to back off. Feds have priority. They trump locals."

"What should we do?"

"How comfortable are you telling him what's happened to you?"

She eased away and her gaze darted back and forth. Panic.

"If you tell me no, that's fine. I'll get rid of him. But if my hunch is right, he knows anyway. Plus, he's got something on Visionary and I'm damned interested if Stennar Pharm is involved in whatever he's working on."

"You trust him?"

He lifted one shoulder. "I don't know, but if he screws us, I know enough people that can make his life hell."

She nodded. "Okay."

He led her back to the living room. Lynx made Boller move to the chair while he and Jillian took the couch. "Agent Boller, we're going to share information with you. We don't know what it means. Could be nothing. We'll leave that to you."

Boller took a pocket notepad from his jacket and held it up. "Do you mind?"

Lynx turned to Jillian. "That's fine," she said. "Since this all started with me, I guess I'll fill you in."

It took fifteen minutes to sum up the various facts of what had gone on between Jillian and Stennar Pharm. When she finished, Boller continued to jot notes. He flipped the page and made more notes. "How do you know where the shipment came from?"

"We saw it—"

Lynx grabbed her hand and squeezed. *Let's not tell a government agent about the hacking.* "You don't want to know."

Boller let out a breath. "Illegally obtained, I presume."

Silence.

The agent shook his head. "Terrific. Moving on." With his pen, he gestured to Lynx. "You're using your contacts to see what they know about Baxtin and Stennar Pharm?"

"I figured if they were suspected of wrongdoing, someone at one of the government agencies had something on them."

"Well, Mr. Lynx, you need to stop making calls. I have agents working undercover and you're endangering their safety."

"Obviously, not my intention."

Boller sighed again. That sigh could have been a rusty saw working Lynx's last nerve. He wanted to wrap his hands around this guy's pencil neck and squeeze. This act of keeping people unsettled had to be Boller's operating procedure. The guy was a freaking ace at it.

He jotted another note and dotted something with a flourish. *Mr. Flamboyant as DEA agent.* "Ms. Murdoch, have you seen any information regarding a company in Vanuatu?"

Vanuatu. Now they were getting somewhere. Gavin had mentioned Visionary being incorporated overseas and Stennar Pharm was under Visionary's umbrella.

"I don't even know where Vanuatu is."

"It's west of Fiji," Lynx said. "I'm told the islands are gorgeous. They have active volcanoes. And liberal tax laws for companies who want to avoid taxes. Strict privacy laws too." He turned to Boller. "Right?"

"Correct. The laws offer privacy to offshore companies incorporated there. The names of company owners and directors do not appear on the incorporation documents. None of that information becomes public knowledge. Even government agencies can't get to it."

Jillian held her hands out. "Perfect for companies with something to hide."

"Yes."

Lynx started mentally putting this puzzle together. Not only did the DEA not want him poking around about Stennar Pharm, they came to his door from halfway across the country to tell him so.

Could they have been the ones putting Taylor Security's three-hundred-million-dollar contract in play to back him off? Maybe the whole story about Stennar Pharm being a contributor was bull?

No idea.

He sat back and stretched his legs. "Stennar is owned by a holding company in Vanuatu that the DEA is investigating."

For a second, Boller said nothing. Not even a nod. Lynx waited.

Eventually, Boller flinched. "We've been watching a particular company in the U.K. for over a year. I'm not at liberty to give you details. Any cooperation or information you can provide regarding Stennar Pharm's connection to overseas distributors would be appreciated."

Jillian sat back and leaned into Lynx. He didn't so much mind and dropped his arm over her shoulder to give her better access.

"Can you tell us why you're investigating them?" she asked.

"He won't tell us," Lynx said. "Open case. He also won't admit he told the local P.D. to stop investigating you getting the shit beat out of you in your own home because they'll bring heat to his case."

And—*whoosh*—Boller shot him one hot-ass glare. No words necessary. The ferocity of that stare told Lynx all he needed. Mission complete. Boller stood, pulled his wallet from his jeans and dug out a business card.

"If anything out of the ordinary comes up, please call me. My cell number is on the back."

Jillian took the card. "Special Agent Boller, it's all out of the ordinary to me."

She threw her head into her hands while Jack showed Special Agent Wacky to the door. The guy looked like something out of a harebrained detective novel. Acted like it too.

Jack dropped onto the couch next to her, wrapped his arm around her shoulder and pulled her close. "You okay?"

"I'm—" She held her hands out, then dropped them. "I don't know. I took this job thinking it would be a great career move. Now I could be in the middle of a federal investigation. Not where I pictured I'd be."

"Stennar Pharm might not—"

"Don't even say it. Of course they're involved. That shipment was documented in a hidden file for a reason. Someone put it there. And my face didn't get like this because they're not involved."

Jack slouched into the sofa and stacked his hands on his belly. "How involved is Ted Ingrams in the day-to-day stuff?"

"Prior to my boss jumping off a roof, it didn't seem like he was involved much. Why?"

"Just curious."

She shook her head. "Please. You have a plan for everything. If you're curious, there's a plan behind it."

He grinned at her and tweaked her nose. "You make me laugh."

She rested her head back and stared at the ceiling. "What am I doing? I should just quit the job. No matter how bad I want to bring them down, it's not worth all this."

Jack hesitated. "You could."

"Oh, no you don't."

"What?"

"You had that if-you-wanted-to-bail-on-saving-the-world tone. "You're the superhero. Not me. All I want is a quiet life. The DEA should not have a part in that."

"But they do."

Again with the tone. She stood. "Screw you."

He flipped his palms up. "It is what it is. You can quit, but what's the point? They'll have scared you off and you'll be left wondering what's going on. Then, a few years down the line, Stennar Pharm will get busted—maybe someone dies because the drugs expired or whatever—and you'll think maybe you could have done something and you'll feel guilty."

This guy was good. Master strategist. She had his number, though. "I will not."

"Yeah, you will. You're the daughter of an alcoholic. You probably grew up in an environment of extremes. Your mother doted on you to balance the insanity created by your father. As a result, you craved the happiness that came with her approval. The more recognition you got, the harder you worked for it. Face it, you like being the hero as much as I do."

How did he know these things?

She snorted and slapped her hands on her hips. "And now you think you know me?"

Jack didn't move. Just sat there on the sofa with his hands resting on his belly like this was no big deal. Two people having a meaningless chat. Or did he know he was reaching inside her, carving up what was left of her emotional scraps and ripping them out?

"I do know you," he said. "I may not be the son of an alcoholic, but I live and breathe for the approval of others. I understand its pull. It is—in fact—one of the drugs I shouldn't have. And you reek of it."

Her pulse banged against her neck and she ran her hand over it. Why would she sit here and let him analyze her? Let him remind her just how damaged she was? She'd done enough of that herself and didn't need the damned superhero laying it out for her. She'd do what she'd done her entire life and sock it away. Just get her things from the bedroom and leave the therapy session behind. "I should go."

"Now you're running because I called you out."

Halfway to the bedroom, she stopped and her mind drifted to the night before when they'd discussed her fears and her need to run from intimacy. She'd promised she'd try harder not to shut him out and already she wasn't fulfilling her end of their truce.

But she wasn't ready to be cornered like this. She turned back and their gazes connected. *Say something.* What could she say? *I'm sorry.*

She didn't even know what she was sorry for. This man confused her and as much as she wanted to believe she would learn to be comfortable allowing him to see her vulnerabilities, she couldn't have that.

He rose from the sofa and walked to her. "You're mad because I understand you and that's scary."

Terrifying. She curled her fingers and her nails dug into her flesh. *Admit it.* When she opened her mouth, nothing came. The words wouldn't break free of that part of her that held her secrets in its greedy grasp.

"It's okay," Jack said. "Don't say anything. I get it. You think someone caring about you means you should care too. It's an obligation and you don't want to be obligated to anyone."

That snapped it. *He knows.* A screaming ball of fury launched up her throat. Nowhere to go but out. "What do you want from me?"

He folded his arms. The epitome of calm as she unraveled. "I want you to be honest with me and admit you'd rather argue instead of thinking about caring. As angry as it makes me, I can't blame you. Why would you want to care about anyone? Every other time you've invested yourself you got a shitload of disappointment."

She shook her head. "I've been through a few thousand hours of therapy. I understand my issues."

"I know you do. You're just not willing to share them with me."

Pressure built behind her eyes and she slammed them shut. *Admit it.* Her head spun and she pressed her fingertips into her thighs. *Hold on.* But the whirling continued and her stomach pitched and rolled and nausea took hold. She opened her eyes, stared at Jack's baby face and kind eyes and wanted to slap him. Just belt him one for making her think about all the reasons she shouldn't want to love him.

Loving him would break her.

The first time he screwed up, she'd be devastated and she wasn't sure, after all the years of fighting her way back from heartache, if she'd recover. "You have enough problems, why take mine on?" She threw her hands up. "Oh, wait. I forgot I'm talking to the superhero. How silly of me."

He unfolded his arms and dropped them to his sides. A few seconds in, he looked at her and his eyes had gone sharp. The look of disgust.

"That's beneath you," he said. "And you know it."

The accusation stung. Fired right through her and settled in her chest. "I'm leaving."

"Yep."

She stormed back to the bedroom. Foolish man trying to get inside her head. He was so wrong. About everything. And even if he weren't, what business was it of his? She'd spent too many years figuring out that she couldn't trust people. Why should she? Emotional attachments never did anyone a damned bit of good.

In her world, attachment meant pain.

Every time.

She grabbed her purse and headed for the front door. The hero was back on the couch with his arms stretched across the cushions. *Bastard.*

She got to the door, grabbed the handle and gave it a yank. Locked. Dammit. So much for her grand exit. Slowly, she flipped the lock and gripped the handle again. Something held her there, kept her frozen in place before she walked out on a man who'd summed up her life in four sentences.

Four sentences.

She rested her head against the door, rolling it back and forth so the cool surface of the door would penetrate.

"You okay?" he asked from somewhere behind her.

Still with her head against the door, she choked out a laugh. "It's taken me twelve years of therapy to figure out what you said in four sentences."

He touched her shoulder and she jumped. He held his hands away. "Maybe I figured out a small piece. The piece that keeps you running from people, but that's not all there is. Not nearly. When things break down, though, that's all you let yourself see."

She turned from the door. "You see it."

"Because I understand it. Maybe my situation is different, but I know what it feels like to want approval. *That's* why I see it. For us, we want all or nothing. And then we're disappointed when our expectations are not met."

"I don't like you analyzing me. I'm not comfortable with that."

"Okay. I won't analyze you. But you have to stop waiting for me to mess up. Eventually, in some way, it'll happen. People who care about each other are sometimes disappointed. That's life. It doesn't have to be a deal breaker."

He was right. She always looked for the escape hatch. She'd just never been accused of it. She leaned against the door, hoping for something intelligent to say. Nothing.

"I don't want you to go," he said.

Thank you.

She glanced up at the ceiling and focused on a tiny crack above her head. *Settling.* Common in structures when the foundation shifts and adjusts to its environment.

Maybe it was common in relationships too.

Walking out would be the easy solution. Just put the whole ugly conversation—and him—behind her. He was the threat. Maybe her own shortcomings got in the way, but without him, her shortcomings didn't matter. It would just be her. Alone. Like she wanted.

She thought.

And yet, she stood at his door, unmoving. Down deep, in that horrible place where she had to face her own demons, she recognized that she'd never be capable of a healthy relationship if she didn't give up this constant expectation of disappointment. Who in their right mind would want her?

An addict with a hero complex, that's who.

We're so screwed.

She gave up on the ceiling. Jack stood there, waiting for —what? "It's not always a deal breaker," she said.

"What? Specifically?"

"I don't know. Specifically. But you just came at me really hard about my biggest hot button and I'm still here. So don't say it's always a deal breaker. I'm resisting the urge to run and I'm scared. Are you happy?"

He smiled. "That you're here, yes. That you're resisting running, that you're scared? No. But one thing I can say is most of the time fear won't kill you. It's what you do with fear that could kill you."

"Yeah, well, let's hope me standing here won't kill me."

"I think you'll be okay. I think we'll both be okay."

17

BY THE GRACE OF SOME ALTERNATE FORCE, JILLIAN MANAGED
to arrive at work by 8:00 a.m. The day already felt as if it had
lasted a month, but she paused in the parking lot to plaster
on the smile of the model employee she wanted her bosses
to see. As much as she despised being there, she wouldn't
give them any ammunition for Operation Nutcase.

After sufficiently convincing herself she could withstand
another day, she swung through the warehouse door and
saw a few of the third-shift crew stacking part of a shipment.
Rick, the shift foreman, a tall, lanky guy in his early thirties,
stood behind a column of totes writing something on a
yellow notepad.

"Morning, Rick," she called.

He glanced up, took a long look at her mauled face and
jerked his head back. "Yikes. What happened to you?"

So much for the huge sunglasses that she'd hoped
would hide the bruises. Without thought, she brought one
of her hands to her face. "Accident. I'm fine."

The rumor mill in the warehouse was a powerful thing
and by lunchtime half the place would know her home had

been invaded. Even if she didn't tell anyone, she was sure someone, somewhere would know.

"Jeez, Jillian, that looks painful."

"It's not that bad."

Even now, her penchant to buck up, to protect her secrets, couldn't be denied. She would have liked to tell him it hurt like hell and that the men who attacked her better never run into her when she had a bat in her hands.

Rick tore off the paper he'd been writing on and approached her. "I was just leaving you guys a note."

A note.

Interesting. Obviously, Rick hadn't gotten the memo that she was persona non grata. She should tell him she couldn't help. After what the company had put her through, she wasn't inclined to do anything outside the scope of her job responsibilities. Which, as of late, was extremely limited.

At the same time, it couldn't hurt to be cooperative.

She took the paper from him. "What is it?"

"We just got a call from a clinic that says they received their shipment, but one of the boxes isn't theirs."

Eh. No biggie. "Did you look it up on the manifest?"

"Yeah. There's no record of it."

That was a biggie. "What?"

"I found their regular shipment in the system, but the tote they have is for Baxtin. I'm not seeing a delivery for Baxtin. It's time for me to clock out. Can you take care of it?"

How her heart went pitter-patter. Considering the drug involved, she'd undoubtedly take care of it. Another phantom shipment. She needed to get her hands on that tote and see what was in it.

"It's only one tote?"

Rick nodded. "Yeah."

Jillian glanced at the warehouse entrance. The

morning shift, including Cliff and Ned, would be walking in anytime. She'd have to beat them to this. "I'll run over and pick up the tote. Then we can figure out who it belongs to."

She'd figure it out, all right.

"That'd be great," Rick said. "I've never had this happen before. Screwy."

"That it is. Which account is it? I'll need the name and address."

He walked back to the stack of crates where he'd written the note, checked his clipboard and jotted the address. "It's Ryder Medical. I can head out?"

"Yes. I'll take care of it. Thank you, Rick."

She waited for him to leave and, with the clinic address in hand, walked out the door and back to her car. On the way, she dug her phone from her purse and called Jack.

This might be the break they needed.

"YOU'RE DOING WHAT?" LYNX ASKED, ROCKING BACK AND forth in his desk chair.

Helluva day so far and it was still early. If he didn't dive into a bottle of painkillers today it would be a goddamn miracle.

"There's a wayward shipment of Baxtin at a clinic. I'm picking it up."

"Why would they suddenly ask you to do this? They've been freezing you out all week."

"They didn't ask. Nobody else knows. Except Rick. He's the third-shift foreman. I was first in this morning and ran into him. He probably doesn't know the freeze is on."

Lynx rubbed his thumb and middle finger across his forehead. "I'll do it."

"It has to be me. I'll just run over there and pick it up. It's only in Skokie."

She'd lost her damned mind. The fact that Baxtin, the drug from the phantom shipments, was involved sent his shit storm meter into the red. "How do you know this guy Rick isn't setting you up?"

"Jack, it's a clinic."

"You don't think an employee at a clinic can be bribed?"

Silence. *Yes, my dear, allow that nasty thought to sink in.*

"Well, hey, I didn't think of that. It's a good point."

"We'll go together. Pick me up in front of my office."

After fighting the tail end of rush hour traffic, they walked into the front entrance of Ryder Medical Clinic and the antiseptic hospital stench that Lynx despised caught him up short. His chest seized.

Jillian, a few steps ahead of him, paused. "You okay?"

He stared at her battered and swollen face, the pixie hair and big brown eyes and thought for a second he might tell her the truth. That, no, he was not okay. But she didn't need that now. If he told her, she'd obsess about him relapsing. *Can't go there, dumbass.* She needed him to focus on the mission and retrieving this box of drugs.

"I hate that smell."

She nodded. "I know. It's stale, right?"

"Something like that. Who do we need to see?"

On the way over, Jillian had called to let the clinic know she'd be picking up the wayward drugs. "They said to talk to the receptionist and she'd escort us back."

Just ahead of them was a winding staircase with a sign pointing up for radiology and left for reception. Jillian's low heels clicked on the tiled floor and echoed through the quiet building. Apparently, there weren't a lot of emergencies this morning because the place was a tomb.

At the reception desk, a heavyset middle-aged woman put aside a newspaper and greeted them.

"I'm Jillian Murdoch from Stennar Pharm. Drew is expecting us."

"Oh, sure. I'll get him up here."

They waited all of three and a half minutes until Drew appeared on the staircase leading from the lower floor.

They shook hands and Drew, being the responsible employee he was, asked Jillian for her Stennar Pharm ID. Old Drew wasn't about to let two people off the street leave with a box of prescription meds.

At least Lynx hoped not, but this guy could be on the take as much as anyone.

After checking Jillian's credentials, Drew escorted them to the lower floor then through a doorway leading to a large storage room. A lidded plastic box sat on a table in the middle of the room and the pouch on the side held some kind of paperwork that stuck out.

"Here it is." Drew held up a length of plastic that must have been securing the lid. "Obviously, we opened it. That's how we knew it was the wrong shipment. The paperwork in the pouch must have gotten mixed up."

Jillian checked the paper in the pouch. "You're missing a box of the blood pressure meds?"

"Yeah. Do you guys have it at the warehouse?"

"I'm sure it's there. I'll check when I get back and send it right over."

Drew nodded. "I don't want to be a dick about this, but how the hell did you people screw this up? The paperwork isn't even right."

But he didn't want to be a dick about it. Lynx let out a long, slow breath. Best to keep his mouth shut and let Jillian handle this one.

"I apologize, Drew. You're right. We did screw it up. I'll figure it out and get you the right shipment."

He shoved a clipboard at her. "I need you to sign this."

Jillian glanced at Lynx, then took the clipboard and signed the form. No way around it, but hell, now there was a trail linking her to this particular box.

She handed the clipboard over. "Thanks."

"Yeah. Sure. Just fix this screw-up."

Lynx had heard enough from this guy. Jillian had apologized. No sense berating her over it. He stepped forward and hefted the box. "I think we're done here. We'll get back to you."

"Make sure you do."

Okay, pal, now I kick your ass. Lynx swung to Drew, but Jillian dug her fingers into his back and pushed him toward the door. Hand signal to get out.

Jillian watched Jack store the tote in her trunk, but her fingers itched to break it open. The answers they craved might be inside and they needed to get someplace where they could open it.

"What are you thinking?" he asked

"We have to open the tote and go through it."

He slammed the trunk and looked around. "Let's find a busy parking lot. We'll head back to that main road. Plenty of strip malls up there."

Minutes later, Jillian turned onto Dempster, where finding a busy spot wouldn't be a problem. They traveled three blocks before Jack pointed to a strip mall with a supermarket and a line of smaller businesses. "Across the street. Right there. UPS store."

The UPS store sat next to a market in a busy strip center.

No one would look sideways at two people opening a box in the parking lot.

The car had barely been parked when Jack jumped out. She popped the trunk from her seat before joining him outside. By the time she'd reached him, he already had his hands on the tote lid, but hadn't lifted it. He simply stood there, hands on the box.

"What?" she asked.

"I shouldn't have touched it. Here or at the clinic. Could be evidence." He shook his head. "Stupid."

"Then I'm stupid too because I didn't think of it. I've got napkins in the car. At least you won't put any prints on what's inside."

A minute later she returned with a wad of napkins and shoved them at him. He lifted the lid and found smaller, neatly stacked boxes within the tote. Using the napkin, he pulled one box and set it on top of the stack.

Jillian craned her neck to see inside the tote. "There should be a plastic bag inside the boxes that's tied with a twist tie. The vials are separated by a foam insert in the bag."

He flipped open the smaller box containing the drug.

"There's your polybag."

Still using the napkin, he undid the twist tie—not an easy task—then slid one of the vials out. Grasping the napkin at the top end of the vial, she took the vial from him and read the label. Baxtin.

Okay, so they knew there wasn't some other drug being shipped under the guise of it being a blood thinner.

"How's it look?"

"I'm not an expert, but everything looks normal." *Hang on.* She brought the vial closer. "Except..."

Jack tilted his head. "What?"

"The rubber looks weird."

Not exactly a shattering crime-solving discovery on her part.

"Weird how?"

"I don't know. The rubber in these tops is usually pristine. After the needle goes in, the rubber heals itself, but this one looks weird. It doesn't look as new as it should."

"You're thinking these drugs have been tampered with?"

She had no idea. Could be. Or maybe there was a defect with the vial. Could be any number of things.

"Jillian?"

Mr. Impatient. "Jack, I don't know. We might be able to check the lot numbers. See if these are stolen. But that means calling the manufacturer."

Calling the manufacturer would trigger an investigation. Could be a good idea that would pressure Stennar Pharm.

"The other night you said the manufacturer doesn't always do recalls. What has to happen to get a recall?"

"Depends. "

"Hell of an answer, Jillian."

"I know, but it's the best I have. Unless the manufacturer recalls the entire lot, there is no way to tell which of the vials were tampered with."

He took the vial from her, wrapped the napkin around it and shoved it in his jacket pocket.

"Wait," she said. "We're keeping that? We'll get caught."

Moving swiftly, he repackaged the remaining vials and rearranged the smaller boxes so the one with the missing vial would be on the bottom. "We'll get this label checked before we get caught."

She put her hands up. "You're banking on something being amiss with these vials so we don't go to jail for pharmaceutical theft?"

He replaced the lid on the box, shut the trunk and turned to her. "Yes."

"Oh, *you* have lost it." And he expected her to lose it with him. A dull ache in her stomach made her queasy. Taking that vial meant putting her trust in him. Believing in him. Her history didn't allow for such luxuries.

He folded his arms and leaned one hip against the trunk. "I'm open to other ideas, but we've been chasing phantom shipments of Baxtin all week. If this vial can tell us what's going on, it's worth the risk."

She stacked her hands on top of her head. "I can't believe I'm doing this."

"I know, but there's not much choice. Time is ticking and you need to get this box back to the warehouse before your boss starts wondering where you are."

"And then what? Hope no one checks what's inside? That won't work. The tote isn't sealed. The first thing they'll do is check the contents."

He brought his hands down and set one of them on the trunk lid. "Then we need to hope we can get this vial tested fast. If it's been tampered with, maybe we can give our friends at the DEA a reason to raid Stennar Pharm's warehouse."

The dull ache in Jillian's stomach turned to stabbing pain. They were about to steal a vial of a prescription drug. If they got caught, they very well could go to jail.

Jack set a hand on her shoulder. "Trust me on this, okay? I have a plan."

Of course he did. "I know you have a plan. You always do. I'm just not sure I like it."

For maximum swaying power, he squeezed her shoulder. This man was *good*. "I understand. Let's give Boller from the DEA a call and let him know what we've got. I'd lay odds he'll want to test the vial. While we're waiting to do the handoff, we'll lock the vial in my office safe."

"I have to take this tote back to the warehouse or they'll know something is up."

"You're going to do that. Not alone, though."

She scoffed. "How are you supposed to come with me?" And if her voice sounded a little shriekish, well, she couldn't help that.

The superhero paused. *Got him there.*

"You take me back to my office and I'll lock up the vial. I'll follow you back to the warehouse."

"And do what? You can't come in with me. How would I explain that?" Now it was her turn to think. "Hang on. You wait outside while I take the tote in. I'll know within a few minutes if they realize a vial is missing. They are so tight on handling the drugs, someone will go through the tote immediately. It just depends on if they open each individual box."

He waggled a finger. "Call me on your cell and leave the phone line open while you're in there. I'll hear everything. If something gets screwed, I'll come find you. I mean, it's not great, but it's all we've got. Are you up for going in there alone?"

She nodded. "I can do it. I may puke my guts out afterward, but I can do it." She patted her blazer pocket. "I'll keep the phone in my pocket."

A car pulled into the spot two down from them and she glanced at the driver. A middle-aged woman. Her paranoia continued to climb. But who could blame her after what had happened this week?

Jack held his hands up for a double high-five. "Let's deliver this box."

"Right. We'll call Agent Boller too."

She dug through her purse for the DEA agent's card and,

when she got into the car, passed it to Jack. "His cell number is on the back."

He dialed the number, then shoved the card in the side pocket of her purse. "Memorize that number and put the card somewhere safe in case your purse is searched."

She smacked her palm against the steering wheel. "You had to say that?"

"Sorry, babe." He went back to the phone. "I got voice mail here."

Never a break. Jillian listened while he left a message then gunned the gas. They cruised down Skokie Boulevard while she frantically checked her mirrors because, well, yes, her paranoia had reached record heights.

"You'd make a rotten spy," Jack said. "Nobody is following us. I've been checking."

"I never said I wanted to be a detective. This whole thing is crazy. My boss jumped off a balcony, we've got phantom shipments, my house was bugged and I my head bashed in. Now, we're stealing medication for the DEA. And we know *nothing*. None of this makes any sense to me."

He reached across the console and touched her arm. "We need one thing to break. That's all. We have a lot of pieces, but not the one that connects everything."

She shoved her sunglasses up and accidentally bumped the spot where the stitches held her face together. A stinging pain shot through her cheek. How had her life come apart so quickly? "Hopefully that missing piece is in the vial."

"Exactly what I'm thinking."

She dropped Jack at his office and circled the block a few times until he called to tell her he was pulling out of the Taylor Security garage.

Her nerves were shattered. She'd have to make it work for her and channel her remaining energy into getting the tote back to the warehouse and talking her way through why *she* went to get it.

No problem.

She glanced in her rearview and spotted Jack's Mercedes, the one he didn't want—and what kind of imbecile didn't want a Mercedes?—two cars back.

I'm not alone.

"I've got this." She gripped the steering wheel tighter. Moisture slicked the surface of the leather and she swiped one hand against her slacks, then the other. She could do this. She knew she could. She jerked her head. One convincing gesture to seal the deal. "I've got this."

18

JILLIAN STOOD AT THE WAREHOUSE DOOR, HOLDING THE TOTE on one knee while she swiped her key card with her free hand.

The green light on the keypad flashed and she pulled the door open. She didn't bother glancing back to the parking lot. Jack was there. She'd watched him pull in behind her and park. Before leaving her car, she called his cell and confirmed the connection. Eventually, someone would come outside for a smoke and wonder whose Mercedes was parked in the lot, but for now he was a directionally impaired guy checking his phone because only crazy people or drug lords drove hundred-thousand-dollar cars in this neighborhood.

Once inside, one of the guys loading a truck in bay one spotted her and jogged over to grab the tote.

"I've got it," she said. "Thanks." Chances of her handing this tote over were nil, but he couldn't know that. "It's the tote from Ryder Medical that wound up in the wrong shipment. I need to figure out where it belongs. I'll take care of it."

She climbed the steps to the first landing, the one where her original office was. Mr. Ingrams's secretary glanced up at her and smiled. "Hi, Jillian."

"Hi, Meg."

No time for small talk. *Gotta run and hide the fact that I stole a vial.* She turned right and entered the stairwell to the second floor.

Sweat seeped from her hands onto the surface of the tote and she gripped it tighter. Last thing she needed was to drop the thing and send it bouncing down the stairs.

On the second floor, she strode to her office, set the tote down to unlock the door then shoved it into the office with her foot. The only noise was the scraping of plastic against the linoleum floor. She tried to embrace the quiet and use it to settle her skipping nerves.

She swung toward her desk, spotted her computer monitor and realized she could have stopped somewhere with Wi-Fi and logged in as Mary to peruse the database for a missing shipment of Baxtin. Still, that would have delayed her and she'd have been forced to explain why the run took so long.

"Good morning," Ned said from the hallway.

His booming voice destroyed any semblance of peace. She spun, smacked her hand on her chest and gasped.

Ned threw his hands up. "Sorry!"

"Holy cow, you startled me." She coughed up a laugh. "It's so darned quiet up here."

The two of them stared at each other for a long minute, each of them knowing about Jack's visit the night before. The air filled with an awkward silence and, despite her nervous energy, Jillian forced herself to stand still. Would Ned bring it up?

His gaze landed on her stitches. "That looks painful. Are you okay?"

Oh, she was not going there with him. "Banged up, but functioning."

Ned nudged the tote. "What's this?"

She motioned at the tote and hoped Jack was paying attention. "That's one screwy problem. When I came in this morning, Rick told me Ryder Medical received a wrong shipment. He couldn't find any stray Baxtin in the system and since he was clocking out, I went to pick it up. I was just about to call Mary and see if she could figure out where it belongs."

Ned bent low, lifted the tote from the floor and set it on the edge of her desk. "It's unsealed."

She nodded. "The customer opened it. When they went to unload the box, they realized it was mislabeled."

Another awkward stare ensued. "I see," Ned said. "Did you check the boxes to confirm all the vials were there?"

There went Jack's grand plan. If she said yes and Ned checked the boxes, he'd know she took one of the vials. If she said no, she'd get in trouble for not following procedure and searching the individual boxes before leaving the clinic. *Operation Nutcase.*

She pumped her fists. "Shoot! I was so caught up in figuring out where it belonged, I forgot to check each box."

Ned pressed his lips together. "Jillian, that's the first thing. Always check the boxes."

"I know. I'm sorry."

To Jillian's horror, he flipped the lid off and went to work on the contents.

Get out.

No. She'd wait. Maybe he'd quit after the top row of boxes. If not, she'd have questions to answer, none of which she had answers for. Her knees wobbled and she leaned against the desk for support as Ned opened the first box and untied the polybag. After ensuring the vials were all in good condition, he placed it on the desk and moved to the next one.

Jillian's stomach dropped and sweat dotted her upper lip. She grabbed a tissue from the box on her desk and pretended to blow her nose. Anything to wipe that telltale nervous sweat. At the third box, his intentions to check the entire tote were clear.

Time to go.

She boosted off the desk. "While you're doing that, I need to visit the ladies' room." She grabbed her purse and headed toward the far corner of the floor. From there, she swung a left and beelined to the staircase.

"Goddammit," Ned hollered from her office, his voice echoing through the cavernous space.

Blood surged and her mouth watered like a bursting dam. *Run.* She blasted through the stairwell door and sent it crashing against the cement wall. Holding on to the metal railing, she flew over the steps. "I'm coming out," she said, hoping to hell she hadn't lost the cell connection to Jack.

At the bottom, she threw the door open. Debbie stood on the other side and jumped back. Jillian shoved past her, skidding down the landing stairs while a couple of the loading dock guys paused to watch the crazy lady running toward the door.

"Jillian," Ned yelled from somewhere behind her.

Don't stop. Pushing herself, she picked up speed, shoved the entrance door open and ran.

*   *   *

No sooner had Lynx slid the car into gear did Jillian burst through the warehouse exit. Damn, she was moving fast. She tripped on the bottom step and nearly did a face-plant on the cement.

"Ho!" Lynx hollered to no one.

She ran toward the car and he drove to the end of the aisle, where she jumped into the passenger seat. At the warehouse's entrance, a woman—maybe late twenties, blonde—saw Jillian and yelled. Whatever she said was muffled by the closing car door.

Lynx lead-footed it. "You okay?"

She bobbed her head, but her breaths came too fast. Panic. He reached for the back of her head and shoved it between her knees. "You're about to hyperventilate. Deep breaths. In and out. Nice and slow."

He shot down the main road of the warehouse complex and turned onto West 35th street. "You okay?"

Still doubled over, Jillian nodded. "I'm okay. Catching my breath. Ned went through the boxes. He must have seen the missing one."

It's over now. After what they'd already put her through, if Ned figured out they took that vial, and if said vial was contaminated or stolen, they'd come after Jillian with the force of the U.S. military. He'd have to get her someplace safe. Her house was out.

Even his place probably wouldn't be safe enough. He needed to hide her somewhere.

Jillian sat up and focused on the road ahead. No move-ment. Just a dazed stare out the windshield and the rise and fall of her chest as normal breathing resumed.

"Who was that woman at the door?"

"Ingrams's secretary. She had to have seen me tearing out of the stairwell. I probably scared the hell out of her."

Or she's in on it.

Whatever *it* was.

Jillian lowered her window a few inches and sucked the moist lake air like a claustrophobic freed from a vault. She needed reassurance. Reassurance that her life hadn't gone to shit and that they'd figure this out. Together.

Only she couldn't go home. Or anywhere she normally frequented. In short, he was afraid to let her be found.

He sat a little straighter in his seat and glanced in his rearview. They needed to get the hell out of this neighborhood before they got jacked. "Okay. Here's the plan. We get that vial to the DEA for testing. Meantime, you can't go home."

"But—"

"Not yet anyway."

This news wasn't what she expected, but she didn't argue. His cell phone rang. Special Agent Boller.

He punched the car's Bluetooth button to put the call on speaker. "Thanks for calling back."

"What's this about a vial?" Boller asked.

Jillian leaned forward as if talking into a microphone. Lynx touched her arm and guided her back to her seat. She cuffed her palm against her forehead.

"It's okay," he said. "Relax."

"When I arrived at work this morning," she said about four decibels too loud, "I was told one of our vendors received the wrong shipment. They got a case of Baxtin, but the tote was marked something else. Plus, there was no record of the Baxtin anywhere, so I—" she glanced at him, "—we went to pick up the tote."

A pause, then finally. "And you *took* one of the vials?"

Jillian winced.

On it, babe. "No choice," Lynx said. "If she brought the

case back to the warehouse, it would have disappeared and we'd have lost any chance at tracking what was in there. Now we have a sample that can be traced and tested."

He stopped at a red light and checked his rearview. No tail. At least he didn't think so. At the green, he drove straight through the intersection, figuring eventually he'd hit Lake Shore Drive.

"You are pushing the boundaries of probable cause," Boller said, his voice strained. "I know you know that."

"Please," Lynx said. "Lawyers and drug cops live and breathe in the gray area of probable cause. Test the vial and see what we've got. Worry about PC later."

Boller sighed. "If the test comes back in our favor, the defense attorneys are going to say you tampered with it."

"And the prosecution will say we didn't."

Jillian held her hand up to stop Lynx from talking. No wilting flower, this one.

"Can we be prosecuted for stealing?"

"We can work around it. If we can prove the vial is a public safety issue, you'd likely be protected by the federal whistle-blower statutes."

She swung her head in his direction. "*What?*" she mouthed.

Lynx shook his head. Mr. Flamboyant had just scared the crap out of her with that whistle-blower status. "Just test the friggin' thing and see what we're dealing with."

Another sigh. "Where's the vial?"

Finally some cooperation. "In my office safe. We'll head there now and grab it. I'll call you back."

He tapped the end button before Boller could respond. Now he had to talk Jillian off the ledge.

"Okay," he said in his best officer voice. "Plan A is in effect and—"

Slam!

Three things registered: his arm going sideways to block Jillian's forward thrust, her head snapping to a painful angle and the *poof* of the airbags deploying.

Something had most definitely crashed into the back of his car.

The airbag slammed into his face, neck and chest like a giant soccer ball. Stinging needles of pain worked through his shoulders and he inhaled the powdery residue from the bag. With the airbag already deflating, he coughed once, leaned back and glanced at Jillian, who battled the airbag with both hands.

The driver's side door opened and someone grabbed his arm, hauling him from the car.

"I'm okay," he said. When his foot hit the ground, he noted a dull throb in his bad knee. *Son of a bitch.* It must have banged into the underside of the dashboard.

"No," Jillian yelled from inside the car, her voice urgent and breathy.

Lynx glanced back and saw her smack at a man.

Shit.

He swiveled back to the guy dragging him from the car. Huge guy with jet-black hair and arms the size of tractor tires.

Boom. Lynx rammed his elbow up and into the guy's jaw, sending him sprawling backward. A car cruised around them and honked, but kept moving.

The guy swung and his beefy hand connected with Lynx's cheekbone. His head jerked sideways. *Yow.* Jillian had gotten hit with that fist. And somehow she was still walking.

Jesus.

"Get her in the car," Tractor Arms said.

Lynx spun back with a chop to the throat. A gagging

sound erupted from Tractor Arms and he stumbled back, clutching his throat.

"No," Jillian shouted again.

Lynx glanced over, saw her folded against the hood, the other guy holding her down. He jumped up, moved toward the front of the car but was flung backward again, his feet literally coming off the ground. He'd never win this fight on strength. The guy was too massive.

Outmaneuver.

Lynx ripped off another elbow shot, connecting with the guy's nose. *Crack*. Blood spurting.

"Stupid fuck," the guy said and blasted Lynx with an uppercut that should have broken a few teeth.

His vision blurred and he swung his head back and forth. Fuzzy. A *whoom* sound filled his head. *Gonna pass out.*

Something hard connected with his bad knee and a shredding agony shot through his leg in both directions. Hot, slick pain consumed him and his knee buckled, sending him to the ground. He rolled and locked his jaw shut. A grunt rumbled in his throat.

Goddamn, that hurt.

He opened his eyes and spotted the second guy standing in front of him with a footlong club.

Sirens wailed in the distance. Police precinct not far.

"Grab her," Tractor Arms yelled.

"Run, Jillian!"

The smaller guy took off, chasing her down. Lynx rolled and shoved himself to all fours, but the knee gave out. *Son of a bitch.* With this fierce pain, his brain should have opened up and started bleeding.

Sirens came closer and Lynx sucked air through his nose to clear the mess in his head. The big guy was just to Lynx's left, but was busy watching Jillian and his partner. Lynx bounced up, held onto the car for balance and rammed the heel of his good leg into the guy's knee.

He went down, but recovered quickly as the sirens reached the next block.

"Forget her," he yelled to his partner. "Let's go."

Two car doors slammed and an engine started. Lynx glanced at the black Lincoln, one of the small ones, making a U-turn. Too far to read the plate number. Maybe an *S*. And a three. He shook his head again and tried to put weight on his bad knee. Nothing doing.

On the next block, the sirens went silent. Pisser, that. The cops were going somewhere else. Life on the South Side.

He glanced to his left—no Jillian—then right. There she was. Running toward him, maybe twenty feet away, her gaze glued to his. "Are you all right?" she asked. "You look a mess."

He snorted. "Probably looks worse than it is. My knee is fried, though. Can't put any weight on it."

Jillian scooted next to him and propped his arm around her shoulder. "That was them. The ones from my house."

"I figured."

"I'll call for help. You're going to a hospital. And don't argue. We'll be safe there and they'll check you out."

A hospital. Where they'd give him painkillers.

Perfect way to fuck up an already fucked-up day.

19

From his ER bed, Lynx stared up at one of three cracks in the faded white ceiling. The longest crack traveled about six inches and hooked at the end. Reminded him of a fish hook. Which was bizarre since he'd never been fishing. Not once.

He lifted his arm and checked his watch. Four minutes of mind travel. Not nearly enough to distract him from the shooting pains bombing his right knee.

Jillian sat in the chair next to his bed, her head back against the wall and her eyes closed. She had to be ready for a nap.

He looked back at the ceiling. A shot of Vicodin would do him some good. Not a lot. Enough to take the edge off. To send him into that nowhere state and dim the tearing sensation in his knee.

The female doc who'd checked him out earlier whipped the curtain back. She didn't look much older than him. She wore her long dark hair in a ponytail and her sunken eyes screamed of exhaustion. How long had she been on shift? He didn't want her screwing him up with Vicodin.

"Mr. Lynx, how's the pain?"

"It sucks."

"We'll get you some morphine." She turned to the nurse. "We need an MRI on that knee."

He slid a look at Jillian, who watched the exchange with big, questioning eyes. Spooked. This is what she'd been waiting for. That moment when he'd have to decide if he'd take the drugs and risk three hundred sixty-five days of recovery. Some fucking irony. His one-year anniversary. None of his plans figured that one.

Morphine.

Admittedly, morphine never did it for him. Vicodin was his drug of choice. A hit of that was like walking into the arms of a lover. It would wrap him up, hold him tight in that place where all pain and anger and heartbreak disappeared. Problem was, the joy disappeared with the pain and anger and heartbreak. All he'd have left was a visit to the land of nowhere.

"No morphine," he said.

The doc raised her eyebrows. "You don't need it?"

"I definitely need it. I'm a recovering addict. Vicodin is my weakness."

She watched him for a moment and her eyes softened. "I see. I can give you Toradol. That's a non-narcotic."

"No."

Jillian scooted the chair closer and grabbed his hand. "I know what you're doing."

"I'm clean almost a year. I'm not blowing it now." He inched his head side to side. No deal. "A non-narcotic will still deaden the pain. The pain and the reminder of how hard I've worked to *not* blow my recovery are the only things keeping me from diving in headfirst. Trust me, I want to, but I can't."

Stabbing agony dug into his leg and he held his breath and locked his jaw against the swirling nausea. If he puked, it'd be all over.

Jillian squeezed his hand and he concentrated on the heat and comfort that came with the gesture. He wanted to prove to her he could do this. That he wouldn't relapse. That he wouldn't disappoint her. Not in this area anyway.

"I don't know what to say," she said, "but please don't do this for me. I don't want you in pain."

He turned to the doctor. "Can you give us a minute?"

"Sure. Let the nurse know if you change your mind. You'll be heading up for an MRI shortly." She spun on her sneakered feet and left the room.

Lynx went back to Jillian. "I've never said this out loud, but I'm terrified right now." He stopped. Took a breath. "You have no idea how hard that is to admit."

"I do know."

"I know I need the meds. This knee is destroying me. But every day for the past year I've woken up and wanted to be high. It never goes away. I think about it for a few seconds and then I put it out of my mind. I make the decision to not go there. Some days it takes everything I have, but I know where it leads and it's not good. I blew up my life on painkillers. And now, I'm lying on this bed like a goddamned weakling and I can't figure out if I want the meds because my knee hurts or because it'll feed my craving."

She leaned closer and rested her chin on her arm. "Why does it have to be one or the other? There's only today and the path you choose to take."

"Exactly. Which is why I don't want the meds."

The door opened and Vic strode through, his big body immediately shrinking the room. *Terrific.*

"Boy Scout, what the hell happened?"

"What are you doing here?"

Vic jerked his thumb at Jillian. "She called me."

Lynx eyeballed her and she held her arms out. "I figured he'd want to know."

"And she was right," Vic said. "Fuck off with the attitude."

Screw him. "Listen, we're doing a-okay without your input."

Jillian stood. "He's in pain and won't take the meds."

Lynx blew air through his lips. What was up with her? Did she *want* him to take the meds? Right. Sure. So she could fall back on him being a disappointment. *Did she even know she did this?* "Thanks. Traitor."

Vic snorted. "Don't be an asshat. Take the meds. Caring for yourself sometimes means making the decision you don't want to. Doesn't mean your life will be ruined. Alleviate the physical pain and don't beat yourself up. You're no use to anyone in this bed."

Jillian held her hands up. "Hang on. You need to back off a wee bit. It's still his decision."

Vic gave her the WTF face and Lynx almost laughed.

Lynx turned to her. "It's okay."

Wrong thing to say. She drilled him with a glare. "No. He's not the one dealing with recovery. It's your decision. Neither one of us should factor into it."

"Damn," Vic said. "I like her."

Lynx pointed at him. "You shut up."

If ever there was a place he didn't want to be it was trapped in a bed between his bullheaded friend and a woman he could easily see himself waking up next to every day while they broke his balls for reasons he didn't quite understand.

The door opened and a nurse came through. "How are we doing, Mr. Lynx? Dr. Rosen asked me to check with you regarding pain management."

Pain management. He needed a whole lot more than pain managed.

"He'll take the meds," Vic volunteered.

Lynx gave him a hard stare. "Back off."

He glanced at Jillian and found her tight-lipped gaze plastered to his face. He didn't know what he was supposed to do. He could fight the pain. He could. But his knee would still hurt like a mother and then his energy would be zapped. None of which inspired him.

"My knee is killing me," he said. "Will you trust me that I won't relapse? That I'll be able to manage this?"

Tears filled her eyes and she closed them for a second. She bit her bottom lip and shook her head before opening her eyes again. "I don't want you to be in pain."

Not exactly definitive encouragement, but it might be the best she could do.

He turned to the nurse. "I'll take the Toradol. No narcotics. Mark my chart or whatever that I'm adamant about no narcotics. And I want to see the bottle it comes out of. Please. It's not that I don't trust you. I need to see what I'm taking and prepare myself."

The nurse smiled. "No problem. I understand."

No, honey, I don't think you do. "Thank you."

The nurse left the room and he set his head back on the pillow to resume his study of the ceiling.

JILLIAN SAT IN THE MISERABLE IMITATION WOOD CHAIR AND watched the nurse push the plunger on the needle. Liquid cruised through the tubing on its way to Jack's veins and at any second the relief would hit him.

Why am I watching this?

Yet, somehow, she couldn't *not* watch. She'd been sitting with him, watching him do mental battle with not only his emotional demons, but the physical ones. Her only conclusion was that she hated to see him in pain. So, she'd done what she thought he needed and offered what little support she could.

She gave him that whole line of crap about taking the drugs if he needed them, but she was a liar. A horrible, disgusting, enabling liar who knew he was suffering and was still disappointed that he'd chosen the drugs.

Ultimately, her fear was he'd get a taste of being high and would want it all over again.

Then where would they be? Each day she'd wonder if he'd used. Was it fair to him? No. Intellectually, she knew he deserved better.

Emotionally, she just wasn't sure she could be fair to him.

Within seconds, Jack's eyes rolled back and a slow smile transformed his face, sheer pleasure so profound that Jillian held her breath. He set his head back on the pillow, that small smile playing on his lips as he closed his eyes.

He's an addict.

Gently, she released his hand and reminded herself the drug was a non-narcotic. But still, the look on his face the minute the drugs hit his system couldn't be denied.

He loved it.

It took a minute for Jack to open his eyes again. When he did, what she saw was the blank stare of an inebriated man.

And she'd told him to do it.

No running from it now. The agony of her decision battered her. Would that little taste, that *hit,* have him craving the next one? And the next after that.

Vic stepped up to the bed. "How're you doing?"

Jack glanced up at him. "I'm very aware that I haven't had painkillers in over a year."

"You had to do it," Jillian said.

He turned to her and glanced at her hand sitting on the bed. The one he held just a few minutes ago. "I know, but it's hard. The addict in me misses it."

"That's the drugs talking."

He grinned. "Maybe. But it's true. The addict wants to be high again. It waits for me to be weak so it can remind me how good the drugs were. Getting that shot makes me realize how much harder I have to fight."

"I'm sorry."

"Don't be. Welcome to my world."

Yes. This was his world. The daily grind. The day-to-day battle of choosing to fight his addiction. She'd had enough therapy in her life to know that addicts were never completely healed. The disease never left them.

They simply chose to take the other path.

She didn't want to spend her life wondering if he'd choose the wrong one.

Two hours later, Jillian remained seated in the chair next to Jack's bed while Vic leaned against the opposite wall. The MRI results showed no major damage, but Jack was still having trouble putting weight on the knee.

He'd need a trip to an orthopedic doctor. For now, they were waiting for the nurse to wrap the knee and give him crutches. Except she got called away to deal with a shooting victim. Probably multiples by the way the ER staff ran by his door.

"Kids," Vic said, "I think we're gonna be here awhile."

"That can't happen," Jack said. "Those assholes who did this to me are probably tossing both our houses as we speak. They want that vial. When they don't find it, they'll come back."

"What vial?" Vic asked.

Jillian ignored his question. "I set the alarm at my house before I left. If someone were there, it would be going off."

Jack turned to her, his eyes a little clearer. "Then they're probably watching for you to get home. At which point, they will shove a gun to your head and force you to tell them where the vial is."

Vic boosted off the wall. "What fucking vial?"

Vic had a tone. A tone that warned all within fifty feet that he could be a very large, very scary man.

Jack, ever so slowly, turned to him. *Yeah, tell him we broke a few laws.* "We took a vial of Baxtin out of a Stennar Pharm shipment. We think there's something screwed going on with it."

Vic cocked his head. "Come again?"

"My idea. Not hers. The vials were there and it might have been our only opportunity."

"Mike talked to you, right?"

What did that mean? Jillian swung her gaze between the two men.

"Yeah. He talked to me."

Vic rolled out his bottom lip. "As long as you know what you're doing."

Jack focused on Vic, but stayed quiet. Here it was, that foreign language of stares only men understood. The blood pressure machine beeped and they all looked at it. "I know what I'm doing."

"Then," Vic said, "I guess we've gotta move."

Shouting from the hallway drew Jillian out of her seat. "This place is a madhouse."

Jack shifted to a sitting position. "All I need is crutches. We can stop and get a knee brace somewhere. I can deal with that."

Jillian shoved him back. "Hang on."

On her way to the ladies' room while Jack was having his MRI, she'd plowed into a nurse leaving what looked like a closet. The supplies the nurse had been carrying went flying.

Lynx held his hands out. "What?"

"I'll be right back."

She darted out the door. *Was it the third door on the right? Second maybe?* She'd have to see. She moved down the hall at a steady, but not hurried pace. In one of the bays, a doctor shouted commands and Jillian spied at least half a dozen people surrounding the patient.

The multiple shooting incident kept everyone busy and allowed Jillian the opportunity to wander the hallways without drawing attention.

She turned right in the middle of the corridor and spotted the door she needed. If it didn't have a lock on it, she'd let herself in.

Please let it be a supply closet.

Two feet from the door, she glanced behind her. A nurse stood outside one of the patient rooms checking a vial of medication. She didn't seem too interested in anything but the bottle in her hand, so Jillian grabbed the door handle in front of her and gave it a gentle turn.

The handle moved—*yes*—and Jillian slipped inside. An automatic light illuminated the room.

Tall metal shelves filled with gauze, bandages of all sizes, rubber gloves and various other nondrug-related supplies lined the walls. She walked along the small aisles. No open spaces for crutches to be propped. Around the other side of the aisle she spotted three pair, lying flat on a shelf surrounded by boxes of padding.

She grabbed the ones that looked longest and hoped they were tall enough for Jack. Either way, she was taking them.

She paused by the door and stuck her ear to it. Some commotion, but she couldn't tell how close. She'd have to go for it. The longer she remained in the room, the more likely she'd get caught. Sucking one huge breath, she opened the door, took three steps and hung a sharp left.

No yelling.

Good.

She turned the corner and spotted Vic standing outside of Jack's room looking seriously pissed off. At any other time, she'd take a moment to feel terrified, but since she'd already reached the point of abject terror, Vic only added to the drama.

He spotted her carrying the crutches and grinned. "Nice."

She swung by him into the room. Dressed in his regular clothes, Jack sat on the edge of the bed. She held out the crutches. "Will these work?"

Vic herded her sideways—not hard, but enough to let her know he'd take it from there—and levered himself under Jack's arm to help him stand. Jack gripped one crutch then the other. The crutches would need a minor height adjustment, but for now, they'd get him out of there.

"Let's roll," he said. "Jillian, remind me to tell you how crazy I am about you."

She smiled. "Will do. I might need to change my pants beforehand, though, because I think I wet myself."

Vic cracked up as he led the way down the hall. Anyone who got in *his* way would be one sorry son of a gun. "I'll bring my truck around. Wait out front."

Minutes later, Jack was safely in the passenger seat of Vic's Tahoe while Jillian sat in the back with his crutches on the floor.

She'd stolen them.

A moment of guilt settled on her, then, like a wisp of smoke, disappeared. She'd had to do it. With no time to waste, stealing those crutches meant getting to safety.

"Kurt?" Jack said into his phone. Obviously he'd called the DEA agent. "I'm heading to my office to get that vial. How can I get it to you?" He paused. "You don't want to know."

He held the phone away from his ear and Jillian heard Agent Boller's voice bashing through the line. "He's *upset*."

Vic, of course, laughed.

"Are you done?" Jack asked. "I just got the crap kicked out of me, so I'm *really* sorry the poor little DEA agent had to wait on my ass. Now, you want this vial or not? Either you're testing it or I'm finding someone else. Today is not the day to fuck with me."

More yelling. Not as loud this time. Men were imbeciles. She waved for Jack to pass her the phone. "Give me that." Jack handed it over. "Kurt? It's Jillian. I'm freaking out here and I need you to tell us what to do. Not only did we steal the vial, I just lifted crutches from a hospital and I'm feeling crummy about that. You screaming is not helping. Just tell me what the hell to do."

"I love this woman," Vic said.

She shoved the phone back at Jack. "Here. Talk to him. He's calm again."

"Thank you."

"Certainly."

"It's me again," Jack said into the phone. A pause. "Yeah. I'd stick with me. You don't want to piss her off. I'll be at my office in ten minutes. The vial is in my safe. Where do you want to meet?" He spun back to Jillian. "Portillo's. That's busy. We'll grab a sandwich, hand off a vial and hope like hell it'll tell us what we need to know."

"I could go for a chocolate cake shake," Jillian added. Might as well. The day had been a disaster and a milkshake made with chocolate cake covered all the indulgence bases.

Jack ended the call and tossed his phone into the console. "Portillo's it is. He can't meet us until five. He's in Indiana. We'll have to stay out of sight until then."

LYNX HOBBLED INTO HIS OFFICE WITH VIC AND JILLIAN BEHIND him. Blinding three o'clock sunlight shined through the large windows behind his desk and smacked off his computer monitor. Typically, the shades would be closed by now.

A reminder he'd ignored his work all day.

He went straight to the framed picture of the American flag, balanced on one crutch and took it off the wall to get to the safe.

"I'll do it," Vic said.

"I've got it."

"I'll be faster."

"Shut. The fuck. Up."

Jillian threw her hands up. "What is wrong with you two? Forget the pissing match and open the damned safe."

Vic did his oh-shit face. "Yeah. I know," Lynx said to him. "I like her."

Me too. Wasn't this always the way? When his friends

were around, the walls between them went down and all the nervousness was gone. They weren't hung up on addiction and disappointment and fear. If they could get past putting those walls up when they were alone, they'd be dynamite. Better than dynamite.

Mike stepped into the office and Lynx thought his entire chest cavity had caved in. Mike's cheeks had that pulled-tight, no-nonsense look that sometimes defined a man who'd built an empire on his own sweat. His eyes shifted from Lynx to Vic and finally to Jillian.

He pointed at the crutches. "What's this?"

"A little accident."

"I see that. How little?"

Where to even begin. Behind him, the safe sat open. Jack ignored the tick-tock of his mental clock, grabbed the stray crutch and moved to his desk chair. "Sorry. I gotta sit a second."

"Sure," Mike said.

Once in his chair, Lynx looked up at Mike and realized this was it. He'd have to come clean about the vial and his continual disregard for a three-hundred-million-dollar government contract.

In typical alpha male fashion, Mike remained standing. Nothing like making a man feel weak by standing over him. But Lynx didn't have room for his ego right now. His knee was shredded and barking at him again, and he had to get that vial to the DEA.

"I don't know where to start, Mike, so I'm just gonna jump in." He pointed to the safe. "In my safe is a vial of Baxtin, a blood thinner that I—"

"We," Jillian interrupted.

"That *we* took from a Stennar Pharm shipment."

The muscles in Mike's jaw twitched. His shit meter hitting launch, no doubt. "Why?"

"I think it's been tampered with and we're turning it over to the DEA for testing."

Mike's eyebrows shot up. "The DEA?"

"It's...uh..."

Mike turned to Vic and held out his hands before coming back to Lynx. "Let me get this straight. We had a conversation about Stennar Pharm, did we not?"

"Yes."

"Mike," Vic said.

Mike didn't bother to look at him, but held his finger up. "I'll deal with you in a second." Vic leaned back on the windowsill. Mike kept his attention on Lynx. "We had a conversation. You assured me it wouldn't be a problem. Now you're telling me you stole a vial of drugs. Gotta be ten broken laws there, so I don't see how that's not a problem." He turned to Vic. "And you're helping him?"

"No," Lynx said. "He's not. He came to the hospital to see if I was okay. Jillian called him."

"How the hell is the DEA involved?"

"An agent came to my apartment early this morning. He wanted to know my involvement in his case."

"An active case?"

"Yes."

Mike pressed his fingers to his temples. "I thought you didn't find anything on them. Why is the DEA in this?"

Lynx sat back. Why indeed? In the few calls he'd made, there had been no indication of an investigation by the DEA. He glanced at Jillian standing quietly off to the side. Mike was steamed enough that he may have forgotten she was there.

Suddenly, her eyes were huge and she rushed to the desk. "Hang on."

"What is it?"

She faced Mike. "Two weeks ago my boss killed himself by jumping off his eighteenth-floor balcony. No one knows why."

Silence descended on the room and Lynx's fuzzy brain circled thoughts of Jillian's dead boss. "Son of a bitch." He picked up his desk phone and dialed Janet's extension. "Hey. It's Lynx. Can you get into those Stennar Pharm files for me again and check—" He held the phone away. "What was the guy's name?"

"Greg Leeds," Jillian said.

He pulled the phone back. "Check any files with the name of Greg Leeds. Call me back."

Mike finally dropped into one of the guest chairs and rested one elbow on the armrest. He swung a finger at Jillian and Lynx. "You think the jumper was involved with whatever is going on?"

"Or he was undercover for the DEA."

Vic whistled low. "That would be a pisser."

Mike held out his hands. "How the hell do my people get into this crap?"

"We can't help ourselves," Vic offered. "It's hardwired."

"Well, we need to figure out a way to *de*-wire it."

Lynx cleared his throat. "Anyway, we're meeting the DEA guy in half an hour to give him the vial."

If possible, Mike's face turned even more solid. Rock hard. He folded his arms and dropped his chin to his chest. A brilliant display of keeping his temper on lockdown. He cracked his neck then straightened. "You'd better have control of this."

I hope I do. First, Lynx had serious maintenance to

perform with his boss. "If I'm right about Stennar Pharm, they're into something illegal. Something big if the DEA is involved. Once they get busted, there's not a politician in the country that'll be associated with them. I'll make sure of that too."

"Mike," Vic said, "this isn't bullshit. You gotta trust him on this."

Bit by bit, the rigidity in Mike's body eased off. "Take the vial to the DEA. At some point, update me. I need to understand what we're up against."

"Yes, sir."

Sufficiently pissed off, Mike headed for the door. "Vic," he said over his shoulder, "stay with them. He's close to useless on crutches."

LYNX HOBBLED INTO PORTILLO'S WITH HIS KNEE BANDAGED and the vial of Baxtin shoved into his jeans pocket. As usual for the dinner hour, the enormous restaurant was packed. There was always an organized chaos to a Portillo's visit. Some folks waited on line to order. Others waited at the far end to pick up food and the rest filled in tables. Good and noisy. And chances of the bad guys trying to make a move on them in here were small.

Too many witnesses.

Right now, they needed to unload the vial, get back to the office, fill Mike in and then get Jillian somewhere safe. Probably the farm, Taylor Security's offsite training facility, literally a farm in Northwest Indiana. It consisted of acres and acres of open land that Vic had converted into a training center where law enforcement, spec ops guys, independent contractors and various other groups came to sharpen their skills.

The farm also had an old house that had been renovated to a ten-thousand-square-foot meeting facility. Mike had built offices with pullout sofas in case any of the guys needed to sleep there.

Jillian would be safe in that fortress.

Lynx commandeered a table while Jillian went to get food. Vic stayed behind to babysit him. Next he'd need a pacifier.

On cue, Vic shook his head. "Anything Daddy can get you, punkin'?"

"Oh, fuck off. You should go with her."

"She can run. You can't."

Way to make a guy feel small. Still, Vic's gaze surveyed the crowded room. If anyone got close, he'd be up and moving.

No one got close.

At least until Kurt came through the revolving door into the crush of people wanting their beef sandwich.

"That's him," Lynx said.

Vic stood. "The guy in the black jacket and Yankees cap?"

"Yeah."

"Jeez, he looks like a goof." Vic held a hand up and waved. The DEA agent nodded and pushed through the line of people waiting to order.

"This is Vic Andrews," Lynx said. "A friend and coworker. He's up to speed."

The two men sat while Vic stood, doing a fine job of pretending to search for Jillian and their food.

From his pocket, Lynx pulled the vial, still wrapped in the napkin, and passed it to Kurt.

Kurt immediately shoved it into his jacket. "I'll check the lot numbers. See if anything has been reported stolen."

"Jillian searched the Stennar Pharm system, but didn't see any alerts from the manufacturer."

"Did you touch the bottle? Leave any prints?"

"No. I used a napkin."

"Good."

Jillian stepped up with a tray of food. "Hi, Kurt. I didn't know what you wanted so you got a burger with fries."

"I can't stay."

She set the tray down and rolled her eyes. "Then I guess you're taking it with you. Maybe you should stay a few minutes so it doesn't look suspicious?"

He smiled at her and Lynx felt a shot of jealousy storm him. Suddenly, other men weren't allowed to smile at Jillian.

"I'll take it to go," Kurt said. "I don't think anyone will notice."

"Suit yourself, but I'm eating." She shoved a cup of soda at Vic. "You. Sit. Eat."

"Yes, ma'am."

She grabbed the seat beside Lynx and handed him a food container from one of the bags. Chicken. That was his. He set the container down. "Kurt, anything we should know about Greg Leeds?"

Kurt's gaze skimmed him then went to Jillian. "Why?"

"Because he was my supervisor who happened to dive off a balcony two weeks ago."

Kurt processed it in silence, then leaned forward so he didn't have to scream over the crowd. "I received a letter from him two days after he jumped. He mailed it the day he died."

"Good Lord," Jillian said. "What did it say?"

"I can't share that with you."

Lynx shoved a fry in his mouth. The painkiller was almost gone and his knee throbbed. Plus, he didn't need

Special Agent Screwball giving him a hard time when they'd just handed over possibly blockbuster evidence. "That's horseshit."

Kurt wrapped his hand around the neck of the open bag and stood. "Life stinks."

"Don't I know it. What do you have on Stennar Pharm?"

"Not enough. I'm not sharing what we do have. Keep funneling me information that might help. That's all I can tell you."

JILLIAN STARED AT JACK. THE PAINKILLER HAD WORN OFF. SHE could see it in the pinch of his lips. The way he focused so intently on his food.

It *was* a non-narcotic.

Hadn't that been the thing she'd been holding on to since she'd watched the plunger go down? She'd sat in that room, holding his hand while the nurse slipped the drugs through his IV. Sat there watching his eyes roll back and the pleasure wash over him.

Pleasure.

He'd admitted it to her. That he liked it. She shouldn't have been surprised, but somehow, the reality of watching the drugs hit his system forced her to accept it.

Her intense attraction to him kept shoving his addiction aside. She enjoyed him. Simple as that. Now, though, she'd spend the next hours wondering if he'd be looking for a fix.

This is how it had always been with her father. He'd get sober and she'd wait for him to fall off the wagon again because that's what he did. Always.

"What's up?" Jack asked her.

She picked up her sandwich. "Nothing. Just thinking."

"Yeah, I see that. Wanna expand?"

She held his stare, thought about admitting her thoughts, but decided against it. What was the point? They had enough to deal with.

Across from her, Vic crumpled his sandwich wrapper in his giant hand. "I think we should huddle up somewhere and go through those files Janet got into. See what's there."

A woman squeezed between Jillian's chair and the one behind her. The dinner crowd thickening. Jillian gathered up garbage, loaded it on her tray and leaned in. "I think Greg discovered something and they knew it. They probably went after him the way they have me. And I don't really know anything."

Jack reached for the crutches on the floor next to him. "Or he was in on it and grew a conscience. I asked Janet to copy any files she found on Greg's drive." He levered himself up and said to Vic, "Let's go through the files at the farm. It'll be safer."

He shrugged. "Sure."

"We need to stop and get the thumb drive. I don't want Janet emailing them."

"Good thought," Jillian said. "Bad enough they have us targeted. We don't need to endanger Janet."

Vic dropped Jillian and Lynx off in front of Taylor Security to save Lynx—cripple that he was—the walk to the building from the parking garage.

"I'll be right up," Vic said as Lynx shut the car door.

Jillian rushed ahead and held the lobby door open for him. The rubber on the bottom of one crutch slipped on the marble floor—*dammit*—but Lynx recovered and steadied himself. He stopped, rubbed the crutch against the door mat in case something was stuck to it and forced himself to center his mind. *Relax, buddy.* Moving fast today wasn't going to happen. He might as well accept it and figure out how to be effective.

At the security desk, Willie, the beefy thirty-year-old night guard, rushed from his post to offer help. "Mr. Lynx, do you need a hand?"

"I'm good, Willie. Thanks. Damned crutches are a pain in the ass."

"Yes, sir. Let me get the elevator for you."

Jillian put her hand on his back and gave him a vigorous rub. Her intention, he assumed, was to offer encouragement, but something felt off. He couldn't place it but her touch was...forced. Cold even. Her lapses into silence since they'd left the ER and her stints of studying his body language were tells that she'd been thinking too much. His guess? She was running from her thoughts. Not unusual for her.

Willie held the elevator door for them. "Thanks, Willie."

"No problem, sir."

The doors closed and Lynx hit eight. In the reflection of the doors, he saw Jillian staring at the overhead floor numbers.

"Nice guy," she said.

"Yeah. He's good." He turned sideways and stared at her. "You wanna tell me what you're thinking?"

A ding sounded and the doors opened. "We're here," she said and followed him out, but an elevator wouldn't keep him from getting answers.

They stood in the quiet hallway outside the executive suite doors. They'd be locked by now and he had a key, but that would have to wait. The tension radiating from her was about to snap his normally controlled temper. Clearly, the painkiller had crapped out. "How about it, Jillian?"

She looked at the floor, shuffled one foot, then the other.

For a solid thirty seconds she did this shuffling thing while he concentrated on the small spikes of hair on top of her head. Despite her torn-up face, the sight of her brought peace and a sense of comfort. Even when she drove him crazy—like now—he was drawn to her.

With one crutch, he nudged her foot. "Hey. Talk to me."

She brought her head up and slapped her hands over her face.

Not a good sign.

A few seconds later, she slid her hands down and tears filled her eyes.

Ah, shit. He knew that look. "It's the pain meds, isn't it? You're worried."

Slowly, she nodded. "I can see the Toradol is wearing off. You're in pain."

"I'll deal with it."

"I know you will."

"Then what's the problem?"

Her eyes stayed on his for a long moment. Too long. "I saw your reaction when the drug hit your system. It felt good, didn't it?"

"Hell yeah. My knee was barking."

"No. It was more than that. It took you somewhere. Somewhere you liked."

An annoying ticking in his ears started. Knee deep in shit and now, when she'd been sitting in that hospital with him, watching him battle with indecision, he had to justify why he'd taken the drugs. "Jillian, my knee was killing me. Of course I liked it. Who wouldn't?"

She nodded. "I know."

"Then what are we talking about?"

She linked her fingers together and squeezed until the veins in her hands popped. "I can't do this, Jack. I know I said I could, but for the last three hours, all I've thought about is the way you looked when you got those drugs."

The elevator dinged, but to Lynx's already ticking ears, it could have been a boom. The doors slid open and Vic stepped off. He stopped, looked at Lynx, then Jillian, then back to Lynx. "What's up?"

Did he have a few weeks? It would take that long to fill him in. Lynx watched Jillian unclench her hands and tilt her head to the floor. Not looking at him.

There it is, pal. The big kiss-off. Maybe it had come sooner than he'd expected, but wasn't this what he'd been concerned about from the first time he'd set eyes on her three months ago? That his infatuation would get him nothing but stress and the yearning to numb himself?

Should have stuck with the plan.

He pursed his lips, thought about his blown one-year goal and decided he needed to start over. Yeah, that's what he'd do. Start from day one again. He'd done it once, he could do it again. At least this time he'd know what he was up against.

Maneuvering the crutches, he started down the hall. "Nothing," he said to Vic. "Just talking. Let's find Janet and that thumb drive."

Jillian, in yet another attempt at running from him, announced a trip to the ladies' room, and Lynx and Vic headed to his office.

Ten minutes later, she was still practicing her disappearing act when Janet walked into Lynx's office. She spotted Vic leaning against the window frame, nodded and held up the thumb drive. "Here you go. Everything I could find—in the pitiful amount of time you gave me, that is—on Greg Leeds."

Lynx took the device from her. "Thank you."

"I'll keep looking. Gavin is gone, so I'll have time tonight."

Jillian swung into the room just as Janet was leaving. "Hi."

"Hi, bye," Janet said, but spun back. "Oh, hey. Where's Willie?"

Vic pulled a face. "The lobby guard?"

"Yeah. I went across the street for a sandwich and when I came back, he wasn't there. I figured he stepped away."

Slowly, Lynx turned his head toward Vic, who gave him the WTF face. "He was down there when we came up."

"Well," Janet said. "I was at the deli when you called me. When I came back, he was gone. Maybe he was getting a pop or something."

Vic moved to the door. "I'll check it out."

Lynx hopped over to the safe where he'd stored the .38 Vic had given him the night of their aborted visit to Stennar Pharm. He might be living up to his nickname and being paranoid, but something didn't feel right.

Janet came up behind him. "What's going on?"

He handed her the .38. "I don't know. Take this and go. Head down the back stairs."

She shoved the gun back at him. "No. You'll need it."

He gripped her arm. "Take it. I'll get another one from the weapons closet Vic keeps. I don't want you unarmed."

"Hang on," Jillian said. She had that spooked big-eyed look about her. "You're freaking me out. If there's a problem with the guard downstairs, why are we standing around arguing about a gun?"

From somewhere outside the executive suite doors the *rat-a-tat-tat* of an automatic weapon filled the quiet hallway and, in unison, their heads snapped up. The silent but potent stream of shock and panic buzzed the room and sparked a blood surge in Lynx.

Gunfire.

Hallway.

Vic.

Every nerve ending lit and sizzled and fried his skin. Vic could be dead, lying on the floor in the hallway while he stood here. On crutches. Doing nothing. They had to get to him. If not them, someone else.

In a fit of movement, Janet lunged toward the door. Lynx grabbed the back of her shirt and yanked. Whatever that firing was, she didn't need to be running into the middle of it. Vic was their friend, but he wouldn't want them throwing themselves into gunfire.

"You can't," Lynx whispered.

But—*Jesus*—he wanted to go just as badly.

Jillian ran to the desk. "I'm calling 9-1-1."

He held his finger to his lips. "Dial and leave the phone off the hook. There's no time to talk. They'll send someone."

Using hand signals, Lynx pointed to the door. He went first, crutches and all, and waved them in behind him. He'd have to clear that hallway. They huddled next to the doorframe in single file. Nothing but silence. No doors opening, no footsteps, no voices. He peeped around the doorframe, looked left then right.

Nothing.

He spun back to Janet and Jillian. "I'll draw their fire. You two get to the exit door at the back of the suite." To Jillian he said, "Go right. The door is on the left."

She nodded, but her eyes darted back and forth and her shoulders shook. Had she even understood? He'd seen this before on battle-weary soldiers. Shock so profound that they functioned on remote, performing their tasks, battling the enemy, but not really absorbing the weight of it. Later, when the shock wore off, that weight would crush her.

He touched her shoulder and waited for her to look at him. *There we go.* "When we get into the hallway, you two run ahead. Don't wait for me. Got it?"

"But—"

"Jillian, I'll be fine. You need to get out." He hobbled into the hall—damned cripple—saw it was clear and waved the women on. "Go!"

The suite entry door swung open and the barrel of an automatic weapon appeared. A barrage of gunfire exploded into the room. Someone yelped—Janet. Jillian hauled ass to the exit door while Lynx dove behind the secretary's desk, hoping to draw the gunman in. He hit the floor, his arms taking the brunt of it, but smacked his knees. Nauseating pain ripped through his right knee and he squeezed his eyes closed for half a second.

If those fucking bullets whizzing by him connected, they'd hurt a helluva lot more. Huddled behind the desk, he peered at the south end of the hallway. Janet lay facedown, her arms sprawled sideways. Blood seeped from under her, darkening the carpet.

Two down.

Goddammit. They might both be dead. He shook it off. No time to think. *Later.*

He shot a look down the hallway. No Jillian. She'd better have run. If he could get to Janet, he could drag her behind the desk for cover.

He gripped one of the crutches. Not a great weapon, but it would have to do. Then the desk flew backward and he swung the crutch, connecting with the meaty part of the huge man's thigh. The man winced, then held his M16 up and—*bam*—something hard slammed into Lynx's head. For a second, everything flashed white and he jerked his head to clear it. His full belly churned and his vision blurred. Nausea consumed him. The carpeted floor loomed, then zigzagged.

Shit.

What a way to die. On the floor with a bum knee.

Useless.

20

JILLIAN TORE DOWN EIGHT FLIGHTS OF STAIRS, AVOIDED THE lobby level in case any bad guys waited there, and burst through the emergency exit door into the parking garage.

Cold, damp air swept in on her and exhaust fumes fogged her thoughts. To her left, shiny black SUVs filled the first aisle. Behind that were rows and rows of empty spaces where daytime employees likely parked. At this hour, only a few scattered cars remained.

Could there be an emergency exit next to the garage door? And would she be able to get it open? A button on the inside maybe?

Breaking into a sprint, she barreled by the row of SUVs. The garage gate loomed, barely fifty yards ahead. She scanned the sides of the garage. Shadows filled the space just inside the doorway. Not enough light to see a button.

Damn.

Her heart slammed and she let out a squeak.

Calm, calm, calm. Over and over she repeated the mantra. What had Jack said? The fear wouldn't kill her, it's what she did with it that would kill her. *Use the fear.*

A small, darkened office sat to the right of the door. Another ten yards and she'd be there. She slowed to a jog and her breath came in quick, deep gasps. If only she'd done more cardio with the yoga. She stopped at the door, studied the wall beside it, then ran her hand over the frame. Nothing.

Other side.

She darted over, did the same routine again.

"Don't bother, baby." The deep, almost amused voice came from behind her. "We got ya this time."

Jillian spun and faced that same menacing man from her home invasion. Another squeak curled in her throat. *Use the fear.* She cut her gaze right, then left. No one. He was alone. She'd eluded him twice already. Maybe the third time was the charm.

She scanned her surroundings. A car wouldn't fit through the narrow aisle to her right, but a person could. Her breath still heaving, she bolted to the aisle.

"Nowhere to go," the man called. "Don't make me hurt you again. Already got your boyfriend. And the big guy. And the skinny bitch. All three of 'em. Got 'em all. Only you left."

In her ears, a soft whistle grew and unfurled to an awful shriek. They could be dead. Jack, Vic and Janet. All dead. Because of her. Because she'd asked Jack to help her with a security system. Because they were good people and wouldn't let someone falter.

Her chest locked and she opened her mouth to release the trapped air. It came out in spurts, a panicked, jerking exhalation, no release. *Can't breathe.* Her eyes burned and she slammed them shut. *Suffocating.* These sons of bitches. A day at a time, they were stealing her life. Snatching all the things she loved. Dammit, if she only had the bat from under her bed. She'd bash this guy's skull in. Just beat him senseless, over and over and over again for the terror he'd put her and Jack and Janet and Vic through. That's what she'd do. She'd beat the fucker senseless.

Maybe they're not dead.

She had to hope. They couldn't kill Jack. They'd want to know what he knew. Somehow, she had to get to him. They'd figure something out. Together. Like they'd been doing all along. That's what she'd do.

Get to Jack.

A siren outside—the police answering her 9-1-1 call—refocused her, brought her senses to perfect, logical alignment. She inhaled through her nose, cataloging the damp smell of the garage, the confined car exhaust, the sight of the SUVs in perfect unison, the sounds of multiple sirens on the street, all of it registering.

Run.

She sprinted to the back wall and turned left. Hide. That's what she needed to do. Make the man search for her until he gave up. Until the police searched the garage. Anything.

Her low heels smacked against the pavement and she dug harder, fighting the fatigue. *Keep running.* Nowhere to go.

Nowhere.

Trying to outmaneuver her attacker, she scooted between two SUVs and dropped to the ground to peer under them. No feet in either direction. No sound either.

Where the hell is he?

And then a foot pressed onto her back, driving her against the cold concrete.

"Gotcha."

No, no, no. Resisting the pressure of that giant foot, her body tensed, every inch rock solid. The thick rubber of his shoes dug into her spine, pressing, stealing what was left of her air. He leaned in and with each compression, her breasts smashed against the damp ground and her ribs jabbed the concrete. Stabbing pain shot down her midsection.

Yet her mind remained on task. *Fight. Don't make it easy.* She craned her neck, searching for a weapon. Anything she could use to bring him down. To hurt his leg enough that he'd have to release her.

"Forget it," he said. "You're mine now."

THE BIG GUY SHOVED LYNX INTO THE TRUNK OF THE SAME Lincoln they'd driven earlier in the day and slammed the lid. Blackness consumed the compartment and Lynx closed his eyes. Stabbing jolts shot from his shoulders to his wrists where his asshole captor had bound them. At least it was rope and not cuffs or zip ties. Rope he had an iota of a chance at untying.

But, crap, his shoulders were screaming. Throw in the aching knee and he was a stone-cold mess. It wouldn't matter, though. He'd dealt with worse.

Which was what he fully expected in the next few minutes and hours. He opened his eyes and let them adjust to the darkness.

He hadn't seen the big guy's partner before being tossed into the trunk. Did that mean he was hunting Jillian? Had Lynx given her enough of a head start to escape?

The car moved forward and Lynx's body swayed with the movement. His guess was they'd take him somewhere local. They'd want to be close in case they found Jillian. If these assholes were smart, they'd play one against the other.

They'd sniff out the weak-minded one. With his military training, they'd most likely focus on her. They'd make her watch while they beat him, choked him, hacked away at his bum knee.

They'd break her by breaking him.

Chances were it'd work. He just didn't know what they were after. Clearly, they knew she knew something and *that's* what they were after. They couldn't get rid of either one of them until they deciphered who told what to whom.

With all the gunshots fired before they'd left the building, Lynx prayed Vic and Janet were injured and not...dead. A racking sorrow punctured his chest and he closed his eyes again. *Work on a plan.* No sense dwelling on the loss of his friend and colleague when he didn't know for sure.

Chances were he'd gotten them both killed.

Plan.

Think later.

Eventually, the car came to a stop and the engine was shut down. Wherever they were, he needed the area to be well lit. He'd get a look around before they threw a bag over his head because, surely, they'd throw a bag over his head.

Or maybe not. Either way, Lynx rolled to his back so he could sit straight up and look around as soon as the trunk opened.

A door slammed and he listened for another. Nothing. One captor. Maybe he had a chance. The trunk popped open and Lynx shot to a sitting position. Large overhead lights shined down on a parking lot he didn't recognize. He cut his gaze left then right. One car in the lot, parked three rows over. That was it. No other signs of activity.

Quiet place.

Loads of trouble.

. . .

BLINDFOLDED, JILLIAN WAS TAKEN FROM WHAT FELT LIKE SOME sort of cargo van and led across a flat, open area—hard ground, maybe blacktop—and up a short staircase with a metal handrail. In certain spots the rail was rusted over. Old building.

The *cha-clunk* of an industrial door sounded and a second later she was shoved inside with such force, she lost her balance and landed on cold cement.

"Jillian?" Jack's voice.

Before she could stop it, a sob broke free. The ride over had been a nightmare of thoughts and visions of Jack and Vic and Janet, their dead bloody bodies sprawled on the floor inside Taylor Security. Now, at least, she still had Jack.

She ripped off the blindfold and blinked a couple of times to bring the room into focus. Twenty feet away, Jack sat in a wooden chair. A thick rope stretched across the front of his body—twice—leaving his arms tight at his sides.

Tears filled her eyes and she ran to him. "I'm so sorry."

Immediately, she bent low to see about the knot on the rope.

"Forget it. They're not stupid enough to leave us here that long."

Still, she'd try. She went to work on the knot, but the rope was too thick and tight. No leverage.

"Where are we?" Jack asked.

She looked around. A warehouse. Not big. Maybe the size of a storefront, but empty. Cinderblock walls surrounded them on all four sides and the cement floor held an inch of grime. She glanced at her hands where some of the floor's dirt transferred when she fell.

"I don't know. It's a warehouse. Or a storage facility."

She worked the knot again, her fingers furiously maneuvering to different spots. "I can't get this knot."

"You're not supposed to."

THE DOOR FLEW OPEN AND THE BIG GUY STEPPED IN. LYNX relaxed his shoulders and concentrated on mentally preparing his already abused body for what might come. Could be bullshit. *Screwing with my mind.* Part of a torture session was the mental distress.

Behind Tractor Arms came his partner. Fierce pricks shot along Lynx's arms, legs, shoulders, everywhere, a current of sizzling shocks. He inhaled, long, slow and deep. *Mental distress.*

In his mind, he visualized each part of his body and willed the discomfort away. Surviving meant keeping his emotions under control.

Jillian, still on her knees, inched in front of him. He appreciated the attempt to shield him, but her eyes were huge with fear. Something he'd never seen on her before. Spooked, yes, but not like this.

"Hey," he said, keeping his voice low but firm. She turned from the two men and looked at him. "Focus," he mouthed.

A third man, one Lynx didn't recognize, entered behind the apes and the heavy door locked into place. He wore a light gray suit with a white shirt and a blue tie. From this distance the suit looked silk, but what did Lynx know? Other than it was an expensive suit.

The man's gray hair was short and impeccably groomed. Of the three, this guy was definitely more accustomed to a spa than a torture chamber.

The boss.

He spoke first and directed his words to Jillian. "I

thought I'd welcome our guests. My dear, you have given my men quite a challenge. I applaud your bravery."

Lynx couldn't place the accent. Nothing stood out. A bit of South Africa. Some Brit thrown in?

A mutt.

The mutt turned to Lynx, inclined his head and went back to Jillian. "Bravery, though, can be a foolish thing. I will ask you only this one time. What you did with that vial?"

She finally stood and faced the guy. He had a few inches on her, but his build was lean. Unimposing. "Who are you?"

Bam. He backhanded her. Lynx jumped at the crack of the slap and Jillian's head snapped sideways. She stumbled a few steps, her hands reaching for something, anything, to cling to. Vicious blow.

Lynx had called this wrong. His heart raced and his arms burned from the tug of the ropes, but there wasn't a goddamned thing he could do. He'd have to sit here, trussed up like an animal, and watch them beat on her.

"One more time," the son of a bitch said. "Where's that vial?"

Tell him something. He jerked his head toward the guy, urging her to say something, anything that would keep them from beating on her again.

She ran the back of her hand over her cheek. The slap had ripped open the stitches there. When her hand came away, a red streak spanned her cheek. "I don't know."

The man tilted his head. He paused as if considering his options. "I gave you two chances. My generosity is limited." He turned to Lynx. "Perhaps you will be the sensible one."

That depended on whose sense they were talking about.

"I understand," the guy said, "Taylor Security has certain government contracts up for renewal."

He's the one. He'd stalled the contracts.

"Contracts," the man continued, "I assume, your superior would like very much to keep."

Jillian drew her eyebrows together, leaving a hard line splitting her forehead.

The man bent over, eye to eye with Lynx. "Don't be stupid. I can give you those contracts. Plus a few more."

Lynx met his stare. "Great. Now who the hell are you?"

The man straightened. "You won't know me. I have politically powerful friends. I keep their greedy pockets fat." He reached into the inside breast pocket of his suit jacket, pulled out a small white medicine bottle. The kind that would hold tablets. He tossed it into Lynx's lap. "Pockets fat and bodies satisfied."

The bottle had no label. Didn't need one. He knew what this was.

A corner of the man's mouth quirked. "I'm told you like the Vicodin."

Yes. "Not lately."

"Ah, that's right." He snatched the bottle back. "If things go well for you here, you won't need them."

"And if things don't go well?"

He shook the bottle. "Then you'll *beg* for it. We're not there yet. I still believe an agreement can be reached on the contracts."

"Jack," Jillian said, "what's he talking about?"

The man jerked his head toward her and his lips spread further into a greasy smile. "He didn't tell you?"

She kept her eyes on Lynx. "What?"

"This is wonderful," the man said to Tractor Arms. "He never told her."

"Told me what?"

He tsk-tsked. "Oh, my dear. Your hero has three hundred

million dollars of Taylor Security's government contracts sliding from his grip."

Jillian turned to him, questioning. "Jack?"

What a way for her to find out. Lynx closed his eyes for a second and reopened them. "When I asked around about Stennar Pharm, Mike got a call that the contracts might not be renewed."

"Oh, my God."

The man spread his arms. "Your god can't help you now. I'm the only god in this room. You tell me what you did with that vial and your contracts stay intact."

"Horseshit."

The man got eye to eye again. "Tell me where the vial is and you keep your contracts, plus a little extra for yourself. A win-win, as you Americans say."

Lynx paused. What he and Jillian needed was time for someone to track them down. But with the only other people who knew they'd been at the office injured—possibly dead—he wasn't counting on being found.

The sight of Vic and Janet sprawled in that hallway, blood seeping from their unmoving bodies, bore into him, and seized his breath. Gina would be a widow all over again, their children fatherless. All because of a few calls Lynx had made.

All because he inserted himself into a situation that was none of his goddamned business.

"Jack?" Jillian said.

And her, staring at him with those big dark eyes, wondering what he was thinking, if he was considering the offer. *Wondering* if she could trust him.

Maybe that was the problem. He'd spent all this energy, energy that should have gone to staying the recovery course, trying to help her and she still didn't trust him. He'd seen it in the hospital when he'd accepted the Toradol. After he'd gotten the hit she looked away because she was sure, despite the doc's assurance the drug was non-narcotic, that he'd relapse.

Now again, she stared at him with those same intense, questioning eyes. Wondering what he'd do.

By now, she should've known. The fact that she didn't proved to be a wicked jab.

Slick suit guy stepped closer. Lynx shook his head, let out an exasperated laugh. *Should have stuck to the recovery plan.* "No deal. Fuck off."

The man continued to stand over him, his face a blank mask. No spark of hesitation, no smirk, no creased forehead. No reaction at all. "I'm sorry to hear that," he finally said. In one fluid, almost elegant move, he faced the big guy. "Get me my information."

Tractor Arms stayed silent, but waved his partner to the door. The three men filed out and Lynx's body roared with energy. Under his skin, his arms and legs flicked and snapped. He fought to maintain control. To relax and keep his mind clear.

Jillian lunged for the knotted rope. "I need to loosen these knots."

"They'll be back any second." He spoke quickly, but his voice was steady. Not a crack or hiccup. No sign of weakness. Couldn't allow that.

She gave up on the knot and squatted next to him, her arms resting on his good leg. He'd have to keep her centered. *Concentrate on the end game.* "They're gonna use us against each other. My guess is they'll come at me first."

She looked up at him, her gaze moving left and right. "What are you saying?"

"They're gonna make you watch."

21

THE HALLWAY DOOR SQUEAKED OPEN AND THE HUGE GUY stepped through carrying a metal bucket. His buddy was hot on his heels, his meaty hand wrapped around the handle of a gallon jug of liquid. The big guy dropped the metal bucket next to Lynx and took the water from his partner. Inside the bucket sat a hacksaw with rusted edges, a black cloth, a hammer and a couple of wrenches.

Here we go.

The second guy grabbed Jillian from behind, locking her arms in place.

"First," Tractor Arms said, "we try water. Then I start taking fingers."

"No," Jillian screamed.

Lynx, his heart racing in full-out ballistic mode, swung his head to her, mentally pleading with her to remember what he'd said. Their eyes connected for a brief second. "Calm," he said. He kept his voice steady, but her eyes were wild again, bouncing all over the place. Already, she was gone.

A cloth bag was thrown over his head, smothering him

in darkness. His chair tipped back and he flinched. Slowly —almost gently—Tractor Arms lowered him to the floor.

Shit, shit, shit. His breathing was too shallow. If he could keep his mind centered he'd probably survive, the midair suspension and knowing he was completely helpless rattled him.

"No," Jillian screamed again.

A drop of water touched his face and he jerked his head. A giant hand pressed his head into the floor, the weight holding him in place. Another drop of water. Then, slowly, a steadier stream. He clamped his mouth closed, but the water filled his nostrils and he gagged. He opened his mouth and more water filled it, smothering him, stealing his air.

All rational thought vanished and Lynx strained against the ropes. A thundering panic filled his mind, his thoughts scattered. *Breathe. Get out. Help Jillian. Save yourself.*

Too much. His heart banged so hard his ribs might snap. The sons of bitches were killing him. Slowly drowning him. Blackness lingered, not quite consuming him, but holding him teetering on the edge of consciousness.

The water stopped. The man released him and violently pushed on his stomach. Water shot out of Lynx's nose and mouth, burning, ripping his throat apart along the way.

"Where's the vial?" Tractor Arms asked.

What was that? Ten seconds? Maybe more. Lynx didn't know. He coughed and breathed. He steadied himself, tried to quiet his paralyzed mind and prayed the next round wouldn't kill him.

JILLIAN'S HEAD BOOMED. OVER AND OVER AND OVER, THE booming continued, ravaging any ounce of self-control left.

This was why they called it mental trauma. All she could do was watch. Her captor was too strong and her mind too weak.

When had she reverted to the helpless female of her youth? The one willing to accept an injustice because it had been forced upon her.

It needed to stop. If they were going to die in this hell, she wouldn't do it without a battle.

She tried to wiggle free, but the man's arms kept her locked in place. Her feet, though. They were free. She lifted one foot and stomped down on the man's toes.

"Ow! Shit." He released his hold to hobble around.

"Jillian? Jillian," Jack shouted.

She scrambled to him.

The big guy held Jack's head in place, but jerked his chin at his partner. "Grab her."

Jillian's captor, still limping around, clamped on to her upper arm and hauled her up. In the scuffle, her foot connected with the bucket and it toppled.

"Stupid," the bigger man screamed. "Pick that up."

And then, it happened. The man released her and bent to gather the items that had fallen out of the bucket. She shifted sideways, letting her weight guide her, and imagined all her strength, all that power and madness funneling into her right heel, and—*voom!*—drove the clunky heel of her shoe into her captor's head.

As if on a spring, his head snapped back, then righted itself, but the man's bulk pushed him off balance and to the floor. The bigger man made a grab for her.

No way.

Again, she shot her foot out and connected with his knee. He howled and spun, searching for the items from the bucket. The tools were still scattered, but she snatched the bucket, swung it hard and the metal base plowed into the huge man's head. The thick wire handle tore loose, leaving her with one sharp end in her hand and the bucket dangling from the other end.

From behind, the smaller guy bear-hugged her and she drove her heel into his right foot. The same foot. A burst of his hot, nasty breath rolled over her cheek and he loosened his grip. She blasted him again.

This time, he released a loud, agonized cry that bounced off the cement and echoed through the empty space. She spun back and—just as they'd done to her in her own house —threw her elbow across his face. A swing of the bucket came next. It connected with his shoulder, but flew off the end of the handle leaving her with only the jagged edge of the wire.

"Stupid bitch," he screamed.

"Jillian! What's happening?" Jack yelled.

The hulking guy came at her, his big fists raised. If he hit her, it would be lights out. He was too big, too strong, too menacing. She tightened her sweaty grip on the bucket handle—*weapon*—sucked in a breath and, with both hands raised it above her head. A loud *whooshing* filled her head. She did as Jack had told her and concentrated on the man in front of her. He kept coming. Hoping for good timing and that her sweat-soaked hands wouldn't slip, she gripped harder and slashed the handle down. Aware of her weapon, he looked up, tried to sidestep, but he was too big and slow to evade her and she drove the jagged handle into his eye.

Screaming agony, louder this time, more piercing, filled the space. Everyone was yelling. An explosion of voices as the man fell to the floor, his hands clutched over his bleeding eye.

Beside her, Jack managed to roll sideways in the chair,

but he was too confined to help. The second man came at her again and she threw the plastic gallon jug at him. Water spilled from the spout and the jug bounced off of him, but he kept coming. She picked up the hammer and held it in front of her.

Somehow, still tied to the chair Jack rolled to his knees and drew the man's attention.

Now!

Moving on her last wisps of energy, and once again, holding on with both hands, she raised the hammer and brought it crashing down on the man's skull. A grotesque thud sounded and the hammer's head recoiled. The man's body swayed and dropped to the floor.

Rage spewing, she turned to the bigger man, now on his feet and getting his bearings. He was much taller. She'd never fight him this way. Too big, too strong.

She flipped the hammer over, took what she hoped was decent aim and whipped it in the general area of his crotch. From the short distance, he only had seconds to deflect it. He brought his hands down, but not quick enough. The hammer caught him just left of center. His face contorted and he let out a burst of air before doubling over. She raced forward, scooped the hammer off the floor and swung sideways. The hammer connected with the back of his head and his eyes rolled.

His body hit the floor with a slap and she stood, hammer in hand, sucking wind. She glanced at the man's still form. *Oh no.* She bent low, propped her hands on her knees, but her heart continued to explode. *Oh no, oh no, oh no.* She'd killed a man. Maybe two.

She opened her mouth to draw a breath. Nothing. Only a scream. An insane grinding in her throat, tearing at her, punishing her. Just below her, directly in her sight line, the tip of the hammer dripped blood. She screamed louder, completely unhinged. She dropped the hammer and held her hands out.

I killed them.

Something moved. She glanced up. *Jack.* Speaking. She stopped the frantic screaming.

"Jillian!"

She ran to him, levered him upright in the chair and worked the soaked hood off of his head. "I'm okay," she said. "I'm okay, but, God, I'm not okay."

"What the hell's going on?"

With the hood up to his eyes, she gave it one last yank and tossed it. "I think...I think I killed them."

LYNX COULD NOT BELIEVE THE SHIT LUCK. TIED TO A FUCKING chair while Jillian got tormented. Again.

Deal with it later.

"Jillian, get the saw. Fast. Move!"

Yelling at her might have been harsh, but he could see the big guy's chest still rising and falling. That son of a bitch was still alive. The other guy? No idea about him. All Lynx knew was they needed to get out. Now.

She ran to the saw—it must have gotten kicked out of the way—and brought it back. He jerked his head. "Saw through these ropes." She hesitated. Shock. "Do it! Now."

He'd bring out the kid gloves later. She stuck the saw between the chair and the rope and went to work.

"Faster, baby. Come on. We gotta move."

She nodded and picked up the pace.

"You're okay," he said. "Doing great."

Again she nodded, but her eyes were...dead. Nothing. And then she started trembling. "Jillian, listen to me." He waited for her to focus on him. "You're okay. I'm sorry. Just get me free and I'll get us out. I'll take care of you. Just get this rope off."

More nodding. She was so gone.

The last braid on the rope tore and Lynx jumped up, grabbed her hand and took a step. His bad knee buckled and the pain drilled so far into his leg he saw spots. Jillian clasped his arm to steady him and he inhaled and exhaled to get his bearings. He glanced around. No crutches. He'd have to work without them. He pointed to the door he'd entered through. The one that led outside. "Check that door for me."

Anticipating it being locked, he picked up the hammer and saw and hobbled to the door the slick-looking guy left through. Each step became an exploration of agony. Yeah, the pain meds would come in handy about now.

The big guy groaned from his spot on the floor. Lynx whipped back to find Jillian, still in her zombie state, moving away from the unconscious men toward him. The shock was setting in, but he needed her to not shut down on him.

"It's locked," she said.

"I figured." He looked up at the door in front of him. "We've gotta go through this one. Any idea what's on the other side?"

She shook her head. "I don't know where we are."

He held out the hammer. "Take this."

"I—I can't."

Tough-love time. He squeezed her hand. "You have to. I know it sucks. I know it scares the ever-loving shit out of you, but the hammer and saw are the only weapons we have." Her face collapsed. Crying. "Hey, stay with me. You just kicked the crap out of those two. You're amazing. You can do this. *We* can do this. I couldn't help you in there, but I can help you now."

He held the hammer to her and she narrowed her eyes. *Come on.* She glanced at the big guy then turned back to Lynx. Slowly, she held her open hand to him. *Atta girl.* He set the hammer in her palm and she wrapped her fingers around it. "Let's go."

Gently, he pushed on the door lever to avoid the *ka-chunking* noise industrial doors made. Inch by inch he opened it until he could peek through. Dark hallway. Only the emergency lighting threw shadows down the length of the corridor. Good enough for them to see where they were headed.

To his right was a wall. Nothing to fear there. The danger would be ahead of them. Unless Tractor Arms came looking. One thing at a time.

Jillian gripped the back of his shirt and he led her down the hall, hobbling on his bum knee, his gaze swinging left then right. Every few feet he checked their six. Nothing. His girl had done serious damage with that hammer.

He eased open the door and peeped through the crack. From his location, he saw a single loading dock. No truck. No people. Bay door shut.

Go time.

One step in and he heard voices. Two men arguing. He halted, shot a look to the right where a couple of doorways lined the dock area.

Jillian went on tiptoes to whisper in his ear and he bent to meet her halfway. "That one sounds like Ingrams. The other one sounds like the guy in the suit."

Using hand signals, he pointed to the side exit door. She reached behind her and tried it. She shook her head and mouthed, "Locked."

Could someone please throw him half a chance to get the hell out of there? They'd have to go out the main door and hope one of the two men didn't spot them.

Good luck.

He switched positions with her and put his lips to her ear. "We'll have to go out the front. They'll probably see us. It'll be a dogfight." She stepped back and he grabbed her hand to hold her in place. "I know you're hurting, but we have to do this."

Almost home. All they needed to do was get down those stairs to the door. His knee had better hold out. Jillian slid her gaze toward the voices, then, being the strong, decisive woman he'd come to know, something in her eyes flicked and she threw her shoulders back. "I'm ready."

Slowly, they crept along the side wall. The voices grew louder.

"You stupid son of a bitch. You've completely fucked us." That was the slick suit guy. The mutt with the combo British and South African accent.

"Your lackeys had nothing to do with it? All they needed to do was deal with her. *Twice* they blew it."

Jillian yanked on Lynx's shirt and he nodded. As much as he'd like to stand and listen, they needed to get out. "Keep moving," he mouthed and continued creeping along the wall.

"What about Greg's files? You got those?" Slick Suit asked.

"We cleaned them out."

Good thing Janet copied them.

"Where is Ned in all this?" the mutt asked.

"He still doesn't know, but after the boyfriend went to his house, he's damned suspicious. It's a loose end we'll have to tie."

"Do we know if Greg told anyone?"

"No."

Oh, he told someone.

"It doesn't matter," Ingrams said. "It'll never track back to the other companies. Vanuatu protects our privacy."

"You fool. The other companies are protected, but we'll lose this one. *You* will take the fall. None other. You cocked it up by not controlling Greg."

"I kept him silent as long as I could," Ingrams said. "How could I know he'd grow a conscience?"

"You're lucky he jumped."

What a couple of schmucks. Pure evil. Lynx checked on Jillian behind him, found her wiping tears from her cheeks. Poor thing. She'd been through a war.

And they weren't done yet.

Using his thumb, he gestured to the door they'd be leaving through. The stairs leading to the exit were directly across from them. All they needed to do was get to the door and they were out.

"Let's go," he mouthed.

He motioned her to head down the stairs in front of him so he could keep an eye on the two men in the office.

Jillian moved swiftly, staying on her toes to keep her steps light and silent as she descended.

At least until Slick Suit exited the office and spotted them.

22

"Bloody hell," Slick Suit yelled.

Jillian spun back and Lynx pointed to the door. "Go!"

He hauled up the stairs, his knee screaming like a son of a bitch, and took a hobbling, barely running start toward suit guy. He grabbed the railing, swung his feet in the air and slammed them into the center of the charging man's chest.

Fire tore into Lynx's knee, the pain so fierce his entire leg burned. The man stumbled, his mouth wide while he gasped for air. Momentum shoved him against the rail where his arms bicycled and bent him backward.

Go over.

Energy crackled inside Lynx, the soldier—the survivor —in him coming alive. He rushed forward, caught him on the jaw with a right and sent him flying.

Ingrams grabbed Lynx, swung with a left and connected on the cheek. Lynx roared back, tackling Ingrams. The two of them hit the floor and something shattered in his knee. Pain radiated in all directions.

He rolled off Ingrams, saw Slick Suit coming at him

again and then, out of nowhere, Jillian jumped on Slick's back.

Goddammit. He'd told her to go.

Slick Suit rammed her against the guardrail, her back taking the brunt of it. She screamed and Lynx leaped up. "Eyes!"

She hefted herself higher on suit guy's back, wrapped her fingers around the front of his face and jammed her fingers into his eyes.

He cried out and made a move to pry Jillian's hands away. She leaped off his back as he stumbled toward the stairs. At the edge, Lynx dove for him, gave him a shove and sent him soaring down the steps, his head bouncing off the cement landing. Nighty-night.

One down.

"Jack!"

He spun. Ingrams was on his feet and heading for Jillian. "Run!"

A second set of stairs was down the hall and she sprinted to them. Ingrams grunted and grabbed Lynx's throat with both hands. Years of training roared back and Lynx locked on to his forearms, yanked and—*boom*—drove his palm into Ingrams's nose. He crumpled to the floor. Heaving, Lynx scanned the area. Jillian was already down the stairs and heading for the door. Ingrams remained unconscious and Lynx, his knee on fire, hauled ass toward the office the men had come from.

On the desk sat an M16. Probably the one from the attack on Vic. Lynx grabbed it, checked the magazine. Ready to go. Also on the desk was a .45. He took that too.

He limped out of the office and checked on Slick Suit. Still out cold on the landing.

Jillian stood by the exit door bouncing on her toes. He

waved her up to the landing and handed her the .45.

"If he wakes up, shoot him."

Her eyes bulged. "What?"

"I've gotta get Ingrams tied up and check the other two. If this guy wakes up and comes after you, shoot him. Center mass."

Holding the gun with both hands, she pointed it at Slick Suit. The way their luck was running, she'd panic and blow him apart. She might do that anyway with the way her hands were shaking.

He grabbed her wrist. "Only if he wakes up and comes after you. Okay?"

She bobbed her head.

It'd be a Jackson Lynx miracle if they got out of this one.

In the office where he'd garnered the weapons, he found a plastic garbage bag filled with pliers, rope, a KA-BAR knife and rags. Among those items were other nefarious-looking goodies, but he stopped at the rope. No sense dwelling on what could have happened.

He hauled ass—as fast as hauling ass could be with a busted knee—back to where Ingrams lay. Once there, he dragged the moaning man to the iron railing and tied him to it with a two half-hitch knot. For kicks, Lynx took another width of rope and tied his ankles together. Good and trussed up.

He spun back to Jillian, still with that .45 on the mutt. Her hands weren't shaking as much. "You okay?"

She slid a sideways glance at him, but went back to her prisoner. "I'm good. Go check on the other two."

Doing his quasi run-limp-walk, he moved down the hallway, toward the back storage area where they'd been brought in. Weapon at the ready, he pushed open the door, swung in and did a quick reconnaissance. The smaller guy's body still lay on the floor where Jillian hit him, but the big guy was gone. *Shit.*

Given that the room was empty, Lynx gave it a quick walkthrough. Nothing. Tractor Arms must have fled. He checked the other guy's pulse.

Dead. He shook his head. Jillian would have nightmares for years.

Weapon still raised, Lynx put his back to the wall and sidestepped to the door that had previously been locked. He leaned against the inside lever. Unlocked. Tractor Arms must have had the key and escaped.

Damn. Should have checked his pockets. Major mistake.

Pressing his weight into the handle, Lynx pushed the door open and, again, weapon ready, scanned the area. No life.

They'd deal with the big guy later. He had a stab wound to the eye. He'd turn up at a hospital somewhere when it got infected.

On his way back to Jillian, he heard a muffled shout and picked up the pace on his quasi hobble-run.

He shoved the hallway door open and saw Jillian with the .45 still trained on Slick Suit, but Ingrams's head was swinging back and forth. "Jack, he's waking up."

"Got it." He stood next to Jillian and checked on her prisoner. Still out. "Do you remember Boller's number?"

She nodded. "I memorized it."

"Nice work. What is it?"

She rattled off the number and Lynx repeated it to himself as he walked back to the office. He held his weapon in one hand and picked up the handset of the desk phone with the other. Dial tone. Excellent. Some of the tension snagging his shoulders released and he cracked his neck. Almost there.

He dialed Duller's number. It rang once before the agent picked up. "Where the hell are you?"

"I have no idea, but we need you here ASAP. Total shit storm. Grab this number off your phone and trace the address. You'll need backup. And a body bag."

With that, he hung up. Lynx had a plan. A plan the DEA agent wouldn't like. Staying on the phone with him would only lead to questions and a conversation Lynx didn't want to have. The way he figured it, he had a good ten or fifteen minutes before law enforcement showed up.

He could do a lot with ten or fifteen minutes.

"He's on his way," he yelled to Jillian. "Stay on that guy. I'm gonna talk with Ingrams."

First, he'd get a chair because his knee was a disaster and he needed to conserve energy for when Slick Suit woke up. He dragged one of the office chairs along the concrete and placed it a few feet in front of where Ingrams was tied.

Then he walked up to him and bent at the waist to see just what state of unconsciousness the man was in. "Hey." He gave his foot a not so light nudge. "You awake?"

Ingrams groaned. Almost there.

Lynx's knee barked at the pressure and he stood tall to shift his weight to the other foot. He studied Ingrams, the guy who'd allowed those animals to terrorize Jillian, and slapped him. One good shot to wake him up.

His head sprang up and he opened his eyes.

"Welcome back." Lynx settled on the chair.

"Jack?"

Jillian shuffled closer, but stopped. She still held the .45 on suit guy and her arms must have been getting tired. For a woman, that gun was not light. She remained steadfast, though, even if her battered face wore the scrunched look of confusion.

"You okay?" he asked her.

"Are *you* okay?"

"I'm great. We've got a few minutes before the P.D. gets here and Ingrams starts screaming about his rights. Right now, he and I are a couple of guys about to square things." He kicked Ingrams's foot. "Am I correct?"

The man's eyes darted to Jillian. "You'll both go to jail for this."

JILLIAN COULD NOT BELIEVE IT. *HE* WAS THREATENING *THEM* with prison? As much as it hurt her face, she cracked a grin. "Really? In comparison to what you've put us through, you think *we're* going to jail?"

Ingrams stayed silent. Good thing too, because with how fried her nerves were, she might march over and clock him one with the cannon she held.

"How's Slick doing?" Jack asked. "He should be waking up about now, no?"

Jillian held his stare a second. Slowly, he lifted his eyebrows and, as if he'd sent a telepathic message, she understood. Brilliant. She checked on Slick Suit and tilted her head. "He's moving a little. Probably anytime he'll wake up and realize we've completely screwed up his plan."

Ingrams tried to swivel to get a look at his partner, but being hogtied, couldn't twist.

"Here's the deal," Jack said, drawing Ingrams's attention. "My guess is your buddy down there is going to wake up and say he tried to stop you. From my perspective—" he plucked at his still-soaked shirt, "—and my recent experience with a jug of water, he's the guy running whatever circus you assholes have going."

Ingrams shook his head in that panicked way people do

when their existence comes apart. Jillian checked on his partner, but the guy was still out. His chest was moving, so she knew he was still alive. Hopefully, he'd stay out until the cops showed and she wouldn't have to shoot the sick bastard.

She went back to Jack. His clothes were soaked and his Boy Scout hair poked in every direction, but with the scary-looking automatic weapon in his grasp, he still managed to maintain his officer-in-charge confidence. The man was beat to hell and yet commanded attention.

A piece—a chunk really—of her heart died. Right there, watching him, knowing he was a good man, a man she'd already fallen a little bit in love with, but couldn't have in her life. Not unless she found a way to let go of her trust issues.

And with the way she felt in the hospital, watching him enjoy that temporary high, she'd never get the image out of her head. If they fought, that image would flash. His biggest weakness, oddly, was also hers. He was the addict and she was the one in love with the addict. Either way, the drugs would control their relationship.

No way around that one.

"So," Jack said to Ingrams. "Before the DEA and the local P.D. show up, why don't you help yourself out?"

"Fuck off," Ingrams said. Jillian felt that last nerve, the one struggling not to burn, incinerate.

She pointed the .45 at him. "Say that again and I'll shoot you myself. Look at my face. This is what your people did to me. You terrorized me. If you don't think I'll kill you, you're wrong. Self-defense. And with the way I look and the police reports I've filed, they'll believe me."

Jack held his hand to her, but stayed focused on Ingrams. "You're screwed. We heard you and your buddy talking about Greg. We know he was involved. And with what the DEA will find when they get a warrant to search Stennar Pharm's files, the ones we hacked into and copied, you'll all go down. Hell, they'll probably be able to prove someone pushed Greg off that balcony."

Ingrams shook his head again, but this time his eyes were big and wide and crazed. Jillian's level of respect for the talented Jack Lynx surged.

He turned to her. "Wouldn't that be a kick? If this asshole threw that poor guy off his own balcony?"

"No," Ingrams said.

Still with his eyes on Jillian, Jack said, "I think that's what we'll go with. And when his buddy here wakes up, that's what he's gonna say." He stood, grabbed the chair and dragged it out of the way. "If Slick Suit down there was smart, he set this whole thing up to look like you were the guy. Am I right or am I wrong? I mean, that's what I'd do."

Brilliant.

Ingrams craned his neck. "*What?*"

Jack laughed. "Dude, you're so fucked. They'll get you a nice cell in Marion. Good news for you is that they've downgraded it to a medium security prison. At least you won't be on lockdown 24/7."

Jillian heard a noise and glanced at Mr. Slick Suit. His foot moved. Just an inch. She brought the .45 up and aimed. "Jack, he's waking up."

"Excellent, we'll have them both awake when Boller gets here." He pointed at Ingrams. "Boller is DEA by the way. And he's had his eyes on you boys."

Sirens sounded, but they were still distant. Ingrams dropped his head. *Thinking.* He just needed another good push. Jillian jerked her head at Jack to urge him on.

Jack limped toward the stairs. "I need to open this door for the P.D. Hold on to your asses. This will be a wild ride."

"It wasn't me," Ingrams shouted just as Jack got to the top of the stairs.

He rushed back. "Tell me."

"Greg Leeds was helping us."

"Who's us? You and the guy on the floor?"

"Yeah. He's Ray Bosnick. He's a drug dealer from overseas. He has legitimate businesses too. He owns Stennar Pharm."

"Wait," Jillian said. "I thought Visionary owned Stennar Pharm. Does he own Visionary?"

Ingrams nodded. "He owns the holding company. It's the parent company for three companies here in the U.S. and several overseas."

"That's the Vanuatu company?" Jack asked.

"Yes."

"Who is D. Smith?" Jillian asked. "We found files belonging to him."

"There is no D. Smith. Bosnick and I are the only ones with access to those files."

"That explains that," Jack said. "What's the story with the Baxtin? Stolen?"

"No. Bosnick owns the lab that produces the drug, but it's not under Visionary. Half of the Baxtin produced is legit, but it's expensive. The U.S. lab produces legitimate medications for big pharma companies, but the Baxtin is the moneymaker. They produce Baxtin the right way part of the time. Then they produce alternate batches where they leave out the most expensive ingredient."

Jillian's mouth dropped open. They were screwing with the meds. "Why? Because it's cheaper to produce?"

"Yes. Legitimate lot numbers are put on the vials. Some

of the vials are used ones they round up from clinics and hospitals."

That was why the one vial looked weird to her. They were recycling the vials.

Jack nudged Ingrams with his foot. "How do the drugs get to the legit market?"

"The lab ships them to distributors owned by Visionary. Stennar Pharm is one of those distributors. Then the concocted drug is funneled into legitimate facilities as the real thing. It's sold at the price of the actual drug when it doesn't cost nearly as much to produce."

"The companies are half-legitimate?"

Ingrams nodded. "They've been hiding the production of the concocted drug under the veil of the legitimate drugs."

Jillian's stomach dropped. She worked for a company that tampered with drugs and probably endangered people's lives. "Greg was in on it?"

"Not at first. We brought him on slowly. He had money problems."

"Ah, shit," Jack said. "You threw money at him to get him on board?"

Ingrams stayed silent. No need to respond. The answer was there.

The entry door flew open and in came a bunch of men dressed in full combat gear screaming at them to drop their weapons. Chaos closed in, voices boomed and cluttered her mind. Jack put his weapon on the floor, slid it away and held his arms up. He jerked his head at her and his mouth moved.

Gun.

She still held it. In a swift move, she set the gun on the floor and pushed it away before raising her arms.

Agent Boller came through the door, spotted Jillian and Jack and charged toward them. "Put your arms down and tell me what the hell happened."

Jack lowered his arms and stepped close to her. "Long story, but you got a body in the back storage area." He looked at Jillian and squeezed her hand. "I'm sorry."

She'd killed a man.

In the back of her mind, she'd feared that man was dead. She knew she'd hit him hard enough. Oddly, she felt nothing. Whether it was shock or her belief that all things come around, she wasn't sure, but she was numb to the thought of having ended a man's life.

Shouldn't it have made her ill? Something? Any feeling at all?

"Down this hall and to the right," Jack continued. "There was a second guy, but he's gone. Took off when we were dealing with these two." He turned to Ingrams. "This guy is Ingrams from Stennar Pharm. He's gonna tell you everything." Again with his foot, Jack gave the still-tied man a bump. "Aren't you?"

Ingrams dropped his chin to his chest and his shoulders slumped. A second later, his body twitched.

"Hey," Jillian hollered. "You don't get to cry. You're a sorry excuse for a man. People are dead because of you. *You* don't get to cry. Greg's wife gets to cry. Not you."

Agent Boller held his hands up. "Okay. You two, outside." He turned to one of the officers. "Get Ms. Murdoch and Mr. Lynx to HQ for questioning." Then he shifted back to them. "Do either of you need medical attention?"

"No," Jack said.

"No," Jillian said.

What she needed was a stiff drink. And when had she ever thought that would happen?

23

LYNX, AIDED BY A CANE—A CANE, FOR GOD'S SAKE—HOBBLED to Vic's hospital room and, as usual, heard the big man blathering. The guy might have had a couple of slugs taken out of him, but his mouth still worked.

All was right with the world.

Lynx breathed in and said a silent thanks that he would most likely regret at a later date when his loudmouthed friend wouldn't stop harassing him. For now, he'd be at peace.

"This is crap," Vic was saying to whoever was in the room with him.

"It's a movie, dipstick."

Definitely Janet.

"I'm just saying," Vic continued. "It's totally unrealistic. Anyone who has ever slid their gun into their waistband without a holster knows the fucking thing won't stay. Especially guys. We're not gonna risk putting a gun anywhere near our peckers unless we're sure it's secure. The gun. Not our peckers. We'd know if our pecker was secure. I'd hope anyway."

"Oh, hell," Lynx muttered. "I gotta shut this down."

He entered the room, found Vic sitting up in bed and Janet lounging in the recliner next to him. She wore track pants with a button-down flannel shirt that covered the bandages from her gunshot wound. Lucky for her, the bullet went through the side of her abdomen and didn't hit anything vital.

"Boy Scout," Vic yelled. "Glad you're here. I was just telling Janet about not shooting our peckers off."

Janet rolled her eyes. "To think I left my nice, *quiet* room to come see him."

Lynx dropped into the metal chair on the other side of the bed. "Apparently, the gunshots haven't altered his line of thinking."

"Never," Vic said. "What's the news? Tell me I'm trapped in a hospital room with Janet for good reason."

"Hey," Janet yelled.

"Chill, sister. At least you don't howl like my daughter." He grinned. "She's cuter than you are, though."

"She's a baby. Babies are always cuter than grown-ups."

"Yeah, but she's cuter than other babies too. She's got 'em all beat."

Lynx laughed. Yeah, all was right with his dysfunctional world. "*Anyway*, Willie is home recuperating from a whack to the head. Ingrams copped to the whole thing. According to Boller, at the very least, they've got Bosnick on multiple counts of tampering with a consumer product and adulterating and misbranding drugs. He's going away for a long time. Ingrams will do time, but it'll be minimum since he's cooperating. The other guy, Cliff, who works at the warehouse, is in on it, but they're still figuring out what his role was. And Ned—Jillian's boss—he's clear. Totally in the dark."

Which meant the chest-pounding visit Lynx had paid the guy had been a total waste of time. Add *that* to his list of screw-ups. The only consolation was, with proving Bosnick was a shithead, Lynx had managed to unkink the Taylor Security contracts with the State Department.

All in all, a satisfactory ending to a train wreck of a week.

Janet sighed. "How are people not dying from this?"

"People *are* dying," Lynx said. "It's just that it wasn't enough people that a pattern was detected. The concocted drug contains an excessive amount of one ingredient and it's caused allergic reactions in some people. Others had their blood pressure drop. The DEA thinks about eighty people died. They just have to prove it."

Janet raised her hand. "And the guy Jillian worked for? The one that killed himself found out people were dying?"

Lynx nodded. "Yes. A couple of years ago, the owner of Stennar Pharm was approached by this Bosnick guy from overseas. He's a drug smuggler and bought Stennar Pharm because he wanted to expand into the U.S. but needed a legitimate distributor."

"I guess overseas wasn't good enough?"

"Apparently not."

Vic shook his head. "And Jillian got sucked into the middle."

Jillian stood outside of Vic's hospital room listening to Jack fill his friends in. She'd only been there a minute and had just about made it into the room, but halted when she heard his voice. All she'd wanted was to visit Vic and Janet and thank them for what they'd done. They'd almost lost their lives trying to help her, the least she could do was say thank you.

I should leave.

As much as she'd missed seeing Jack these last two days, she couldn't make herself step into that room. It wouldn't be fair to either of them. She'd told him she couldn't handle being with a recovering addict. Telling him she missed him would only confuse him and he didn't deserve her playing mind games. Not after all he'd done.

"The bogus drug trade is a seventy-five billion dollar a year racket," Jack said from inside the room.

"Well, shit," Vic said.

A nurse came down the hall, spotted Jillian's death grip on the chair rail and stopped in front of the doorway.

"Are you okay?"

Not wanting to speak and risk being heard by Jack, Jillian nodded.

"Are you looking for someone?"

Jig's up.

Jillian sighed. "Yes. Mr. Andrews. Thank you."

"Who's that?" Vic called.

No choice. She breathed deep and swung into the room.

"Oh, hey," he hollered, his pale face lighting up. "Look who's here."

Jack grabbed hold of a cane—a cane?—and levered himself up. "Hi," he said, offering her a small smile. But his eyes were focused in that way that instantly brought heat to her cheeks.

"Hi." They stared at each other in silence. *What to say?* Finally, she tore her gaze from him and bent low to hug Janet. "I'm so happy to see you up and about."

"Eh," Janet said. "What's a little gunshot? Now I can brag about my scar."

Vic snorted.

Jack maneuvered out of the way. "Here. Take my seat. I was just telling them about Ingrams."

Jillian nodded and waved him back to the chair. "I heard. I can't stay long, so you should sit."

"I'll sit when you leave."

"Christ sakes," Vic said. "Someone sit in that fucking chair so we can finish the story."

Jack grabbed her hand to guide her to the chair and the two-day ache in her chest turned to a violent rip. Even that bit of contact hurt.

"You finish it," he said to her. "I was telling them about Bosnick."

Knowing exactly where he'd left off, she picked up the story. "Bosnick brought in Ingrams when he bought Stennar Pharm. Ingrams hired Greg. At first, Greg didn't have any involvement with the bad drugs. Ingrams slowly brought him into it. Little by little, he paid him more money. He'd have him handle a shipment for him and tell him not to mention it to anyone. If an extra few thousand dollars showed up in an envelope, Greg didn't mind so much. He was a young father with bills and a family to support. According to his letter to the DEA, he thought the drugs might have been stolen rather than tampered with. Somehow, I guess that justified it—he didn't think anyone would get sick from a stolen product."

"Right," Jack said. "Until people started dying. Vendors complained to Greg about the Baxtin shipments he was asked to manage. He went to Ingrams, who told him it was a fluke. When more people died, he pressed Ingrams. Ingrams got scared and went to Bosnick, who started putting pressure on Greg and threatening him."

Jillian held out a hand. "They made it look like Greg was in charge of everything. Ingrams's name wasn't anywhere.

No reports, no bills, nothing. Greg was convinced he'd go to prison. Plus, this drug smuggler threatened his family. I guess that's what did him in. Then the guilt got to him and he couldn't stand it anymore, so before killing himself, he sent the letter to the DEA."

"His way of absolving himself," Janet said.

"Jesus. That's a helluva thing."

"Yeah," Lynx said.

The small hospital room descended into silence. Unable to stand it, Jillian reached into her tote and pulled two gift bags. "Here." She handed them to Vic and Janet. "These are for you. Just some cookies I made. Nothing lifts the spirit like cookies."

"Oh, hey," Jack said to Vic. "You're sharing those."

"My ass, Boy Scout. You ate my meatloaf. I'm the guy who got shot."

Jillian laughed. It dug into her soul and filled the emptiness of the last two days. Jack's friends were now her friends too. She suddenly wondered how much they knew of her history.

She supposed it didn't matter. They weren't treating her any differently than they had before the shooting—and what kind of people could be that forgiving? Truly, Jack's peeps were special. In their own demented way, they took care of each other.

I need people like this. Friends who didn't judge and who loved her for all her flaws. Friends who understood.

She glanced at Jack and the remaining chunk of her heart died. She could have had all of this. The man, the friendships, the love. All of it could have been hers if she hadn't pushed it away.

She cleared her throat. Janet turned to her. "You okay?"

Again she cleared her throat, but no good. Dry as a bone.

Except for the tears filling her eyes. *Don't cry now, don't cry now.*

"I'm fine." She pointed to her throat. "A tickle."

Vic tossed a sealed cup of apple juice at her. "Take a drink."

She caught the juice and stood. "Thank you. I should be going anyway. I have a call with a recruiter in a little while. Gotta find a new job."

Jack shifted in front of her. Not necessarily blocking her, but not letting her by either. "You got right on it, huh?"

"Had to. Got a mortgage to pay and Stennar Pharm was shut down." Looking at Jack only tore more holes in her. She swiveled to Vic and Janet. "You guys take care, okay? And thank you. For everything. It meant...so much to me. You're extraordinary people. Jack is lucky to have you." She backed toward the door and blinked away the tears still threatening. "I'm sorry. I have to go."

Once she hit the hallway, she speed-walked down the hall.

"Jillian?"

Jack.

Please no. She couldn't do this. Not today. Not when she wanted so badly to tell him she'd made a mistake. That she missed him. And if he'd have her, she wanted to try. With him, all the things she craved and needed and dreamed of, she could have. Despite his addiction.

If they could promise each other to try, maybe, just maybe, they could work.

"Jillian," he called, "slow down. I'm a crippled old man here with my cane."

Again, she was running from him. Hadn't she promised him she wouldn't? She stopped and spun back. Jack limped his way toward her, so she met him half way. "Did you go to the doctor?"

He smiled. "Yeah. It's pretty banged up, but no ligament damage. Should be good to go soon."

"Good. That's good."

An orderly wheeled a gurney behind her and she nudged closer to the wall.

"You doing all right?"

A spot on the wall drew her attention and she focused on it. Anything to avoid him. "Yep. How about you?"

"Back to my routine. Meetings every day for a while, just to be cautious."

Such a good man.

In a matter of days, she'd blown into his life and torn apart his yearlong effort to stay clean. A tremendous weight bore down and her head became too heavy to hold up. She leaned against the wall and finally looked at him. "Jack, I'm so sorry."

"You didn't do anything."

"I dragged you into this mess."

"I could have said no."

He'd never have done that. Wasn't that one of the things she loved most about him? His willingness to put his needs aside to help someone in trouble? "Yeah," she said. "I guess you could have."

Their eyes met and held for a few long seconds. *Talk to him. Tell him you miss him.* A slew of thoughts about what she should say bombarded her mind. But he'd said he was trying to get back to his routine. That's what he needed now. She didn't have the right to impede again.

"What are you thinking?" he asked.

"Nothing." He raised his eyebrows in that I-so-don't-believe-you look and she laughed. "Just...stuff."

"I've been thinking about *stuff* too. In fact, can you walk out to my car with me? I have something for you. I wanted to give you space for a few days before I called. Figured I'd let things settle."

Space. In the past two days, she'd had more space than she'd ever wanted. Sure it was the same pre-Jack Lynx space she'd had before, but somehow it felt different. Now, when she walked through her front door, the only thing she could think was that he'd never be there again. The loneliness she'd chosen for herself suddenly left a void.

Before Jack, she hadn't been obsessed with her loneliness. She'd recognized its existence, but chose not to dwell on it. Now, that old life seemed...well...tragic.

"Sure," she said. "I can walk out with you."

In the hospital parking garage, where the damp cold of late March had permeated every inch, Jack led her to an ancient sedan in surprisingly good shape. The car he'd told her about. The one Mike didn't want him driving. "So, this is the car you love?" She stuck her tongue in her cheek and bumped his shoulder.

He laughed. "Hey, this car is loyal. Ten years, I've had it. Hell, it was used when I bought it and it still runs like a champ. I love driving it. Makes me feel like myself again."

Like himself. Perhaps, in the chaos of the last couple of weeks, she'd helped him get there.

Jack tapped the trunk lid. "Mike hates it, though. He called the body shop and told them to put a rush on the Mercedes."

"He did not."

He held up two fingers and grinned. "Scout's honor."

The Boy Scout. Her chest heaved as though it was being torn open. Just one big fissure in the center of her body. She'd felt that agony before, but only allowed herself to experience the ailment commonly known as heartbreak on several occasions.

She held her breath and her eyes watered and—*dammit* —she couldn't do this. Not in front of him. Couldn't let him see how much she wanted to go back. Just change it all. Ridiculous. They were too far gone for that.

Their lives simply didn't mesh.

Tears tumbled from her eyes and she swatted them away. He stared at her. Not commenting, not judging, not giving her the pity face.

So freaking Jack with all this understanding. She smacked her hand into his chest. "I hate that you're a great guy."

He nodded. "I know you do. And not to be too pushy, but *you* were the one who dumped *me*."

"I know."

"Just saying."

He stuck the key into the trunk. That's how old the car was. He needed a key to open the trunk.

I love him.

Inside the trunk was a medium-sized plain white shopping bag. "I picked this up for you."

She wrapped her fingers around the handle and gave a jiggle. It had some weight to it. Jack shut the trunk and she set the bag on top of it.

"Can I open it now?"

"Sure."

Inside the bag was a gift-wrapped box and she smiled. Couldn't help it. "You bought me a gift."

"Don't freak. It's not a big deal. I just thought—" He shook his head. "Doesn't matter. Open it."

She untied the big white bow on top and set it inside the bag before starting on the bright pink paper. She tore the tape on the bottom of the box and spread the paper apart. Jillian gasped. He'd bought her the newest Nikon DSLR. And a lens.

"Oh, Jack, I can't accept this."

But how she wanted to. She flipped the box over and read the description. Not only had he replaced her stolen camera, he'd gotten her the upgraded version.

"Sure you can. You never got the old one back, and I know you love taking pictures." With one finger, he nudged the box closer to her. "I want you to have it. It's important to me."

Pulling the box against her, she clutched at it, wanting something—anything—to hang on to. She dropped her head and slammed her eyes closed because, yes, she was about to cry. The pressure inside her was too much. Too much hurt and agony and loneliness had built up and she couldn't stand it anymore. Release. That's all she needed. A way to get past this heartbreak.

Jack stepped closer and dropped his hands on her shoulders. "Please don't cry. I thought you'd be happy."

"I am happy. That's the problem."

"I don't understand."

"For two days, I've been missing you. Trying to convince myself that you and I will not work. That our *issues*—which, frankly, is just one big issue—will be too much to overcome. It's been killing me. All I've wanted was to call you. Tell you that I screwed up and that I do trust you. But I don't trust myself. I'm confused and it's not fair of me to throw my confusion at you. Not when you're trying to stay clean." She smacked him in the chest again. "Then you go and buy me a camera. A camera! You know it brings me comfort and you've given it to me. God, Jack. You're making this hard."

She stepped back, sucked air through her nose and

focused on him. The man who desperately tried to control his features because, yes, he was about to laugh.

She shoved him. Hard. "Seriously! I'm having a moment here. A total freaking breakdown and you're laughing at me. What the hell is that?"

He put his hands out before she shoved him again. "I don't know what you want me to say. I give you a camera and suddenly you hate me, but you don't hate me. You're a lunatic right now. It's kind of funny."

She gritted her teeth, but he looked so darned cute standing there—his slightly messy blond hair, the baby face, the ridiculous cane—that she stepped up, threw her arms around him and kissed him. A good smack right on the lips.

That'll teach him for laughing.

With his free hand, he pulled her closer and returned the kiss. This couldn't be considered bad. Not when it felt this right.

Slowly, she backed away from the kiss, but stayed close. Close enough to feel his breath. "What do you think?"

"About what?"

Dope. "*Us.* I've missed you. Everything in my life has changed. I'm starting from scratch. I need a new job, which definitely stinks, but it's more than that. The last two days have been empty. Without you, the little life I'd created, feels vacant."

He shook his head, faux somber. "Vacant is not good."

"Vacant sucks, Jack. *Sucks.*"

"I know. Look, I'm not the one fighting this. I gave up the fight when we made love the first time. I blew my one-year plan. I'm okay with it. Because of you, I feel like myself again. Before the addiction, I was a responsible guy who cared about others and got shit done and faced every day like something great would happen. That's where I am again, and I don't want to lose that. I've been miserable these last two days, but I've been going to meetings, making sure I take care of myself. I wanted to be able to come to you, though, and tell you that I'm still clean. I planned on waiting a week or so to give you time. That's when I planned on giving you the camera. When you showed up here, I figured life was throwing me a bone."

"So the camera is bribery?"

"If it works, why not?"

Ass. She smacked his chest again. Lighter this time. At least she hadn't knocked him off his old-man cane.

But he got serious again. The pensive, frowny face that was so much a part of him. "Jillian, I wish I could tell you I'll never relapse, but I'd be crazy to say that. I can tell you that every day my focus will be on not using. Every day. And if I'm having a bad day, I'll talk to you about it. If I need a meeting on an off day, I'll tell you why. I'll be as honest as I can because I never want you to wonder. I don't want that for either one of us."

"You're such a good man, Jack."

"But—"

She sighed. "There's always a but."

"You have to trust me. You can't run every time things get rough. I've accepted my situation, but this is a relationship. Relationships are never perfect. If I'm talking to you about my issues, you need to do the same. When you're scared, you need to tell me you're scared. And you need to introduce me to your family."

She swallowed. Her family. Wow.

He grabbed her hand and squeezed. "You don't have to hide them from me. I get it. If anything, I understand a little of what your dad faces."

A burst of heat exploded inside her and her shoulders

felt...light. Finally. Someone who understood the mess that was her family. "I'm gonna love you, Jack Lynx. It'll hurt us sometimes, but I know we'll take care of each other. I know that and I want to risk it."

He squeezed her hand again. "I'm in. All the way."

She stepped closer, snuggled into his neck, and he rested his cheek on top of her head. After fiddling with the zipper pull on his jacket, she felt his chest rise and fall with a deep breath. In the odd quiet of the garage, they stood in silence, for once not running from each other. "Then let's do it. Let's take a chance."

ALSO BY ADRIENNE GIORDANO

PRIVATE PROTECTORS SERIES

Risking Trust

Man Law

Negotiating Point

A Just Deception

Relentless Pursuit

Opposing Forces

THE LUCIE RIZZO MYSTERY SERIES

Dog Collar Crime

Knocked Off

Limbo (novella)

Boosted

Whacked

Cooked

Incognito

The Lucie Rizzo Mystery Series Box Set 1

The Lucie Rizzo Mystery Series Box Set 2

The Lucie Rizzo Mystery Series Box Set 3

THE ROSE TRUDEAU MYSTERY SERIES

Into The Fire

HARLEQUIN INTRIGUES

The Prosecutor

The Defender

The Marshal

The Detective

The Rebel

JUSTIFIABLE CAUSE SERIES

The Chase

The Evasion

The Capture

CASINO FORTUNA SERIES

Deadly Odds

JUSTICE SERIES w/MISTY EVANS

Stealing Justice

Cheating Justice

Holiday Justice

Exposing Justice

Undercover Justice

Protecting Justice

Missing Justice

Defending Justice

SCHOCK SISTERS MYSTERY SERIES w/MISTY EVANS

1st Shock

2nd Strike

3rd Tango

STEELE RIDGE SERIES w/KELSEY BROWNING

ACKNOWLEDGMENTS

With every project there are people to thank and I'll start with my readers. Thank you all for coming along on this amazing journey with me.

Thank you to Amy Remus, who won the Name a Hero contest and finally, after five stories that included him, gave Lynx a first name. Jackson Lynx. What an awesome name. To Wendy M., I can't thank you enough for your patience with me as I worked out plot details. Your input on this project was invaluable. To my friend Sara McCaw, who sat with me at Starbucks and helped me with organizational charts, thank you for the laughs. Brandi Prazak, thank you for helping me understand the differences between specific prescription drugs.

I cannot forget my usual suspects who keep me sane and grounded and laughing. Misty Evans, thank you for always answering the "brainstorming" call when I'm stuck. I love your devious mind. To the wonderful LJ Charles, who bravely takes on the challenge of reading my early drafts, you're a wonderful friend and author and I'm so glad we have each other. John Leach, you always seem to come up with an answer that will save my plot. Thank you! Milton Grasle, you always make writing action scenes so much fun that I'm in awe over my luck at having you in my life. Thank you to Nicole Mannis for giving me the incredibly funny "helmet" line. A special shout-out goes to the Dangerous Darlings, you guys rock!

Theresa Stevens, Kelsey Browning and Tracey Devlyn, my sisters of the heart, I'd be lost without your constant and unwavering support. We are an awesome team.

To my editor, the fabulous Gina Bernal, who somehow crawls into my brain and knows exactly what I'm trying to do even when I mess up a scene. You're the best.

To my stepdaughter, Julie, who has overcome so much in her life, thank you for keeping me well stocked when it comes to swag for my readers.

Finally, to "my guys" who make my life the wonderful place it is, I love you.

But wait, there is one person I cannot forget to mention. To Rich Picerno, who told me it would be nice if I mentioned him in a book and said something nice, thanks for always making me laugh. There you go. I mentioned you and said something nice. I've held up my end.

A NOTE TO READERS

Dear reader,

Thank you for reading *Opposing Forces*. I hope you enjoyed it. If you did, please help others find it by sharing it with friends on social media and writing a review.

Sharing the book with your friends and leaving a review helps other readers decide to take the plunge into the world of the Private Protectors. I would appreciate it if you would consider taking a moment to tell your friends how much you enjoyed the story. Even a few words is a huge help. Thank you!

Want to find out what's coming next?

Sign up for my newsletter

Follow me on Facebook and Twitter

Happy reading!
Adrienne

ABOUT THE AUTHOR

 Adrienne Giordano is a *USA Today* bestselling author of over forty romantic suspense and mystery novels. She is a Jersey girl at heart, but now lives in the Midwest with her ultimate supporter of a husband, sports-obsessed son and Elliot, a snuggle-happy rescue. Having grown up near the ocean, Adrienne enjoys paddleboarding, a nice float in a kayak and lounging on the beach with a good book.

For more information on Adrienne's books, please visit www.AdrienneGiordano.com. Adrienne can also be found on Facebook at http://www.facebook.com/AdrienneGiordanoAuthor, Twitter at http://twitter.com/AdriennGiordano and Goodreads at http://www.goodreads.com/AdrienneGiordano.

Don't miss a new release! Sign up for Adrienne's new release newsletter!